TORN
between **TWO**

MIA KAYLA

Visit my WEBSITE at: *www.authormiakayla.com*

Cover Designer:
Sommer Stein, Perfect Pair Creative

Cover Photography:
© 2017 Scott Hoover

Interior Design & Formatting:
Christine Borgford, Type A Formatting

Developmental Editor:
Megan Hand

Copy Editor:
Jovana Shirley, Unforeseen Editing

Proofreader:
Shawna Gavas, Behind the Writer

TORN
between
TWO

To my friends that turned into family…
From twenty one, to dirty thirty and now into our fab forties—
Thanks girls for teaching me about life.

chapter ONE

I WAS A STALKER.

Not the scary kind. Not the stick-her-in-the-jailhouse kind. But I was guilty of stalking a certain rock star. A rock star that was so fine, any fangirl would drop her thong on his command.

When I was a teenager, I'd had posters of his hot bod plastered on every inch of my walls. Now, at twenty-three, I had T-shirts that sported his band's logo. But I wasn't ashamed. I'd yell it loud and proud. I was in deep lust with Hawke Calvin from Def Deception.

Chloe grabbed my hand and pulled me through the crowd of Club Rex. The loud music, people screaming in each other's ears and laughter filled my ears. I'd never been to any place like this before.

Growing up in my small town of Carbarny, Illinois, clubs had been nonexistent, but what we'd had was music. Music was everywhere. Playing on the radio, on the speakers at a restaurant, or on my phone. And where there was music, there was Hawke Calvin of Def Deception singing his soulful rock tunes into the receiver.

"Sammy, speed it up." She tightened her hold and jerked me forward. "The band's got to be here. They just have to be."

"Chloe, that concert was freaking awesome!"

"Yes, it was, girlfriend. Yes. It. Was."

My first concert at Chicago's United Center had been one of the best experiences of my life. The absolute best.

Their music was like no other, and every word Hawke had sung spoke to me like words in a romance novel. I swore, it did. So, when

Chloe had found out where the band would be after the concert, I couldn't miss the opportunity to meet him in person.

Chloe propelled us all the way to the front of the line at the base of the stairs. The VIP lounge was on the second floor.

I glanced around, taking in the half-naked women hanging around men in tight-fitted muscle shirts, feeling totally out of my element. "Chloe, I doubt your intel. Why would they be at a club that plays rave music? They're a rock band."

Chloe ignored me and tugged down the hem of her shirt, exposing some of her cleavage. The tall, tatted-up bouncer's eyes flew to her breasts, like a puppy eyeing his Kibbles 'n Bits. I wondered if his tongue would drop and if he would start panting like a good boy.

"We're on the guest list." Chloe offered him her sweetest smile, the smile that could melt Ebenezer Scrooge's heart.

God, I wished I'd had her boldacious charm. Internally, I applauded her. I would've given her a thumbs-up if the bouncer weren't looking.

Guest list? How the hell did we get on some sort of guest list?

"Are you now?" He quirked an eyebrow, and a sly smile crept up his face, but his eyes stayed fixed on her chest, as if he were in a conversation with the twins.

She placed her hand on the guy's muscled arm and angled closer to peek at the clipboard in his hands. Chloe's short jean skirt hitched up, and half of her cheeks hung out. "Chloe and Sam." She tapped the list with her weekly manicured red fingernail.

It was hard not to notice the difference between us—me in my regular boot-cut jeans with a yellow belt that matched my sandy-blonde hair and my white Def D tank twisted into a knot on the side and the bombshell brunette beside me in a hot, tight-as-hell tube top and jean skirt. I was more cheery, happy princess, and she was more sexy vixen. I guessed it was true what they said; opposites did attract because she was my best bud for life.

He pointed to the list and smiled down at her. "You're on here."

She squeed in his face, her I'm-so-cool act disappearing like water dousing a tiny match.

When she stepped in front of him and walked up the stairs, I followed behind her.

The top floor was not as crazy crowded as the bottom floor of the club. The cloud of mist from the fog machine swirled around us, and the scent of cigarettes entered my senses. I thought smoking had been banned in Chicago. Who knew? And there was one other familiar smell—weed. It reminded me of high school—the crowd, the loud music, the drugs. Not like I was into that stuff, but if we were here long enough, we'd get high just by being in the room.

Most of the women were wearing Def Deception shirts or the signature tanks that they'd sold at the concert for fifty bucks. A piece of material for that much money was not worth it, but the logo had me charging toward the shirts super fast, like the whole nation would sell out of them.

"I'm this close to flipping and fainting." I threw one arm around Chloe and pulled her close. "Selfie time! We have to have proof that we were actually here. Smile."

Pursing her lips and giving a peace sign, she smiled. I followed in the same pose.

If my mother were here, she'd have done the same. She was a modern hippy and had exposed me to all the greats—The Beatles, Aerosmith, Bon Jovi, and Def Deception. My heart rate slowed almost to a stop at the thought of my mom, but Chloe's next words started my heart racing again.

"Look, there's my drummer boy, Cofi!"

My eyes followed her line of sight, and holy cannoli, she was right.

The drummer of DD sat on a long black leather couch that rested against a wall. Two women were chatting him up. He had a drink in his hand and a chick on his lap. I was surprised Chloe had even seen him with it being so dark.

"God, he's gorgeous, isn't he?" Her eyes turned all googly-gaga, just like when we'd been teenagers gawking over Haden Lewis, the head quarterback of our football team.

I wasn't any better as my insides swirled with excitement.

"If he's here, Hawke must be somewhere." My mouth turned dry, and my palms slicked with sweat. I raised my arms and placed them on top of my high ponytail to give myself some air. All I wanted was a glimpse of him close up, and then Christmas and my birthday would be made.

Le sigh.

The bar was situated in the middle of the room. Shot glasses lined the bar, waitresses were filling orders, and men were waiting for their drinks. But that wasn't where the crowd was. My eyes flew to the people congregated against one section of the room.

Through the darkness, I spotted a guy in the corner, sitting next to a girl. She was laughing at something he had said, and his hand caressed her upper thigh.

I squinted and then stiffened because it couldn't be. But it was. *Hawke.*

It was him. Not the Hawke Calvin who had been a million yards away on the concert stage, not the Hawke Calvin being interviewed on TV, not even the Hawke Calvin in my magazines. It was Hawke, in the flesh.

My sweaty palm reached into my back pocket and plucked out my five-by-seven card with the band's picture. All I wanted was a signature and to pick his brain about every song he'd ever written. And maybe just to touch him . . . to say that I'd touched him. That was all. That wasn't being too greedy, right?

First, I wanted a glimpse of him up close, then I needed an autograph, and now, I wanted to touch him? Which was it, Samantha?

I'd settle for the autograph, given I couldn't even hear myself think above the music blaring in the background. I knew we wouldn't be having a long, drawn-out question-and-answer session in this type of atmosphere.

"Where are you going?" Chloe asked.

I pushed past the crowd of mostly girls around me, squirming myself in between the small spaces of their bodies, trying to make my way to the couch where Hawke was sitting.

"I'm getting his autograph." I flipped toward Chloe, who was trailing right behind me. "Do you want something signed?"

"Yeah, my boobs." She laughed her Chloe carefree laugh.

I didn't know if she was serious or kidding. With Chloe, I never knew.

The bass of the sound system pounded under my feet, and the laser lights illuminated the dark room in streams of fluorescent blues and reds and pinks. I rapidly blinked, debating on my next move. I went on my toes but couldn't get a good look because about twenty girls were in front of me, vying for his attention.

But, oh, was he a dream, even from this distance. I'd worshipped him from afar, and now, I was within feet of him. His hair was a dirty-blond, wavy and it twinkled against the light.

My hand fluttered to my lips, reluctance filling my veins. There was no way I could approach him. He was beyond unattainable.

But, in the next second, I decided I'd have to at least try.

New city. New adventure. New Sam.

Gritting my teeth, I forced myself out of my shy shell.

When would I ever be this close to the lead singer of Def Deception again? Probably never.

I craned my neck and huffed. He was only a few feet away from me, but the women had formed a barrier between us.

There was no way I was going to get in front of these groupies, so I started to yell his name obnoxiously loud, "Hawke!"

And then Chloe joined in. It was as if Chloe had been born with a built-in microphone in her throat, her voice loud, screechy, booming.

Suddenly, a woman in a tight minidress turned around and threw me the dirtiest look. Her hair was a fiery red that matched the fire in her eyes. I flinched, but in the next second, I didn't care.

Be bold, or go home.

"Hawke!" If Chloe and I screaming at the top of our lungs wouldn't get his attention, I didn't know what would.

When the redhead said, "Listen, bitch, wait your turn," Chloe yelled louder, turned up her nose, and smirked.

If there were going to be a girl fight, I knew she would throw down. My best friend looked sweet and innocent, but she could bite. Bite like a predatory lion ready to protect her cubs.

And then it happened.

Finally, Hawke tore his gaze from the woman in front of him, and our eyes locked.

Deep green eyes bore into my boring brown ones.

Holy wow!

Electricity sizzled in the air between us, and I staggered and stepped back, blinking a couple of times. He squinted and leaned toward my direction, really seeing me. A numbness fell upon my body, as though I were going to faint, but I was frozen in my spot.

"Don't let that witch stop you." Chloe pushed at my back until I knocked into one of the girls.

Brown hair whacked me in the face, and she flipped around and gave me the bird. Her eyes narrowed, and I swore, she was about to throw a punch when a bald guy, who must've been close to seven feet tall, stepped between us.

The bodyguard.

I took a step back, ready to call defeat, when he tugged at my elbow. Scared, I tried to jerk away from his grasp. "Let go of me! I'm going, all right?"

His hold on me tightened, and Chloe grabbed my other arm. My body was in a tug-of-war between the two of them.

"Let go." Chloe squinted her hazel eyes and her voice lowered to a menacing growl, like a bulldog ready to pounce. "We're leaving. You don't have to physically attack my friend here."

"No, come with me." With one flick of his thick wrist, he turned my body toward the couches. "Mr. Calvin would like a word."

Chloe's eyebrows shot to the ceiling. "Mr. Calvin? Hawke Calvin?" Her grip was tighter than the bodyguard's but now for a whole different reason. "Oh my God," she squealed.

And, all of a sudden, it was like a dizzying dream.

My heartbeat sped up, and then in the next second, I was in front of the lead singer of Def Deception. I stood, unblinking, my eyes taking in every detail of him from his chiseled jaw to his sparkling eyes to the scar right above his eyebrow. He tipped his head, sporting a crooked smile. A smile so panty-dropping gorgeous that the teenage butterflies in my stomach fainted and then were brought back to life again, causing a frenzy in my belly. All from his crooked smile.

Le sigh . . . again.

The magazines did not do him justice. He was most definitely more handsome than my calendar that Chloe had gotten me for Christmas. His eyes were the greenest of greens, just like emeralds or as vibrant as a newly manicured lawn.

The bodyguard released my elbow, and I stepped closer, my left yellow Converse hitting his black leather boot.

"Name?"

I heard him clearly, yet it was as though my mouth had been wired shut. I lost all ability to speak, think, or utter my own name.

Chloe nudged my shoulder. "I'm Chloe, and this is Sam."

He didn't tear his eyes from mine as he shook Chloe's hand first and then reached for my waist where I had to bend down to hear what he had to say. "Is Sam short for Samantha?" His warm breath tickled my skin and caused goose bumps to spread down my neck.

Hawke is touching me. Hawke. Is. Touching. Me.

I pulled back and nodded, still mesmerized by his beauty and trying to keep my cool. I inhaled deeply and coughed because I had, at some point, forgotten to exhale. I guessed breathing normally in his vicinity was not possible.

His fingertips grazed the bare skin at my waist and he pulled me onto his lap. One minute ago, I had been a girl just hoping to see her rock idol, and now, I was straddling him, knees on either side of his waist.

That seemed to break me from my trance, and I pushed at his chest. "Wait."

"Relax." He planted his hands on my hips to keep me still. "Sam, relax."

Like that was even possible. I was straddling Hawke Calvin. And there I was again, dazed and confused at the sound of my name falling from his lips.

"Is there something you wanted, sexy?" His eyes smoldered, and his tone dropped an octave lower.

Me, sexy? Okay, sure. What did I want?

I gulped. My thoughts were a jumbled mess, like mixed-up computer code.

He licked his lips as his fingertips drew tiny circles on my hips, triggering tingles throughout my body. From the look in his eyes, I knew what he wanted.

But I couldn't. We wouldn't.

I snapped myself back to reality.

"No . . . it's not what you're thinking." I shifted forward to get the postcard from my back pocket and froze when I felt his hard length against my inner thigh.

Any sort of reasoning flew out the door. I wasn't a virgin. I'd been in two long-term, failed relationships, but I didn't sleep around. One-night flings were not in my vocabulary. Even with a rock star.

Breathe. Just breathe.

Who knew if he was aroused by me? For all I knew, he wore a

rock-star boner from the moment he woke up until his head hit the pillow.

"Never mind." Forget the autograph. I tried to wiggle off, but his hands only tightened against my waist. "Can you let go?"

"Is that what you really want?" His crooked smirk was enough to melt me again, but I was not *that* girl.

"No, I wanted an autograph, but I'm not really comfort-able . . . right now." Something snapped within me, through all the weed and smoke in the air and the loud music. Yes! Clarity and san-ity and virtue had arrived.

He was a gorgeous face and had a beautiful voice, but I was a re-lationship kind of girl. My stomach dropped at the total letdown in meeting him. I'd had such high expectations. I'd wanted to pick his brain about his music, about his songs and the inspiration behind the lyrics to his tunes.

But the typical rock star only wanted one thing. Crushing disap-pointment seeped into my skin.

"What do you want me to autograph?" The glint of the strobe lights caught the green in his eyes.

Because his voice didn't have that same sexual intonation as it had a second ago, I pulled the postcard of the band from my back pocket and handed it to him. "This."

He tipped his chin toward his bodyguard, and the big guy hand-ed him a pen. It was like they could communicate without actually using words.

He held the pen in his hand and sucked in his bottom lip. "See, I don't give anything up without getting something in return."

My eyebrows jumped to my hairline. "Right here? Sorry, it's not happening." My response shot out quick, steady, automatic. I wasn't going to have a public exhibition for everyone to see.

"No." His eyes danced with amusement. "One kiss."

My body tensed. I didn't like being forced into something. Never had. But this was a no-brainer.

Did I want to kiss one of the biggest rock stars in the world?

Forbes's richest entertainer? *People's* sexiest man alive? The lead singer of Def Deception?

I nodded, my heart leaping into my throat, and then before I could say anything, it happened. He leaned forward, his lips meeting mine, and a flame ignited my whole body. His kiss was overwhelming. Warm at first but fire the next. Tingles initiated at our connection, even reaching to the tips of my tiny toes.

A moan escaped him as the pen slipped from his hand and hit my arm. One hand reached under my shirt to my bare back while the other grabbed the back of my neck and pulled me closer, flush against him. My pulse raced, and my skin warmed as he groaned and deepened our kiss.

Sanity had left, and so had clarity. Soon, my panties would be next.

With one flick of his tongue, I opened and breathed him in, his musky cologne with a hint of spice. His tongue intertwined with mine. His hard mouth devoured my softness.

My hands reached for his hair, lying just above his neck. It was soft and silky, and I gently tugged at the strands.

His touch and the scent of him were like drugs lulling me toward nirvana.

When he forcefully moved my body against his erection, my breathing labored, and my body heated. I pulled back, and my heart jumped into my throat. Our eyes locked, both of us a little dazed and a lot breathless.

He leaned in again to meet my lips, but I pressed him back with one hand to his chest.

Without giving myself another second, I scrambled from his lap, almost losing my footing in the process. He reached for my hand, but I pulled away, biting my lip, the stinging pain snapping me back to the present.

I pressed a hand to my thumping heart as it all became so real.

I had just made out with Hawke Calvin, doing the Humpty Dance on his crotch.

And, now, I was leaving with my clothes on and my integrity intact.

Go me.

I staggered a little and glanced down. Somewhere between sitting on my idol's lap and feeling his tongue in my mouth, I had dropped my postcard.

I took two steps back toward him, bent down to pick it up, and stuck the five-by-seven card in his face. "You can make it out to Sam." I forced a calm coolness in my smile even though my lips were on fire and my heart was going to fly out of my chest.

He blinked, momentarily stunned. For once, his eyes were unreadable, his sexual innuendos gone. I lifted an eyebrow and wiggled the postcard in his direction.

I wanted to ask him so many questions, but I knew I had to go. I smelled like weed now, and I sensed a whole bunch of danger in Hawke Calvin's eyes, as though he would devour me for his meal and swallow me whole. No part of me would be left unscathed.

With one tip of his chin to his bouncer, the pen was back in his hand. He balanced the card on his knee and scribbled his name along with his number on my card. Even his signature had personality.

When I turned to leave, he stood, reached for my waist and spun me to face him. "I need to see you tonight." His tone lowered, and his alert gaze was set on mine, his fingers grazing my hip.

His body language promised me more than dinner and a movie. Hell, I doubted that would even happen at all.

I smiled, turned and reached for Chloe as my cheeks flushed pink. Any normal girl would've dropped her panties right then and there, but I wasn't a normal girl. And maybe if he'd had some manners, quite possibly had said, *Pretty please*, I would've considered it. But, no.

His hands circled my waist and pulled my body into him, my

back now flush against his hard chest. My nipples pebbled from his touch, betraying me.

He bent down and nibbled the top of my ear. "I don't beg. Not normally." His voice was warm against my skin. "I'm in Chicago for a few days. Call me tonight. Please," he whispered.

And there was that one word I doubted he used often.

Despite me not being *that* girl, everything inside me tingled with want. But I brushed it off and snapped back to Sensible Sam.

I had to go, or I'd be giving him more than a kiss. I had a feeling that this guy would stomp on my heart, and I couldn't afford to get sidetracked from my ultimate goals in life, especially since it was only recently that I had gained some normalcy.

I stepped away with my pretty panties still on, integrity intact.

chapter TWO

CHLOE'S EYES HELD SO MANY questions, but it was too loud for me to think, too loud to talk. While I was still on a high, we went downstairs and shook our tails to the rave music blaring on the speakers. When my feet felt like they were going to fall off, we strolled out of the club and into the parking lot, laughing like lunatics.

"What did he taste like, Sammy? I need to know." Chloe linked her arm through mine, dragging me toward the car.

With my free hand, I lifted my long blonde strands that were sticking to my back, sweaty from our dancing session. The humid August night air didn't help. "He tasted like cigarettes, beer, and one hundred percent bad boy."

She stepped back, bounced on her toes, and threw me a you're-so-cool look, as if I were the famous one. "Do you know what you just did in there?" She pointed back to the club. "You kissed Hawke Calvin." She batted her eyelashes, and the inflection in her voice took on a dreamy tone. "His tongue was down your throat. Do you know how many women would want to be you?"

With my shaky hand, I touched my lips and laughed. "Yeah." I pulled the postcard from my back pocket and took in his unreadable signature. "I kinda wish I'd had more time than our less than five minutes make-out session." Even though I had been the one to walk away, disappointment surfaced. "He wasn't what I'd expected."

"What did you expect?" Chloe smirked as she pressed the button to unlock her Mercedes. "You don't like the super-hot kind?"

"No, I just thought he'd have more"—I shrugged—"substance." Yes, he was hot, but I guessed I had hoped for the non-typical rock star who didn't have only one thing on his mind.

Only in my fairy tales.

"What? Were you going to pick his brain?" Her voice turned incredulous.

I turned toward her, smiling. "As a matter of fact, I was. I wanted to know what his inspiration was for his song 'Death by Life.'" It was such a beautiful song that spoke about a woman who had to die to feel alive. Deep, moving, and powerful.

She flipped her brunette locks over her shoulder, mid eye roll. "Only you, Sam. You're so odd."

I opened the door, slipped in right next to her, and laughed. "I'm a pastry sous chef. We're all odd."

After she pulled out of the parking lot and veered right, she braked to a halt, causing me to buck forward. My palms slammed against the dashboard. A SUV limo had purposely stopped in front of us.

"What the fuck?" She threw the car in park, flew out the door, and approached the black Hummer limo in front of us that had dangerously cut us off.

Before she got herself in trouble, I stepped out, muscles tense, eyes cautious.

The limo was shaking from the music playing inside, causing the windows to rattle.

"What the hell is your problem?" she yelled, stepping in front of the vehicle

I tugged at her shirt. "Chloe . . ." I said in my calm mama-bear voice even though my pulse was racing.

She pounded at the driver's black-as-night window. "Are you trying to kill people tonight? Open the fuck up!" Her tone could have cut metal.

My adrenaline spiked, and I pulled at her arm as hard as I could.

I didn't want to go to jail tonight—or worse, be a statistic. "Let's go."

I desperately tugged at her, yet she wouldn't budge. She was on a mission to beat some ass, and I was on a mission to stay out of trouble.

When the rear window rolled down, she jerked back, and her eyes widened.

My fingers flew to my parted mouth, and a low gasp escaped me.

Hawke was inside, a cigarette between his lips—the lips that I'd had against mine hours ago. The chatter of the people partying inside his vehicle echoed through the open window.

He tipped his chin. "Hey."

Chloe blinked, her face totally shell-shocked, and answered with a, "Hey."

His eyes were on me the whole time.

A dizzying current took over my body, and I focused on the soft breaths leaving my mouth.

Holy smoking-hot rock star.

Maybe he had no substance, but he most definitely made up for it with his sex appeal.

Even if I still wasn't *that* girl, only a blind person wouldn't be able to appreciate his fineness.

His eyes were like a laser-light beam against mine, unwavering. Now that we were no longer in the club, I took in his strong features—his dirty-blond hair, his prominent nose, the electric-green eyes that seared through me.

I swallowed. Hard.

"Sorry about that. I was trying to get your attention." His voice was calm and smooth, as though his driver hadn't almost caused an accident.

He held this demeanor, like nothing fazed him. I bet nothing did.

"Well, you got our attention." She smiled, cheeky-Chloe style, and her eyes ping-ponged from Hawke's to mine.

He flicked his cigarette out the window and blew out a long puff of smoke that fizzled into the night air. "Wanna get a bite to eat?"

Before I had a chance to contemplate if I should go or figure out what to say, Chloe interlocked our arms and answered for the both of us, "Sure, we'd love to."

He let out a low chuckle. By the look on his face and the fact that he couldn't stop staring at me, I didn't think it was a joint invitation.

This was a bad idea. Bad. Bad. Bad. Especially considering the way my body was reacting to him. "Chloe, I don't think—"

He pushed open the door. "Let's go."

"I've gotta park my car." Chloe waved me toward the limo. "Sam, jump on in. I'll be right behind you."

Chloe turned and headed to her vehicle, and I sucked in a breath, focusing on her retreating back. Focusing on anything but the green-eyed male and his intense stare.

He stepped out and tipped his head toward the door. "After you."

The full moon was out tonight, and I knew, if I got in the vehicle, a whole lot of craziness was about to come, but with Hawke sporting his cocky, crooked smile, I couldn't resist.

I hopped in, and he slipped in beside me.

Black leather seats spanned the whole vehicle, and fluorescent lights lit up the bar behind the seats. The bar was stocked with beer and hard liquor and the party had already begun.

Every spot was taken. There must've been over a dozen people in the car. I recognized two of the band members, who were preoccupied with the women—multiple women—on their laps.

"Hey there." Two words. Simple and seductive. Hawke's fingers pressed against my waist.

Warmth spread through me from where his hands touched my body, and the nervousness I had been feeling jumped up twenty notches.

"What do you want to eat?" he asked, his hot breath brushing against my skin. "I know what I want to eat, but it's not food."

I didn't know why his abrasiveness had surprised me, but it had. I wasn't used to men being so forward. Instead of fighting it, for once, I decided to play with him to calm the jitters stirring inside of me.

When I smiled and leaned in, his lips parted at my proximity.

"Oh God . . . I want . . ." I breathed heavily. "I want . . ." I forced a sexiness in my voice that made his eyes flash with lust. "Chicken nuggets and fries," I whispered back in the most seductive tone, sweet and sexy soft.

He reeled back, looking confused at first, and then his lips twitched at the corners until a small laugh escaped. "You're cute, you know that?"

"I'm here," Chloe said in her peppy voice.

And I was glad for her arrival.

I pressed at Hawke's chest, needing the room to breathe.

Hawke scooted in to let her jump in on his other side, but because the limo was crammed like a bus of football players going to an away game, he pulled me onto his lap, one hand resting on my hip. I didn't protest.

Chloe's eyes brightened as she scanned the limo. "Where are we headed?"

"Apparently, somewhere that has nuggets and fries." Amusement leaked from Hawke's tone.

"Let me guess; that was Sam's suggestion." Chloe laughed. "She eats nuggets and fries like it's a five-star meal."

"And her wish is my command." He laced his fingers together around my stomach, pulling my body flush against his.

It took all my energy to keep my face level and not melt into his touch. All the while, I was thinking, *This is so not happening to me. So not.*

Chloe dreamily peered up at Hawke. I wouldn't be surprised if she started pawing at him and petting him as if he were a real live pet. Goodness . . . we could take turns.

"Guys," Hawke announced, "say hi to my friends. This is Chloe, and right here is Sunshine."

Murmured greetings echoed through the vehicle.

"Sunshine?" I turned to face him.

His crooked smile was on display, the same smile that had stared at me from my bedroom poster and fueled my teenage dreams.

"Cheery and bright," he said, amused by his own nickname for me. Then, he grabbed a strand of my sandy-blonde hair. "Sunshine."

My hair was a natural yellow. My mother used to describe it as being as yellow as the brightest sunflower.

A broader male with a crew cut, right in front of Chloe, spoke up, "How about you? Are you cheery and bright, too?"

In the dim light, Chloe blanched. We glanced at each other with recognition, her eyes widening. When Cofi, the drummer of Deception, smiled his devastatingly beautiful smile, I knew Chloe was a goner.

"Not cheery and bright," she said. "More like sweet hard candy."

He laughed and beckoned her over, patting his knee.

Without hesitation, Chloe hopped onto his lap. The woman sitting right next to him scowled at Chloe, but Cofi ignored her and whispered something in Chloe's ear that made her giggle.

"Sunshine, you're going to make this hard for me, aren't you?"

I swallowed. "What?"

He reached for my hand and placed it on his jeans. The length of him hardened underneath my palm, and my breath caught in my throat. Someone needed to press the Pause button. Stat. Super stat.

Playing the game, I squeezed, knowing he was well endowed, and I rubbed against the ridge in his pants. He leaned back, and his eyes filled with a lust so strong, my heart raced.

I creeped up, close enough to whisper something in his ear, "It's too bad what they say about rock stars isn't always true. Such a shame really." I released him, pinching my finger and thumb together, and shrugged.

He smirked, tugged at my shirt, bent down, and trailed his tongue from my neck to my ear. The wetness of his tongue against my skin caused warmth to pool between my legs.

"Oh, I'm going to show you, that's far from the truth. I'm the epitome of a rock star in all things."

My stomach fluttered, my pulse skyrocketed, and my breathing hitched. I pulled back and stared at him, still pretending to be unaffected by his proximity, which was the opposite of the havoc happening internally. There was no doubt his words were true, judging by his cocky smirk.

"I doubt that." My tone shook like a glass on top of a washing machine.

He flicked his tongue against my lips. "Better watch out. I might take you and never give you back."

I smiled, but in the next second, I pressed my hands against his chest and turned toward AJ, the bass guitarist. I needed to focus my attention on something, anything, anybody else because my cool demeanor was slowly fading in front of Hawke.

Breathe, breathe, breathe.

"Where are we eating?" AJ asked.

"Wherever we can get nuggets and fries," Hawke called out.

"Like chicken nuggets?" AJ asked. "McDonald's!"

"Yeah"—Hawke nodded, meeting my eyes—"McDonald's, it is."

I rubbed my cheek against my shoulder. "Aw, our first date at McDonald's. Calorie-infused foods. What can I say? I like what's bad for me." Somehow, Sensible Sam turned into Playful Sam.

"You're a good girl, but you're into bad things?" Hawke's eyes darkened.

I had no idea where all this flirting was coming from.

Who knew I had it in me?

I straightened and smiled, fully knowing I was playing with fire that would burn me to ashes and leave nothing behind. "If you define bad as greasy and artery-clogging, then yes." It was hard to keep the googly eyes off my face because, seriously, the rock star was hot. Not pepper hot. Not curry hot. Hot-sauce-burning-your-tongue-off *caliente* hot.

No wonder he had gained the massive fame that he had. The band was insanely talented, and their leader was crazy gorgeous.

I couldn't stop staring.

Painfully tearing my gaze from his, I turned to the tinted windows. "Rock 'n' Roll McDonald's. Is that where we're heading?"

We were in the middle of downtown, stuck in late-night rush hour. It might be a while.

"Who knows?" He shrugged. "Our driver will know."

"Don't tell me, you're just going to get out, stroll into McDonald's, and buy a burger. You'll start a riot."

He laughed. Even his laugh was sexy, hoarse, deep, and delicious. I wanted him to do it again.

"No, we're ordering food and going back to the hotel."

I blinked and raised both eyebrows.

Back to his hotel?

Well, Sam, what did you think was going to happen?

Did I think we'd drive around in his limo, pigging out on nuggets, and he'd drive us to our car afterward?

I shook my head through the fog. "Wow. Presumptuous, aren't we?"

He shrugged. "This guy gets everything he dreams of." There was no hesitation in his tone. He spoke as though it were a known fact.

"I don't doubt that," I said. "It looks like you're living the dream." I motioned to the people in the limo. "Right Chlo—" I stopped mid sentence because I had just caught my best friend riding Cofi, the drummer boy, like she was at the rodeo. Dry-humping, of course.

She still had her clothes on, but his hands were on her ass, and her fingers were threaded through his hair. Even with the jam-packed car, she did not care.

"All righty then." I cleared my throat.

"Jealous?" Hawke whispered, thoroughly amused at my reaction.

"Actually, yes." I sighed, feigning disappointment. "I've always fantasized about Cofi and me. Together. Having passionate—" I paused at Hawke's abrupt change in his demeanor with his clenched jaw and eyes flashing with jealousy.

His arms tightened along my waist as he angled closer, and with one hand at the base of my neck, he pulled me into a kiss so fierce, I forgot where I was.

He captured my lips with possessiveness, with a want that was evident by his hard length pressing against my thigh. I might have moaned against his lips. I might have pressed my breasts against his chest. I might have opened my mouth to feel his warm tongue against mine.

After a beat, against all those warnings screaming in my head, my hands slowly moved along his firm, toned abs to his pecs, and then I slowly pushed him away. I broke our kiss, needing to find my bearings.

"How many dates?" he asked, his eyes darkening, his breathing labored. "What date will you give it up, Sunshine? I'm here tonight for another sold-out show."

My mouth dropped, and I lightly placed one hand on his chest, just so I could continue to touch him even though the question annoyed me. His heartbeat raced against my hand.

Rock star or not, he shouldn't assume I was like every other girl he had access to.

"Wow. You've got nerve." My body tensed.

"That's nothing I haven't heard before."

When I went in for another shove, he reached for my hand and intertwined our fingers. "Then, I'll be traveling for a few weeks before we head to Europe. "How many dates?" he pressed.

When I stared longer into his eyes, the cockiness in the green slowly disappeared. I witnessed something deeper that surprised him as well because he leaned back, giving himself some room.

I swallowed. "If I say twenty dates, are you going to fly me all over the world until we hit the twentieth McDonald's?"

"Maybe," he admitted with a chuckle.

"Oh, you want to get in my pants that badly?" I was still annoyed but also shaken that he seemed to even care, to want me that badly.

He leaned in, his warm breath laced with the scent of cigarettes brushing against my face. "You have no idea." And then he kissed my lips again without hesitation and without apology.

His kisses were hot and intense, making me squirm in my seat, my whole body rising in temperature.

"You taste so good," he said through his kisses. "I can only imagine how it feels to be inside you."

His fingers trailed under my shirt, touching the bare skin right above my hip, inching up to the middle of my back. When he unclasped my bra, I placed one hand on his chest and broke away from him.

"Sorry, you're not getting that kind of action." My voice shook with arousal.

I was using all my self-control not to take off my bra and toss it at his face—which I was certain happened often. The crowd in the limo was a good deterrent though.

The music died down as someone yelled from the front of the limo, "Orders! We're almost there."

A couple of pads of papers along with pens flew down the aisle. The lights flipped on, and there were echoes of complaints.

I welcomed the lights and the distraction and the interruption.

I rested against his chest, catching my breath.

The sooner I was out of this car, the better.

chapter THREE

COFI'S ARM WAS SNAKED AROUND Chloe's shoulder as we strolled with Def Deception's whole crowd into The InterContinental Chicago hotel on Michigan Avenue. A crowd formed a red carpet line on either side of us, but the bodyguards kept the gawkers and fangirls away.

My arms were preoccupied with multiple McDonald's bags. I had volunteered myself and Hawke to take the bags into the hotel, giving his hands something to do other than touch my body.

Sweat formed along the inside of my palms as I walked in step with Hawke. Since our kiss, he'd been silent, reserved. I didn't know if I had offended him by denying his advances or if he was going to try again later.

Being with Hawke, the band, and their entourage was awfully awkward. I didn't like being the center of attention, and all eyes were zoomed in on me because I was with Hawke.

I suddenly wanted to retreat to my two-bedroom apartment that I shared with Chloe, but I couldn't leave her and break the girl code. If she was going to get it on with Cofi, I'd stay and wait until she'd had her fun. Chloe was like a carefree bird, but I didn't care because she was a fanatic about protection.

We strolled toward the rear of the hotel to a secluded elevator bank, and I moved to the back of the elevator as everyone piled in.

Hawke stood beside me, leaning in, his warm breath brushing my face. "You're awfully quiet."

"I don't see you chatting it up." I focused on the bright

fluorescent lights above us, covered by plastic panels.

"The truth is, I'm really hungry." His tone was softer this time without its usual flirty flair. He displayed his signature crooked smile.

I quirked an eyebrow, waiting for some sexual innuendo to come but it didn't.

"Really." He laughed. "I needed nuggets and fries thirty minutes ago."

The elevator pinged and opened to a massive penthouse. My jaw nearly dropped as I took everything in. Black marble floors beckoned us forward, like an infinity pool. The room was adorned with arrangements of white hydrangeas and roses and peonies, a contrast to the black tables they sat on. A circular white leather couch that could sit twenty was centered in the room. Floor-to-ceiling windows surrounded us, giving us a wide, open view of the city below. The glimmer of the lights from the Chicago skyscrapers blinked in front of us like stars against a dark night.

"Wow." I staggered mid step to a stop.

I had only seen the city in its finest at the top of Willis Tower, but that was in the middle of the day.

I readjusted the bags of warm food and walked closer toward one of the windows overlooking the beautiful buildings. The tiny cars looked like moving ants from this distance. Chicago was even more breathtakingly beautiful in the evening. It seemed like everything was twinkling.

"Let's go." Hawke held my elbow and maneuvered me toward the table in the corner. He dropped all but our two bags on top of the table and intertwined our fingers. "Get rid of the cargo. I've got our food." He lifted the two bags he held.

After I dropped the food, my eyes searched the room for Chloe. "Where's my friend?"

Music blasted through the wall speakers as the whole entourage dispersed.

"She's fine," Hawke said, walking us through the penthouse.

"Where are we headed?" I spotted a couple of leggy brunettes sitting on another white couch backed against the wall, but none of them were my best friend.

"We're eating where it's less crowded." He winked, and his sexy, crooked smile popped on display. "My room."

I extracted my hand from his. "I really need to look for Chloe."

Rock star or not, he was still a stranger, and I was in unfamiliar surroundings.

He intertwined our fingers again, tugging my hand along like I hadn't said anything.

"Hey." My face meant business.

I needed to know she was okay. We'd been in one too many situations before to just leave each other without checking in.

"Relax. I'll take you to her." He smiled, but that didn't curb the uneasiness stirring inside me.

He led us down a hall, past a grand piano and kitchen area, further down another hall, and up some stairs. Full white hydrangeas sat on every table we passed.

He stopped at a door at the end of the hall and banged on it. "Cofi, open up."

When no one responded, Hawke's hit the door harder, fist closed. "Open the fuck up, man."

The door flung open, and a shirtless Cofi stood at the doorway. "What the hell?"

I drove past him, and my eyes scanned the area. "Chloe," I called out.

She was sitting on the couch, eating a fry. She had a humongo grin on her face, as though she was in the happiest place on earth, and she stared at Cofi as if he were Mickey Mouse.

"Can I talk to you for a second?" I asked.

Her smile momentarily slipped, and her eyebrows pinched together. "Why? Is something the matter?" Her eyes flew immediately to Hawke, a shoot-to-kill look crossing her features. Superstar or not, if he stepped out of bounds, there was no doubt that Chloe would kick his ass to the next country, travel to that country, and kick his ass to the next one.

"No." I shook my head. "I just need to ask you something."

She stood and tilted her head toward the bathroom where I trailed behind her and shut the door, locking us in.

She flipped to face me, her eyes hard. "Did Hawke try something?" She shook her head and elaborated, "Something you're not comfortable with?"

"No, not at all. That's not it." My eyes moved to the shut door. "You didn't tell me where you were going."

Why did it feel like Hawke and Cofi were listening beyond the door?

She slapped her head. "I'm sorry. Ugh. My brain is mush from being around that muscled hunk." She stuck out her pinkie. "Never again. I'm sorry."

I wrapped my finger against hers, feeling much more at ease after our girlie pinkie promise. "It's okay." I shoved down memories of our past, one where she had gotten so drunk that I'd had to step into the situation when a jerky guy had overstepped his boundaries while she wasn't of sound mind. Since then, we'd promised that we'd never get that wasted, and we'd know where each other was at all times. "Are we staying long?"

"Good God, I hope so." Her voice rang with excitement, taking on a dreamy tone. "I hope he's not a one-minute man. You can totally leave if you want to, but I'm going to hook up with that sexy bod." She licked her lips and glanced at herself in the mirror. With one finger, she rubbed below each eye, fixing her eyeliner. "And I'm going to tell the world that I hooked up with Cofi Cole, the hottest drummer from Def Deception." She batted her eyelashes with exaggeration.

"He's the only drummer of DD, dummy." I rolled my eyes. "And I'm not leaving you. I'll just hang out till you're done."

"But, girlfriend"—she gave me a amused look—"little drummer boy could last all night. I'm officially releasing you from your girlfriend obligations." She pointed at the door. "How about Hot Hawkey?"

I jerked my head back and assessed her face. "What about him?"

"He's hot, hot, hot for you, baby." She flicked her index finger against my arm. "You need to let loose with the sexiest man alive. Seriously? I get the drummer, but you . . . you, Samantha Sunshine . . . get the lead."

"Please." I averted my gaze. "Not going to happen."

She squinted her eyes and placed one hand on her hip. "Why the hell not? Are you planning on getting married tomorrow?"

"Of course not."

"Listen, I know you're not into the temporary-fling thing."

I could read the pity in her eyes. Pity for a girl who hadn't had action or satisfaction in over three years.

"You've lived your life, acting as a parent to your own parent. You moved here for a reason, Sam. To get away. To start over. To forget." She placed both hands on my shoulders and leaned in, speaking softer, firmer, clearer, "But you're twenty-three, Sam. We're in the prime of our lives and out of school. This is the time to let loose, girlie pie, before we're stuck with one dick for eternity. Don't think too heavily on this. Just have fun."

When she pulled me in close, I tightly wrapped my arms around her. Chloe had the emotional makeup of a man; she could separate the emotional and physical whereas I, on the other hand, could not. And, yeah, my childhood had been a rocky one. I had come to Chicago to forget and move on, but I had also moved to Chicago to work as a sous pastry chef and to apply to culinary school. I couldn't let anyone or anything deter me from achieving my goals.

Boom, boom, boom.

The door shook behind me.

"Time's up. We want to join in on the girl fun." Cofi's voice filtered through the door.

Boom, boom, boom.

Chloe kissed my cheek and squeezed my hand. "Don't overthink this, okay? If anything, just be safe."

I stepped to the side, so she could get to the door. Her hand lingered on the knob before she said, "Have fun, Sam. You're in your twenties only once. And I'll text you, so you won't worry. Do you have cab money to get home?"

I nodded.

She threw the door open and tossed her wavy caramel locks over her shoulder. "We're right here," she said, mid flip.

She pinched his nipple and kissed him, hard, and I blinked at the heat of their interaction.

He lifted her from her butt, and her legs wrapped around his waist as he walked them back into the room.

All righty then. I don't want to rain on her mating match.

Chloe had changed and peed in front of me with no problem. I wasn't ready for our relationship to jump to a whole other level. I'd be blinded for life.

Hawke intertwined our fingers again. "I'm hungry, Sunshine. Let's eat."

I let him lead me down the hall and up the stairs to another room. I wondered how many rooms they could fit in the penthouse suite.

When the double doors opened, I knew that Hawke had the master bedroom. The bed spanned half of the room. The pillows alone looked like they could swallow me whole. More floor-to-ceiling windows encompassed another wall. The room was big enough to have a full sitting room, center table, couch, love seat, and recliner. A massive television was hung on the wall.

Oh, the things that money could buy.

He dropped the McDonald's bags on the center table in front of the TV and plopped on the couch. "Shit, I'm starving."

I dropped my purse on the couch. When I sat next to him, my stomach grumbled at the smell of and sight of fries. "I'm sure you could've ordered anything. Room service if you wanted," I pointed out, still surprised that he was slumming it with me and my McDonald's.

He shrugged. "I haven't had Mickey Dee's in forever." He took out the box of fries, flattened the bag and dumped the fries on top of it. "And, right now, this greasy shit will hit the spot."

He grabbed the remote and turned on the TV. The news showed on the big screen. He opened packets of ketchup and mayo, and I made a face when he twirled his fingers to mix the two sauces. I watched red and white blend into a light pink.

He dipped his fries into the mixture and stuffed them in his mouth. Then, he nodded in my direction. "What are you waiting for? Eat."

"I'm observing. I could do a whole documentary on how the rich and famous eat."

He dipped the fries into the sauce and stretched his hand toward my mouth. "Open up for me, Sunshine." His voice was teasingly sexy.

"Nah, I don't think so." I cringed. "Ketchup and mayo? Not my thing."

"Don't knock it before you've tried it," he shot back, faking offense. "You have to try everything at least once." He angled closer, pushing the fries toward my mouth. "Take it."

His eyes darkened when I opened my mouth, and he slowly pressed the fries between my lips. The move was methodical and deliberate, and it was the most sensual thing. I shifted in my seat, chewed, and ducked my head into my pile of food. I felt his eyes on me the whole time.

I opened my box of nuggets and the small tub of honey-mustard sauce.

"Here." He extended another fry dipped in his ketchup-mayo

concoction and placed it against my lips.

I opened for him and took the fry into my mouth, slower this time, our eyes never breaking contact. He surprised me when he leaned over and kissed my lips. Just a quick kiss, but nonetheless, the kiss packed a pleasurable punch.

When he pulled back, I read pure lust in his green eyes.

"I'm hungry for something other than fries now." He licked his lips and focused on mine.

Seconds ticked by, and heat spread from my toes to my chest before reaching the tips of my ears.

"Me, too," I said, my tone seductive and silky, as I tore a piece of chicken within my fingers. "Nuggets. I'm hungry for nuggets," I said. I chomped on the nugget, chewing on it like I hadn't eaten in days. Nervousness bubbled in my chest, so I took a different approach, going for unattractive.

A small smile crept up his face as a deep chuckle escaped him. "Funny, Sunshine." He reached for my waist and tugged me toward him. Easily lifting my body, he set me on his lap in a straddling position, as he had done in the club—except, now, no one was watching, no one could stop us, no one would know.

I breathed him in as my heart pitter-pattered in my chest, like a timed bomb ready to explode.

Hawke was the epitome of a rock star. From his tight jeans to his fitted white tee to the way his hair was wavy and wild. He was dark and dangerous, intimidating yet enticing.

He threaded his fingers through my hair and tugged, exposing my neck. When his warm tongue licked a path up the side of my neck, I released an uninhibited moan.

I closed my eyes as he lapped kisses up and down my neck. With his free hand, he cupped the front of my shirt, stroking my breast, causing my nipple to pebble against his touch.

And, right then, I knew I'd let him take me. I knew I'd throw my no-one-night-stands rule out the window. It had been a three-year-long dry spell, and I suddenly wanted to end that dry spell with him tonight.

I wanted sex. I wanted Hawke. I wanted to feel wanted.

Chloe was right; I didn't need to overthink things. I'd never had a one-night stand, but there was a first time for everything, right?

And maybe I was in denial, but my last two relationships had ended badly, so this was exactly what I needed. A one-night fling. I wasn't looking for a relationship, and I sure as hell wasn't dumb enough to think this was going to end in anything more than pure, uninhibited, raw sex.

With a sudden need, I grabbed the edge of his shirt. I wanted to feel the firm span of his stomach beneath my fingertips. His skin was taut and perfect.

When I grazed his bare skin under his shirt, he shifted and captured my lips with his. His tongue was hot and insanely talented as it intertwined with mine—no hesitation, no restraint. It was as if, once he'd sensed my change in mood, it unleashed the sexual beast inside him, and he only advanced with more fervor.

I moaned into his mouth, and my hands moved to undo the buckle of his belt. There was no stopping now, not when my body was on fire.

In one swift movement, he stood, bringing me up with him and not breaking contact. My legs wrapped around his waist as he walked backward, holding me by my ass, pressing me against his growing erection.

I pulled back and stared into blazing emerald-green eyes. "Where are we going?" I asked, gripping the tips of his hair.

"I want to fuck you on the bed," he said, his tone husky, horny, hot.

"Romantic," I joked.

He bit my lip. *"I'm going to love you and worship every inch of your body."* Then, he continued whispering the lyrics to "Love You Hard," one of their Grammy Award-winning hits. There was no inflection in his voice as he recited the words to one of the best-written love songs of all time.

"Nice. Who did you write that for?" I asked, my voice breathless.

"For a woman I've never met before. For my future wife." He flicked his tongue against my lips. "Enough talking."

I closed my eyes as I threaded my fingers through his hair that ended at the base of his neck. I matched his kisses, tongue for tongue, heat for heat.

He gently guided me onto the bed. Through hooded eyes, his stare never wavered from mine as he lifted the back of his shirt and tossed it across the room. My mouth watered as I took in the art that covered every inch of his chest and arms. A real-life living mural of pure perfection stood before me. Black tribal art wrapped around both his arms and down his torso with colorful Chinese characters adorning each pec.

He tipped his chin. "Your turn. Off with it."

With all the lights on, my cheeks flushed, and I stilled, motionless beneath him. Nervousness hit me at the enormity of what was going to happen next. Us naked. Him inside me.

When I didn't move, he went on his knees on the bed and dropped his hands to the edge of my shirt, gently lifting it above my head and tossing it to the side.

He bent down and sucked on my breast through my lace bra. Thank the heavens I was wearing my pretty black undergarments. My head fell back as he sucked my nipple and bit down, the pain shooting straight to my core.

My breathing labored when his kisses trailed up my neck and back to my lips.

"I love the sounds you make." His voice was rugged and rough and on the verge of losing control.

Kneeling above me, he unbuttoned my jeans, and the anticipation was almost too much to take as I lifted my bottom, so he could tear off my pants. When he cupped my sex, wetness dampened my lace panty. My breathing accelerated as he slipped off his jeans, and his cock sprung free before he began stroking it.

My eyes widened, and a light sheen of sweat formed above my brow. Being fully in the light embarrassed me, for no other reason than feeling inadequate, given I knew he'd been with beautiful runway models before.

"Can you turn off the lights?" My tone was fragile and soft, opposite to how I'd wanted it to sound.

He paused and flipped the lights off along with the television. The only light in the room now was from the skyscrapers shining through the floor-to-ceiling windows.

The sound of a condom ripping had my pulse racing, my palms sweating, and my heart stammering. As I peered up at his glorious body, I swallowed and pushed down all that anxiety because today, for once, I would live in the moment.

He shifted above me, and a silent moan escaped my mouth as I felt him at my entrance.

"Wait," I said, breathless.

"What?" He sounded equally breathless.

"Uh . . ." Nervous butterflies stirred in my belly as the reality hit me hard. I was going to have sex with Hawke Calvin. My mind raced.

Would he know it'd been a while for me? What if I sucked in bed? Shoot, would this classify me as a groupie?

"Sunshine, I'm fucking hard as a rock over here," he moaned, his tone deeply desperate. Want was written all over his face. "Do you want this or not? Because I really want to be inside you."

"Okay," I whispered.

He moved my panties to the side and entered me without hesitation and without restraint, not even giving me a chance to let out a breath. I clenched my eyes as the fullness of him rocked inside my body.

He dropped his head into my neck and lifted my ass, so he could drive deeper. "Shit, please don't tell me you're a virgin. Because you feel like a virgin."

"No," I exhaled. "It's just been a while."

He pushed into me from tip to balls, and low moans escaped from his lips. My fingertips wrapped around his neck, feeling the sweat against his skin, as he pumped harder and faster and deeper into me with every thrust of his hips. My teeth clenched with the impact and the feel of his satin skin against mine.

"You feel so fucking good, Sunshine," he said gruffly. "So tight."

I had no words because there was no doubt that he wasn't a virgin.

He was screwing me raw, his movements animalistic.

A moment later, his thrusts intensified, and a familiar sensation began in the pit of my belly, like the first of a small spark at the top of a firecracker that was ready to explode.

"Hawke," I moaned, on the verge of combustion.

I was close . . . so close. He must have felt it, too, because he shifted and quickened his pace. With the pounding of his hips, I closed my eyes, and my toes curled as pure sensation ran through my body.

And then it happened.

Sparks. Explosion. Fireworks.

Hawke did not stop pounding into my flesh, causing the orgasm to last forever and ever, convulsion after convulsion. After one final thrust, he stilled and collapsed on me. My whole body was hyper-sensitive to touch as the sweat off his chest stuck to mine.

Holy wow.

He didn't move and was still lodged in me. We waited for our breathing to even out and our pulse to slow down.

A one-night stand in my twenties. There. Check. Done.

Extra points for having sex with the most attractive man on the planet, according to seventy-five percent of the female population.

He flipped over as his chest heaved from exhaustion. After he disposed of his condom in the garbage next to the bed, he turned on his stomach and conked out, his head still facing mine but his eyes closed.

I hugged the sheets closer to my chest, feeling uncomfortable in my own skin, not knowing what to do next.

Did I leave now or wait for him to kick me out tomorrow morning?

Then, he opened his eyes, still lazy, and extended his hand toward mine, intertwining my fingers with his.

"Sleep, Sunshine." His voice was groggy, tired.

I turned toward him and inched over. The heat of his body radiated against mine. I breathed him in, and for a moment, I basked in the glow of amazing sex.

I let what had just happened sink in. I was lying next to the man I had been drooling over since I was a teenager.

After a few more minutes, my breathing slowed, and I closed my eyes.

Tomorrow, I'd do the walk of shame, but tonight, I was going to sleep next to the sexiest rock star alive.

chapter FOUR

I COULDN'T SLEEP. WHO COULD blame me? I was in an unfamiliar place with a very familiar stranger.

I glanced at the digital clock on the nightstand and noted the time—three thirty in the morning. The noise of the partying had disappeared and been replaced by the hum of the air conditioner echoing through the room. I snuggled closer to Hawke, dimming the chill.

Sighing, I stared, openly gaping at the beautiful man beside me. His long eyelashes fluttered with each soft exhale.

I could pinch myself.

Last night, I had been like every other woman at his concert, one of the twenty thousand people screaming his name. And, last night, I had screamed his name for a totally different reason—glorious, gratifying sex.

I touched his cheek because I could and because I wouldn't have any other chance to do so. Thoughts of Chloe filtered through my head, and I slowly extracted myself from Hawke's hold to look for my phone. I snuck out of his bed and walked to the living area.

My feet brushed against the Persian rug underneath the low coffee table, and my eyes stopped on the gossip magazine on the table. Hawke's mother was on the front cover.

BETRAYED AND HURT BY HER ONLY SON!

Who knew what was real or what was used to sell papers?

I only knew what he'd gone through from the tabloids, that his mother was suing him for money. At one time, his mother had been his manager, but then Hawke had fired her. Hawke had never come out with a statement.

I glanced back at the bed where he was soundly sleeping. I guessed people with money weren't without their own problems.

I reached for my phone by the television and swiped at the keypad to read Chloe's texts.

I'm okay. Took a cab home. Don't worry about me. :)

Have fun and be safe, but most of all have fun!

That eased my mind, and I dropped my cell in my purse and slipped back into bed.

Automatically, warm hands encased my waist, bringing my internal temperature to rise.

"Where did you go?" Hawke lifted his head and peered up at me through sleepy, sexy eyes.

"I needed my phone."

He inched closer and buried his head into my neck, like a big, lean, toned teddy bear, and I couldn't help but smile.

I could get used to this.

But I shouldn't get used to this.

He was a rock star, and I was a pastry sous chef. He traveled the world. I'd only ever been to Canada. It would never work.

"Everything good?" His voice was rough, groggy.

"Yeah," I replied, all the while trying to talk myself down from my princess fairy tales, ones where I married the rock star.

"Good." His hand trailed lower until he cupped my sex.

I pulled his hand up. "Wow. No lead-up? Just going for the gold there, huh, buddy?"

He shrugged and started to draw kisses up and down my neck, which ignited a flame deep in my belly. There was no shame in his game. A game he knew very well.

"I'm still . . . I'm still recovering from the first round of after-shocks." It was hard to formulate a coherent thought in his vicinity.

His lips were silky soft against my skin. He didn't stop his advances. When his fingers entered my body, I grabbed his wrist, needing a time-out.

"Let's chat for a bit, shall we?" My husky voice didn't sound too convincing, but I pulled him up to face me anyway.

He groaned. I knew we had only a few more hours together, and I wanted him again—no doubt. But I also wanted to remember this morning for more than passionate sex. I wanted to *talk* to him because, soon, this night would only be a memory.

He kissed my mouth and drew back to assess me, the sly, crooked smile heavy on his lips. "We can communicate without words."

When he pinched my nipple under the blanket, I let out a moan.

"But I like using words. I'm an adult." I tried to lift the sex fog from my brain, but it was hard when I very much wanted the same thing.

He shook his head and inched closer to me, getting nose-to-nose.

My goodness, he looked glorious while half-asleep and horny.

"What do you want to talk about?" He propped his head on his hand while his other hand made circles across my ass.

"Your songs. Your goals. Your life." I wanted to know something deeper, something I couldn't read in the magazines, something no one else knew.

He scrunched his face. "This early in the morning?"

I counted down the hours until sunlight. Before I knew it, our moment together would be gone. "Yes."

"We play your game, but then you have to play mine." His devilish smile awakened every nerve in my body.

"Okay," I said nonchalantly, as though his games consisted of Scrabble and checkers.

"Go. Shoot. What do you want to know?"

"Do you write all your own songs?" I didn't know why, but I assumed he wrote all his music.

"I did." He averted his eyes, staring above me. He was masking something that he didn't want me to see.

"What do you mean, you *did*?"

"I used to, but I stopped a long time ago. I haven't written anything in years. Now, Cofi is the writer in our group. He's insanely talented."

"'Beautiful Girl'?"

"That's Cofi's."

"'Tuned Out'?" I started spitting out songs currently on the radio.

"No."

Disappointment seeped into my skin, the kind where you found out that the chocolate cake you'd been eating wasn't made from pure chocolate.

My smile faltered. "Oh."

There was an internal satisfaction to being an artist and being in charge of everything you produced and sent out into the world. It seemed wrong in a way, as though the songs he sang didn't really belong to him.

"Why did you stop?" I asked.

He shrugged, as if it didn't bother him at all. "Because Cofi . . . he's better at it, and it's kind of a habit now."

"Do you write at all anymore?"

He cocked his head, assessing my reaction. "Is this a deal-breaker for you?"

Deal-breaker for what?

I was afraid for him to elaborate, so I just said, "No, I'm just curious."

"Yes, I do still write my own songs." His fingers rested on my hip, the tips drawing circles. "Mostly when I'm depressed and need to let go of my feelings, but those songs will never be published."

Though his tone was casual, his words caused a pinch in my chest.

Was he depressed often? .

"Why not?" I had always been the annoying little girl who asked, Why? I guessed that part of me hadn't changed because I was still curious.

"Because I don't want them to."

Before I could stop myself, I blurted, "It's like he's the brains, and you're the brawn. It seems unfair that he doesn't get the credit." I bit my tongue, wishing I hadn't just insulted the biggest rock star to ever grace the planet.

Blunt honesty—another fault of mine.

"I'm not just the brawn, Sunshine. I *choose* not to write the songs. He writes the music, and I choreograph every tour. I approve everything—from the marketing to our clothes to every tiny detail when it comes to our brand. I'm the one who got us together." He raised his chin a tad, a fatherlike pride heavy in his eyes. "I'm the one who got our first gig. I'm the one who harassed every record company."

"I'm sorry." I didn't know their day-to-day. "But I don't understand why you wouldn't just release your work."

His jaw tightened, and he shifted uneasily from my one-too-many questions. "It's too personal."

"The stuff you write?" The question of *why* was on the end of my tongue, but I swallowed it back.

"Yes." Now, it was his turn to look away. He pulled back, and one hand ruffled through his hair. "I write for release. No one else needs to hear it."

"Is it about your mom?" As soon as the words left my mouth, I bit my tongue before another question could fly out.

His lips pressed together, his demeanor flipping like a light switch turning off. "Wow, Sunshine. You've got balls." He tipped back his head, his eyes hard. "That's a bad word around here. Everyone wants me to talk about it, but all I want to do is pretend that she isn't my mother. She checked out on me. Picked her dealers over her son and never looked back."

Though his voice was bitter, I sensed the hurt in his eyes, the vulnerability of his younger self. That pinch in my stomach heightened to unbelievable heights.

In that instant, I wanted to hold him, to comfort him, to let him know I knew where he was coming from.

"I'm sorry." I was. And, of all people, I understood.

"For what? You didn't do anything wrong. People should stop apologizing for that kind of scum." Anger seethed from his tone, and he glanced out the window, into the night sky.

"I can imagine." I knew what it was like to feel the burn from someone who had just checked out on your life.

His mouth slackened, and for a brief second, his eyes were unguarded, exposed again. Then, the moment was gone, fizzled into the air like smoke.

"No, you can't possibly understand," he said bitterly, jerking up into a sitting position. "You don't know how she is. She isn't a mother. She used me, and I'm still paying her off." He pushed his legs to the side of the bed, and without glancing in my direction, he said, "I'll tell Tilton to drop you off. You need to go."

I stared at the mural on his back, noting the perfection of tribal art that made up the words *Def Deception*. My face fell, and all of me wanted to wrap my arms around him and tell him I was sorry again, but that would only make things worse. Ultimately, I'd crossed some invisible line that I shouldn't have.

I stood and retrieved my clothes that were scattered on the floor. "I'm sorry." The words flew out automatically, and I cringed.

"Stop saying you're sorry!" he roared, turning toward me. His face pinched with irritation.

I flinched and slipped on my clothes and shoes, reeling in my own feelings because I understood. She'd hurt him. The tabloids made it seem as though his mom was the victim, but he was the injured one.

I was going to say more. I wanted to say that I was sorry he was hurting, that I was sorry I had stuck my nose into something that was none of my business. He was a stranger to me, as much as I was a stranger to him.

It still ached to talk about it, but I found the words coming out of my mouth anyway. I slouched on the bed and murmured, "My father abandoned my mother and I right before I went to college. Upped and left us for another woman. But, before that, he had torn my mother down, bit by bit, and before she . . ." My voice trailed off. I breathed through my next words, forcing down the ache in the center of my chest, biting back the lump in my throat. *"I'm sorry doesn't make it better; I get it. But maybe coming from someone who knows what it's like when your parent just leaves you behind . . ."* I shrugged, unable to finish.

Our eyes locked, and I read the ache and torment and memories in his eyes, a pain so familiar to mine that I had to tear my gaze away.

I slid my mini purse over my shoulder and walked to the door.

When my hand went for the knob, Hawke was already beside me, his eyes torn and hands at my waist. "Don't go," he said, whisper soft.

"Why?" My voice cracked with emotion, and I searched his face for an answer.

He could have picked anyone. I was sure women were camped outside the hotel, even in the wee hours of this morning.

His eyes broke right before he said, "Because . . . I'm lonely."

And then my heart cracked, split in two by his words. He was adored by millions around the world, admired by all those in his industry, yet he was lonely. It made no sense.

Nothing was ever as it seemed, was it?

His fingers found mine, warm and soft and pleading. "Stay." He let out a jagged long breath. "Tell me about him." There was a need in his eyes that told me how badly he wanted to hear my story.

I'd spoken to numerous counselors, but talking it out with people I could relate to had always helped the most. It was the best kind of therapy.

"I'll tell you about my scum if you tell me about yours." I threw him a weak smile.

His lips pressed together in a rigid grimace, and for a second, I thought he'd deny my offer, but he nodded and led us back into the room.

My stomach tightened in a double knot because I knew I'd have to recall memories I'd been pushing down for so long. I bit my thumbnail and sat on the edge of the bed, watching him as he went through the dresser. He threw one of his T-shirts in my direction, and I caught it midair.

When he went to the bathroom, I slipped out of my clothes, into his shirt, and under the covers to get comfortable.

He hopped back into bed beside me, and although we were both in the room, in the same bed, where I could feel the warmth from his body radiating against my skin, a familiar icy sensation spread through my heart. The chill formed every time I thought about my childhood. The distance between Hawke and me was palpable, like I could taste it, feel it, touch it.

If he was lonely before, I doubted I was making it better because I felt the same.

I held my breath and was the first to break the silence because I needed to get the words out. "He was verbally abusive over the years—not toward me, but toward my mom. When he lost his job, it got worse. I remember times . . ." I swallowed and paused but needed the next sentence to come out. "He'd be so out of it that I'd walk into a room, and he wouldn't even see me. So out of it, he couldn't even answer her when she asked what he wanted for dinner. He drank himself to oblivion every night. Every. Single. Night."

Anger filled his eyes. Eyes that held pain and rage behind his fame. "Why didn't you just leave, the both of you? Get up and walk out on him?"

My stomach hurt, physically hurt, but I knew this kind of ache would never go away. "Because I loved him; we both did." I tore my gaze away from his. My voice was soft as I whispered, barely audible, as if the words were only for me to hear, "And because . . . because she wouldn't leave. She didn't want to give up on him, and I didn't want to give up on her."

I'd seen my father destroy her until he'd left her in a pile of ashes, unrecognizable. She hadn't left him because she couldn't. Because her love was deep. Her love was unconditional. Her love was strong. But not strong enough to keep him from leaving.

I clenched my jaw. Good God, it had been years. Years since it had happened, yet the pain was still so fresh, like an open wound. And reliving the past forced me to rip the Band-Aid off, causing the hurt to surface, forcing me to see the blood.

It was only when I heard the hardness in Hawke's tone that I turned back to face him. "Everyone knows I emancipated from my mother when I was sixteen. That's no news. No one knows what she's like in real life." He ran one hand through his hair, sighing up at the ceiling, unable to look me in the eye. "She's sold her sob story to every tabloid outlet that'd pay her. *The good mother who helped Def Deception rise to greatness.*" He clenched his hands together, his knuckles white from the tension.

"She's telling everyone we had practiced in her garage, and when we hit it big, we kicked her to the curb." The distant look in his eyes had the hair on the back of my neck standing at full attention, like needles on a porcupine's back. "Did I ever tell my side? Like how, when we rose to fame and she had access to everything, she lived in excess. How she liked to shoot up in front of us and then beat me because I was her kid and she had the right. How about when she cut herself and almost committed suicide in front of me?" His voice shook with rage, the type of anger that could not be contained.

"Hell no, I didn't. Because it's none of anyone's fucking business. They all think they know my story . . . me." He pounded his chest. "But they don't. They don't! I don't owe anyone anything.

Not one fucking—"

I threw my arms around him, needing him to stop, needing him to calm down, needing him to forget, because I knew what anger could do. It could choke the life out of you and keep you from living and moving on. Even though it still hurt, I'd stopped being angry with my father a long time ago. What was left in his wake was only the raw pain and sadness. He had hurt my mother, and my mother had wronged me in ways she didn't even realize.

I pushed those memories down. All the way down to the pits of hell because that was where I had to go when I recalled those memories.

His body was tense, but I held him in silence because, sometimes, that was all anyone needed. Slowly, his shoulders relaxed, and he ducked down to rest his chin against my shoulder.

When his lips touched my skin, I peered up at him. He lifted his head and kissed me, slow and sensual at first but building into a roughness that scorched my insides.

When he guided me onto my back, I didn't resist because I knew this was what he needed. And maybe I needed this, too. We both needed to forget.

I STOPPED IN FRONT OF my apartment and let out a huge breath. Hawke's bodyguard, Tilton, had dropped me off. With the limo gone, I took in my five-story apartment building.

Last night almost seemed like a crazy dream, but I knew it wasn't because every single one of my muscles hurt from exhaustion—or what I'd like to say was *sexhaustion*.

With a tired but happy sigh, I walked through the door, took the elevator to our floor and strolled to our unit. When I opened the door to our place, Chloe stood from the couch, eyes wide and questioning. Voices from the television played in the background.

"And? So?" Her eyes gleamed with the kind of excitement seen in the eyes of a child, full of questions and wonder.

But what I had to tell her was not for children to hear.

I threw my purse on the counter and tried to bite back my grin, but failed. "We had mind-blowing, spine-tingling sex, and I'm glad you convinced me to give the no-attachment experience a try."

She squealed and tightly gripped my hand like a vise. That was what best friends were for, after all. She tugged my hand toward the couch with such force that I almost tripped.

"Everything. I want to hear everything—from what he smelled like to what you two talked about. Every single thing!"

I pulled my knees up, hugging them against my chest. There were some things I couldn't tell her, of course. The intimate details that Hawke had revealed were not meant to be repeated. "He was sweet and rough and talented and, O-M-goodness, so unbelievably hot. I still can't believe last night happened."

If Chloe had not been there to witness it—well, the before-sex part—I doubted anyone would believe me.

She shook her head and straightened. "The sex! I want to know about the sex."

I shifted with unease and bounced on the cushions of our gray microfiber couch. Usually, I was always on the receiving end, hearing about Chloe's great adventures in the sack. Now that it was my turn to share, my cheeks warmed.

"I don't have a lot of experience in this field, but yes"—I nodded profusely—"he made me come multiple times." I wasn't an easy comer either. I had faked it one too many times with my ex-boyfriends, but Hawke . . . I knew he was experienced because sex with him had not disappointed.

"Is he going to call you?" she asked, breaking me from my sex-filled thoughts.

I chewed on my bottom lip and let out a low sigh. "He has my number, but I'm not going to hold my breath." I sounded confident, but it broke my heart to hear myself say those words out loud.

I shouldn't pretend that it was more than it had been, and I shouldn't hope for more, but I was *me*. Because of my broken home and messed up childhood, hope was all I had. Marrying Hawke Calvin and sailing into the sunset would never happen, so I needed to stop believing that it would.

Changing the subject, I tilted my head and asked, "Hey, what happened with Cofi?"

She reeled back, her eyes narrowing, her smile disappearing. "That asshole invited another girl to play, and sorry"—she screwed her face and wrinkled her nose, as though there were garbage nearby—"I don't share."

Apparently, Cofi was a player, big and bad and without apology. I'd known guys like him in high school. Those were the type Chloe had always been attracted to, not me. I preferred the good boys who ended up breaking my heart.

"What a jerk."

Cofi was a cocky jackass. Cliché as it seemed, all rock stars were probably the same, but I'd like to believe Hawke was different.

"Yeah, he is, but forget Cofi. We're talking about Hot Hawkey." She pinched my side so hard, it made me yelp. "I'm pinching you, so you know it actually happened. You, my best friend, slept with the lead singer of Def Deception." She lifted her hands in the air. "Touchdown, girl! If this is the last thing you do on earth, you have it made! *Ah!*"

I chuckled. "I highly doubt I have made it quite yet." As great as last night had been, I had higher hopes than banging an über-hot rock star. "But, yes, it's definitely something I am going to tell my grandkids someday." I squeed, my knees bouncing with excitement.

"Their ears will bleed!"

"That's the goal." I laughed, and we high-fived. "And, now, real life hits. I have to get to work in a few hours."

She groaned, and I scrunched my face and then dragged my butt into the shower.

Back to reality.

chapter FIVE

WHEN I FINALLY ARRIVED AT Sheldon's Italia, I shuffled into the locker room, slipped on my white apron, and strolled into the kitchen. The sight of the kitchen—the white linoleum flooring, the stainless steel industrial appliances, a hanging rack with dangling pots and pans, and three oversized sinks.

I let out a happy sigh. I loved this place. I loved the people. I loved my job. This was where my life was. This was where I shone as Samantha Clarke, pastry sous chef extraordinaire.

Baking had been my thing with my mother during her better days. She had been my partner in crime when we set up our make-shift bakery in our kitchen. It was our way to make a few extra bucks, selling baked goods to our neighbors.

"Yo, Sammy, you made it." Todd's voice snapped me from my thoughts.

I glanced down at my watch, noting I was only a few minutes late. "Yes, and I'm ready to rumble." I averted my gaze.

Last time I'd seen Todd, he'd asked me out on a date, which had caught me by surprise. I'd told him I didn't want to mix business with pleasure since we worked together, but that still hadn't made anything less awkward between us.

"That's my girl." The way he'd said it dampened my mood.

If I could wish for a spark between us, I would. But my insides didn't flutter every time he talked, my knees never felt weak when he walked into a room, and he didn't give my heart the bumpety-bumps.

"Is it crazy busy out there?" I asked, finally looking up.

As he was over six feet tall, I had to crane my neck to look up at his face. His short brown hair was parted to the side, his glasses at the tip of his nose. "Not too bad."

With one weird wave of my hand, I said, "Okay, better get to it before boss man, Kyle, has my head." I smiled and walked toward my station.

With everyone busy working, I heard the chaos of the kitchen—the loud voice of the head pastry chef, the clanging of pots and pans, the fryer sizzling in the background, and the shuffle of people's feet. Every scent imaginable bombarded my senses—garlic and ginger and basil and rosemary. When I moved closer to my station, the scent of cinnamon, pumpkin spice, and cocoa entered my nose.

I smiled. The happy mojo that always hit me when I was here filled my veins. All that time baking in my mother's kitchen and at the local culinary school had led to this.

Candice—my cute coworker with her long, curly black hair and hips that didn't lie—stepped into my line of view, handing me a list of orders. "I'm cooking a fresh batch of chocolate chip cookies. Take them out in five minutes. I'm all caught up, so I think you're good with the new orders."

Candice was also my partner in the kitchen. She was the first sous chef on duty. When she wasn't working, I was, and vice versa.

"Sam! I need two chocolate soufflés!" someone yelled in the background.

"So"—Candice smiled with her natural full cheeks, as though she were storing food for the winter like a chipmunk—"did you find a date?"

I walked to the fridge where I took out two ready-made soufflés and placed them in the oven. Candice had prepared the soufflés in batches this morning.

"No, not yet. I think I might go stag." I shrugged. "Who knows?

Maybe I'll meet someone at your wedding." A part of me even hoped for it.

The heat from the oven caused me to sweat, which dampened my shirt, and I swiped my hand over my forehead to wipe off some of the sweat forming at my brow.

"I found my wedding dress." Her eyes lit up with an inner glow.

Candice had known her fiancé forever—since high school—and they'd been engaged for almost a year.

I reached for her hand and squeezed tightly. "That's awesome, Candice. You'll make one beautiful bride."

The smile she sported was contagious.

Her upcoming nuptials was the highlight of the restaurant's year. Practically the whole cook staff had been invited. The event would be black tie. Everyone here had been talking about what they were going to wear. Me, on the other hand? I still didn't have shoes to match a gown I'd bought online.

"I seriously cannot wait," she squeed.

"Sam!" Kyle peered over in my direction. "Those soufflés?"

I gave him a thumbs-up. "Already in the oven, boss."

Kyle, the gray-haired old man who was my boss, tipped his chin and continued along.

My phone buzzed in my back pocket. When I saw the text from the unknown number, I almost dropped my cell from shock.

I'm thinking of you, Sunshine.

I would have sworn on my dead grandmother's grave that I would never hear from Hawke again. Maybe I had hoped, but here he was, texting me.

My shaky hands gripped the phone tighter, so I wouldn't drop it. I texted him back with a smiley face.

I'm awfully tired at work because of you.

Hawkeypoo, I silently added.

Goodness. I'd just nicknamed him.

This was bad. Way bad. Over-the-top bad.

Do not have hope, Samantha. Do not have hope.

Candice snapped her fingers in front of my face. *Snap. Snap. Snap.* "Earth to Samantha."

I blinked back to the present and stuffed my phone back into my pocket even though I was holding my breath, hoping it would buzz again.

Candice bounced on her toes. "Before you know it, it will be here—the wedding."

I nodded, but I had checked out of the wedding talk. I needed to immerse myself in work today because I didn't want to be *that* girl, waiting for a call that wasn't going to happen.

Been there. Done that.

"You going shopping for your shoes soon?" she asked.

"Maybe after work," I said distractedly.

Maybe that would also keep my mind off a certain rock star who was still in Chicago.

AFTER WORK, I ENDED UP at the dreaded department store. I blinked as I took in the rows of shoes lining an aisle at Nordstrom. Shoe shopping was more Chloe's forte, not mine.

I had one real pair of heels, and they had green polka dots. Quirky and fun. I'd worn them with my floral dress for my high school graduation and rocked them well. My favorite pair of shoes was my yellow Converse that I wore nonstop, but I couldn't wear those to a wedding.

So, seeing all these shoes at once, in every color and possible style, made me want to hide in a corner and cower.

"Seriously, can I just go up to a salesclerk and say, *Hey, I want a pair of black heels?*"

Chloe laughed on the line while I lifted my shoulder to hold the cell against my ear.

"Sorry, babe," she said. "I wish I could be there to help you out. You're like a lost kitten, aren't you? You could've waited for me."

"I just want to get this over with." I lifted a black pump and compared it to another black pump right beside it. There was no difference. "I give up, Chloe." I was tired and shoe-shopping defeated. This was pointless.

"Buying shoes should not be a horrendous ordeal, friend. What you need to do is get a sales attendant to help you. Try them on, okay? And walk around in them. If you're going to be shaking your booty at the wedding, make sure you can, at a minimum, walk in your shoes."

Chloe knew all, I swore.

I peeked up and scanned the area, looking for anyone with a name tag, when I spotted a short redhead carrying a stack of shoe-boxes. Already, I was on a mission to be her best friend, her next customer.

"Okay. Will do. I'll call you later." I ended the call, stuffed the phone into my purse, and rushed toward the salesclerk before someone else reached her. "Excuse me?"

She lifted her head from the pile of boxes in her arms. "I've got four more ahead of you, sweetie."

My shoulders wilted with disappointment, and I found myself pouting, which was so unlike me. My eyes perused the area, but practically every salesclerk was assisting other customers.

I huffed. If it were any other person than Candice, I'd be sending a gift and a card and calling it a day.

"Hi, do you need assistance?" a male's cool voice echoed from behind me.

I turned and swallowed back the next words that I had been about to say. My breath caught at the male's compelling warm brown eyes, the confident set in his shoulders, his boyishly good looks, and his J.Crew/Gap style. . He had a little wave to his short dark hair, but what was amazing was his smile—a Crest White, double-dimple smile.

"Do you work here?" I asked, crossing my fingers, my toes, and practically my eyes.

Both dimples deepened on his cheeks, and he pointed to his name tag. "Josh Stanton." He studied me a little before letting out a slow, low breath, his eyes taking me in.

"But you're a guy." I cringed at my response.

No shit he was a guy. Great. Now, I sounded like a total idiot. Guys could obviously work wherever they wanted. What a sexist comment.

He dropped his eyes toward his package. "Yeah"—he nodded—"I'm pretty sure of that."

My ears warmed. "I mean, do you know anything about women's shoes?"

He let out a rich masculine laugh. "I do work here."

His smile widened, and then so did mine, which curbed the uneasiness in my stomach. I wasn't usually attracted to guys in suits, but he held a certain appeal, as though he'd just walked out of a *GQ* spread. He sported a smile like he had no cares in the world, his happy aura contagious.

I straightened my shoulders, ready to get down to business and check one more item off my list. "Okay, so I need black shoes."

He glanced around the area, his eyes searching the rows and rows of shoes. "Is there a certain brand? Heels? What height?" His eyes locked back on mine again.

"Yes, to a heel. Two and a half inches? And I'm planning to wear them for a wedding." I hoped that was enough information to get me going.

"Yours?"

I sensed disappointment in his eyes, but maybe I was imagining it.

"No, a friend's. It's a black-tie event. I'm wearing black. Is that weird? Black to a wedding?"

"I think you'll be okay." His eyes raked me in, as though he were committing every one of my features to memory, and slowly, his smile dimmed. Another small exhale escaped him.

I shied away at the intimacy of his stare, dropping my gaze to my yellow Converse.

"Well then, let's look around. First, give me your hand," he said.

I blinked at his outstretched fingers. "What?"

"I can determine the size of your shoe by your hand size."

His face turned serious, but I'd never heard of such a thing.

"Whatever . . ." I clasped my hands together against my stomach, protecting them from his touch.

He curled his fingers forward, urging me to comply. "I'm being serious. You can measure your waist by the size of your neck and your shoe size by the size of your hand." He looked amused but still totally serious.

"Really?" I scrunched my nose, but I decided to trust him, so I placed my hand in his.

He flattened our palms together, his palm over mine. My skin tingled where it touched his, and I wanted to jerk my hand back, the feeling oddly intimate for buying shoes.

"Wait." He took his thumb and lightly traced the inside of my palm, inching up to brush against the inside of my wrist.

The movement was soft yet weirdly sensual. Our eyes locked as his thumb rested on my wrist, just above my racing pulse.

And my whole world seemed to stop. The people shopping around us, the noise, the time—it all fuzzed to a blur in the background. It was as though a spotlight was focused on just the two of us.

For a brief moment, I drowned in his eyes, noticing how his warm-brown irises had specks of green in them, submerging in their depths. I couldn't help but compare the differences to Hawke, whose beauty was instant and ruggedly hot compared to this stranger in front of me.

Josh's appeal wasn't like that. You would notice him at first glance, but the longer I stared at him and took him in, two words formed in my brain. Not hot, but *beautifully handsome*.

"What's your name?" His voice came out barely above a whisper, his breath gentle and soft.

He radiated a vitality that drew me in like a magnet, a force that had me leaning toward him.

I inhaled deeply and slowly retrieved my hand. A coldness hit as soon as I withdrew my hand from his. "Samantha." My heart beat louder in my ears, like a clock ticking.

"Size seven and a half?" He smiled, dimples on display.

And then I reciprocated. It was as if, when Josh smiled, there was no way I couldn't. The gesture was automatic.

His smile snapped me out of my semi daze. "Wow, Mr. Josh. I'm impressed."

He was spot-on with my size.

"You should be." He smirked. "I totally pulled that out of my ass. You can't tell a person's shoe size from the size of their hand." He looked just a bit embarrassed for admitting his game, but in the next second, his features relaxed, and he laughed.

"You tricked me?" I laughed along with him.

I shouldn't have believed that crap, but he'd said it with such a straight face.

He shrugged, unapologetic. "I just wanted to see if your hands were as beautiful as you were." He turned away, as though he wasn't supposed to let that comment slip. "And they didn't disappoint, Miss Samantha. They didn't disappoint."

The blush from my cheeks spread to the tips of my ears, and I was glad he couldn't see.

"Follow me," he said. "We've got shoes to shop for."

This was where you didn't judge by looks alone. His appearance screamed seriousness, good boy, guy next door, but he was a jokester through and through. Not to mention, a big flirt with his shoe-size game.

He gestured to a plush bench. "Sit down, Princess. I'll be back."

He sat me next to a bunch of black pumps, and I dropped to the seat.

A little later, he emerged from the stockroom with a stack of boxes. Shoe after shoe, Josh kept on pulling out more from the back. Just when I thought that I'd found the pair, he'd tell me he had another for me to try.

"I think you're having fun doing this." I tugged on another pair—black platforms with a red bow in the middle.

"Fun?" he asked, face set, tone serious. "This is my job. Fun and work don't mix."

"Uh-huh. Sure," I said, my voice heavy with sarcasm.

When he headed away for another pair, I groaned. "Seriously, Josh, the salesman, please! I just want a pair of black shoes." The whine in my tone could rival a toddler's. I was butt-tired from my rock-star experience last night, then work, and now, shopping. I was ready for bed.

"What's your date wearing to the wedding?" he asked.

"I don't know how that's relevant."

His dimple set deep on his cheek. "See, that's where you're wrong. Whatever he wears has to match whatever you wear, and shoes matter." He nodded toward my platforms. "Say he's wearing a red tie. Then, the shoes you're wearing now would match perfectly."

"Well then, issue solved. I don't have a date. I get to wear whatever I want."

He leaned in, so close that I could smell the mint on his breath "So, what do you want me to wear for the wedding?" He winked, playing for cute.

I tried to bite back a smile but failed. "That was smooth. Are you this debonair with all the women you sell shoes to?" I guessed, last night, I had improved my previously nonexistent flirting skills. "You got the sale. You don't need to use your best lines on me."

He laughed and averted his eyes, seeming sheepish, his game a little off. "I'm not usually this upfront."

When his stare met mine again, his smile faltered, and the noise around us quieted to a light hum. What filled the noise was a shared intimate stare between us. His eyes were compelling, magnetic, and familiar, as though I knew him from somewhere, but he was a mere stranger.

I swallowed hard, and my pulse picked up speed.

Breathe, Samantha.

I cleared my throat and broke us from this trance we were both under.

With his pointer finger, he tapped his chin and tilted his head. "I have the perfect pair." He walked past me to the back of the store, behind the register.

A moment later, he strolled back, holding a black shoebox. The white lettering on the box could have been a designer name; I had no clue.

He knelt down in front of me and trailed his skilled fingers down my calf. His strong hand cradled my ankle and slowly slipped off the previous black heel. I swallowed hard, letting out a long, silent sigh, from the sensual nature of his tender touch.

After he opened the box, he took out the oddest-shaped pair of shoes I'd ever seen. "Here's your shoe."

When he slipped it on my foot, I flinched from the coldness, but he rubbed my ankle, bringing warmth back to my foot.

"It's a glass slipper," he said, his brown eyes staring at me.

The corner of my lips tipped up, and a low laugh escaped. "And let me guess; you're supposed to be my Prince Charming?"

"How did you know?"

My insides swooned a little because he was just that adorable. "I bet you have a book filled with those pick-up lines. You played the superhero when you were younger, didn't you?"

He laughed. "Not really, more like the villain. I used to paint my face and pretend I was The Joker from *Batman*. But you . . . I bet your childhood bedroom was filled with stickers of Cinderella and all the other princesses."

I shrugged. "Yeah, me and every other little girl in the whole world."

I did believe in fairy tales, even after everything I'd gone through.

Fairy tales had been my escape as a kid, what I'd hung on to. My parents' story had been made for the books, their own little fairy tale—until it wasn't. But . . . but what if it was all for nothing? That all this hope deep inside would only end with tragedy. I was sure my mother would never have predicted that my father would leave her for another woman.

"What if none of that stuff ever happens? What if I don't believe in all that bullshit?" I wasn't able to hold back the thoughts in my head.

"Ridiculous," he scoffed. "What kind of woman doesn't believe in fairy tales?" There it was again—this undeniable connection, like an electric wire strung between us. "Maybe you haven't met your Prince Charming yet."

My breath caught, jammed in my throat like a piece of bread. The very air around us seemed electrified.

"What are you doing tomorrow?" he asked, hope in his eyes, the very same hope that was terrifying me right now.

I blinked. "What?"

He shifted, looking a little nervous now, but he blurted out, "Forget tomorrow. What're you doing for forever?"

The corner of my mouth lifted, slowly at first, and then the smile turned into a full-on chuckle. His corny question made my lips twitch. "Please tell me you don't roll these lines out to every girl who's shoe shopping?"

His eyebrows scrunched together. "No. No, I don't actually." It was as though he were speaking to himself.

With one hand on my heart and the other one fanning myself, I said, "So, I'm special, Josh Stanton?"

He stood and extended his hand. "Special? Yes. Beautiful? Definitely."

His stare never left my face, even when I slipped out of the glass slipper, almost forgetting it was on my foot.

I picked up the black shoes with the red bows. "I'll take these." My ears burned from his intimate stare that made me want to kiss him and dart away, like a girl playing Spin the Bottle.

"You never answered my question," he said.

I smiled, and my eyes dropped to the ground. I was never one for rejection—on the receiving or giving end.

"That was on purpose." I walked to the register, and he followed. "I can't."

"Are you not into men who sell shoes by night and are in law school by day? Are you only into the rich and famous rock-star type?"

I staggered to a stop and studied his face, wondering if he had intel.

Had he been at the hotel last night in the mass of people?

No. It had to have been a random comment.

His voice sped up as I approached the register. "Are you dating someone?"

Seriously, things like this never happened to me. Two good-looking men asking me out in a matter of a day? That was Chloe's life, not mine.

If I looked into his face one more time, I'd most likely give in. "Maybe," I said. I wasn't dating anyone. But it didn't feel right, jumping from a one-night stand into a date with someone else.

When his gaze met mine, my heart turned over and over again, like a gymnast doing cartwheels.

After a beat, he released one low whistle. "Whoever he is . . . he's one lucky guy." He set my shoes on the counter, still smiling, but there was a hint of disappointment in his eyes. "It was nice meeting you, Samantha."

"You, too," I said softly. "Thanks for helping me."

I went to shake his hand, but he brought his lips to the top of my hand instead.

"Have a great night." And then he winked and was gone.

After I paid, my eyes did a search of the area, secretly looking for the boyish salesman with the killer smile, but he was nowhere to be seen.

With a sigh, I swung my bag over my shoulder and walked casually out of the department store and onto the street, heading for the bus, when my phone rang in my pocket. Again, it showed up as an unknown number.

I never picked up for unknown numbers, but this time, I picked up on the first ring.

"Hello?"

"Sunshine."

Loud music blared in the background. The bass and chaos of people filled my ears.

"Hey." I tried to sound cool and collected, pretending like my heart hadn't just leaped from my chest, onto the floor, and back again.

When a rock star you'd just slept with told you he'd call, you were supposed to believe he wouldn't. Even with my little girl hopes, I never believed he'd call for real.

"What're you doing right now?" he asked.

"Shopping."

"Something for me?" There it was—the flirtatious tone in his voice that turned my breathing erratic.

"Do you need something?" I asked, flirting back.

"You." Blunt, no hesitation, no humor, no shame.

Silence filled the air between us. He must've ditched whatever party he was at or moved to somewhere quiet because the ruckus around him ceased.

"Sunshine, come to my concert tonight. It's the last night I'm in Chicago." His voice dropped, subtly sweet. "I got you and your friend VIP tickets, front row."

Don't hope. Don't. He'll break your heart.

"I can't. I have to work tomorrow." I looked to the sky and threw up one hand. I couldn't believe those words of rejection had flown out of my mouth.

Wow.

"You had to work today. What's the big deal?" His voice turned seductively soft. "Don't you want to see me?"

If I saw him, I knew what we'd be doing tonight.

"Do you want me to beg, Sunshine? That's not my usual style, but I would. For you."

I closed my eyes and tried to block out the way the sound of his voice affected me, but I was failing. Failing and falling for a rock star.

Chloe's life theme rang loudly in my head.

You only live once. Don't live for anyone else.

I had skipped part of my childhood, functioning as a mother to my own mother. Chloe was right. I had come to Chicago to start anew and follow my dreams. There was no reason I couldn't have fun along the way.

I found myself agreeing to his little get-together simply because I wanted to see him. "Okay."

I didn't know how long this ride would last, but I wanted to hang on for as long as I could.

"Good," he said.

I could sense the smile in his voice, his signature crooked smile.

"I'll have Tilton pick you up at eight. Be ready."

"Sure." I bit my bottom lip, still shocked at the thought of seeing him again.

"I cannot wait to see my Sunshine."

My heart skipped a beat at the *my*. I wondered if he'd meant that or said it as a slip, but his nickname reminded me of that classic childhood song. The way he'd said it, however, was anything but innocent.

chapter SIX

TILTON PICKED CHLOE AND I up exactly at eight. I stepped into the stretched limo in jeans, a pink top with a large flower embroidered on the side, and my favorite yellow Converse. Chloe, on the other hand, was dressed to the nines in her sparkly tank top and designer DKNY jeans.

The limo was fit for a party of ten. Wraparound leather couches spanned both sides of the vehicle. Sporadic white LED lights on the ceiling created an ambiance, as though we were sitting under a dark night filled with stars.

I'd be lying if I said I wasn't nervous. I bit all my nails down to the flesh, and by the time we strolled into the United Center, I was about to throw up.

When I'd done the walk of shame this morning, never in a million years had I thought I'd ever see him again. Never, ever. But here we were, being ushered past two sets of double doors and through security by Hawke's head bodyguard himself. The bald white man had shoulders bigger than boulders. He was a walking brick wall.

Tilton did not smile, nor did he speak or make eye contact unless Hawke gave him orders. The most I ever got from him was a tip of his chin, as if that were his way of saying hello.

"What time's the concert?" I asked. You couldn't say I wasn't trying to crack this guy's wall of silence. "Are they backstage? Or are they on the stage now?"

Chloe rolled her eyes, as if telling me there was no point in trying.

Chloe and I were two steps behind him. She walked with a smoothness to her step while I was trying not to trip in my Converse. It was amazing—what Chloe could do in heels. I bet she could run a marathon in stilettos.

"So, what's the next leg of their tour?" I pressed.

Still no response.

Despite our efforts, Tilton forged forward, and we trailed behind him and into the massive arena.

The crowd was chaotically loud, almost deafening.

The lights from the stage blinded me, and when he led us up the aisle to the front, my pulse ticked up in tempo.

Here we were, front and center of the action, and I could see everything—the huge speakers, the amps, the microphones on stands. The stage was lit with multicolored spotlights shining at the crowds of thousands.

The third act was already onstage, and everyone was waiting for the main act—Def Deception. Though the room was cool around us, the scent of sweat permeated the air from the amount of people packed into the huge venue.

Chloe tugged my arm and screamed into my ear, "We're here! Can you believe this?"

I winced at the way her nails were digging into my arm but laughed at her giddiness.

No words came out of my mouth. I was shocked and silent and still. Although I had been at one of his concerts last night, I'd been sitting in the far corner of the arena, at the tippy top. Any higher, and my nose would've bled. But this? This was unreal.

Lights from camera phones and the strobes from the ceiling lit up the room. This was insane. My thoughts of Def Deception's star power were only amplified by taking everything in. The screams of adoring fans filtered through my ears. When everything went dark, the crowd roared.

Chloe jumped up and down in a continuous motion. "Oh my

God! They're coming out!"

I'd been the same way last night but not today. Today, my hand flew to my heart as I waited for their entrance. I knew why I was nervous. It was because of last night. Because I was here on his special request. Because I was seated in the front row, and he could see me, *really* see me, this time. I was no longer an adoring fan from afar but an invited guest, close and personal.

Last night, I'd been more excited, screaming at the top of my lungs, almost losing my voice.

Today, I was silent. Waiting with bated breath.

And then it happened.

It was like hearing them for the first time. One spotlight focused on the lead singer—*my* lead singer. Though he wasn't really *mine*, mine.

He belted out one single line, soft yet clearly and distinctively Hawke. The crowd's roar drowned out his voice, but it didn't matter because I could recite the lyrics to their Grammy-winning song by heart.

"Her face . . . is all I see."

God, his angelic voice . . . I still had yet to meet a living being not moved by his voice.

Then came the strings and the next line sung by Hawke. His tone was packed with emotion and slowly dragged out, as though they were drawing out the concert on purpose to torture their adoring fans.

Then, percussion chimed in. Cofi banged on the drums, and the music halted. If I'd thought the arena couldn't get any louder, I was dead wrong. I couldn't even hear my own thoughts.

My heartbeat raced in my chest in anticipation. My breaths became slow and impatient as I waited with the herd of thousands.

Then, the lights flashed on, and the whole band rocked the stage.

I was up on my feet, on my toes, straining my neck to see them, looking up instead of down. All my inhibitions disappeared, and

I joined in the fun. I was jumping and dancing and singing with Chloe, like we were one with Def Deception and were onstage as their backup singers.

Her wide smile matched mine. I was in utter awe. Pure wonder at how talented they were. Their music forced you to move, and Hawke's talented voice oozed everything masculine and sensual and rock star.

Suddenly, the noise quieted to a buzz, like a bee in my ear, yet I couldn't move because I was entranced with Hawke walking toward our side of the stage. His eyes found mine through the crowd, through the darkness, like the spotlight was on me instead of him.

In his cool and suave way, he bent down and sang to me. It was as though we were the only two people in the room, and no person or thing, even the chaos around us, could break our connection.

And then I died. I died and went to heaven in eternal bliss because the most famous rock star in the world had just sung to me.

I was sure he had done this a million times as he toured around the nation, around the world. And those women had probably swooned, and some might have fainted as he played the part and sang to them. Maybe it was all a part of the concert—the practiced, orchestrated part. But I hadn't seen him sing to anyone last night.

When he took my hand in his, my insides melted like milk chocolate.

Every part of me believed that, this time, maybe he wasn't playing a part. It wasn't just an act, and he was seeing me for real. Just maybe.

BEFORE THE LAST SONG, TILTON tapped my shoulder and nodded toward the door. It was our cue to leave, but I wasn't ready. I wanted to see Def Deception's grand finale.

He tapped my shoulder harder and leaned in. "We have to go," he said in his you'd-better-listen-to-me tone.

His bald head shone against the flickering strobe lights, and I wondered if he shaved his head or if he was just plain bald.

I glanced at Chloe. She looked oblivious, engrossed in the music and dancing. I reached for her hand and tilted my head toward the exit.

"Why?" Her pout could rival a three-year-old's sullen face.

"Because Daddy says we have to go." I pointed to the bodyguard, who was already standing by the exit, his eyes expectant. If we stayed in our spot, there was no doubt he'd carry us out, flailing and kicking and screaming.

"Don't get Daddy mad." My comment seemed to lighten Chloe's mood.

With one final boom and Hawke's clear voice thanking Chicago for their love, the concert was finished.

Insane was an understatement. We proceeded to the exit. Everyone rushed behind us, pushing to get out, like the place was on fire.

Someone shoved me forward.

"Hey!" I lost my footing and almost tripped.

Chloe gripped my hand as a stampede of fans charged toward the doors. "Oh my God, really? We're all headed the same way."

I tilted my head up to find Tilton a few feet ahead, in front of the door. He tried to make his way toward us, but it was like swimming against the craziest river current.

When he finally reached us, he wrapped one arm around my shoulders and one around Chloe, and then he led us toward the exit. His massive upper body was able to get us out, and he flashed his tag to another Hulk Hogan-looking guy, who let us pass.

Once we entered another set of double doors, everything turned eerily calm. It was as though, one second, we were running with the bulls in Pamplona, and the next, we were on the beach in utter silence with only a few people walking around.

Four people walked down the narrow hall, wearing the same VIP pass. I could only assume we'd made it backstage.

"I'm glad we made it out alive," Chloe sighed. "I mean, the concert was over. What the hell did everyone have to get back to?" She swaggered behind Tilton, trying to get his attention.

"They're going outside to wait for them," Tilton said.

I cast Chloe a look of victory, and she shrugged.

This was the most I'd heard him say without Hawke around. She had cracked the Hulk.

"Figures," she huffed, casting Tilton a look of camaraderie. "They're waiting to follow Def to their hotels. But they're not leaving anytime soon, right, Tilly?"

I laughed at her nickname for the seven-foot giant.

He ignored her comment, but she kept going. "I'm sure they have a secret passageway or some getaway car tucked underneath the arena, right, Tilly Willy?"

When she slipped her arm through Tilton's, I widened my eyes. *Balls. Chloe had balls.*

He stopped and turned toward her, and for the first time in my life, I saw Chloe cower.

"Do not call me that," he said in an even but surly voice.

Her face blanched, but when he turned back around to lead us down the hall, giggles escaped her.

I bit my tongue to prevent a laugh from escaping. My girlfriend was crazy, and I thought that was one of the main reasons I loved her.

When we rounded a corner, we stepped into what seemed like their dressing room. Clothes were scattered on the tables and on the couches and on the floor while others were neatly hung up on a rack. Against one wall, there was one long mirror and chairs, where I assumed the band got their makeup done or whatever they did to get ready.

"They'll be back. Stay put," he said with a flat and even tone, opposite to his eyes that said, *Cross me and die.*

When Tilton shut the door behind him, Chloe sprawled out on

the couch and threw her feet up, like she was in her own personal living room. "So, this is where rock stars get ready before their concerts? We should totally write their documentary."

"We'd make millions." I smirked.

Everything was white—from the walls to the couch to the round lights above the long mirror. Their dressing room was a large contrast to the beautiful artistry they created onstage.

When the door flew open, I jumped. One by one, the band filtered in—AJ, the bass guitarist; Max, the lead guitarist; Cofi, the drummer; Carl, on piano; and finally Hawke.

My heart beat so loudly in my ears that I thought it would bust an eardrum. When our eyes met and his sexy smirk was thrown my way, I was a goner.

His hair was slicked back and he was shirtless since he'd tossed it into the crowd. Some woman was one happy fan tonight.

He went straight for me without hesitation, and in front of everyone, he wrapped one arm around my waist, brought me in, and kissed my lips so deeply, I felt it to the tips of my pinkie toes.

My whole body tingled. There was no lead-in. Nothing. No words exchanged, just a slip of his tongue.

After a moment, he pulled back. "Hello again," he said, his tone suave, sexy, and smooth.

"Hey." Goodness gracious, I was not only starstruck; I was *Hawke*-struck. Sounded stupid, but it was true.

He threaded his fingers through my hair with one hand and gripped my waist with the other, embedding his fingers into the span of skin between my jeans and my shirt. I'd definitely have a bruise by morning, but it was worth it.

"What did you think of the concert?"

I feigned nonchalance and shrugged. "It was okay, I guess."

He pulled back a tad and laughed. "Just okay?"

I caught the sight of his glistening chest. Who knew if it was water or sweat? But, at the sight of him, my mouth fell dry.

"Well, I have to make up for that mediocre concert, don't I, Sunshine?"

I gasped when he lifted me by my ass and wrapped my legs around his waist.

He tipped his chin toward Chloe as his greeting, all the while walking with me attached to him. "We'll be right back."

I locked my hands around his neck to keep myself steady.

When he walked us into the restroom and shut the door, my whole body flooded with warmth, and my breath quickened.

He was going to take me, right here, right now, right away. It felt forbidden, knowing that everyone was just outside that door and they knew what we were doing.

He rested me against the sink, my butt touching the basin.

He nipped at the tender spot on my neck, not quite a bite but hard enough to leave my skin pink. The motion sent a current straight to my core.

"Just okay, huh?"

When my lower back hit the mirror, my legs automatically parted to make room for him. His fingers through my hair, his lips trailing down my neck, and his hardness rocking against me—it all ignited a fire in my belly.

Our lips made contact, and it wasn't a sweet reunion; it was the clashing of tongues, the hot breaths of mine against his, and the moans of wanting more.

And then I decided I didn't care about the people outside.

His fingers moved to the button of my jeans. "Why are you making this so hard for me?"

I didn't know if he was talking about the logistics of getting me out of my pants or his erection pressing against my thigh.

I lifted my bottom, and our lips lost connection for a brief moment as he shoved down my jeans.

Then, with a frenzy, we were back at it—hands on skin and lips on lips.

The rip of the condom wrapper and rustle of his zipper being pulled down was like the sound of the lunch bell.

Ding, ding, ding.

A hunger deep in my innermost being was about to be fed.

"I've missed you, Sunshine."

He entered my body without restraint and filled me with a possessiveness that made my insides quiver.

"Tell me how good I feel."

If he weren't inside me, I would've rolled my eyes.

Rock stars and their egos.

Loud noises escaped my mouth as he rocked against my body.

"Tell me," he urged, pounding into my center.

"You feel so good," I whimpered. It was the truth though his ego didn't need to be inflated any more than it already was.

As I fell deeper into ecstasy, my head rested back against the mirror as he slammed into my body, taking me higher and higher on one of the best rides of my life.

chapter SEVEN

MY HANDS WORKED THE TORCH, caramelizing the top of the crème brûlée order at Sheldon's Italia. The kitchen was busy with our regular Saturday patrons, but my concentration was shot.

Two weeks.

It had been two weeks since the last concert. Two weeks since the last time I'd seen Hawke. Two weeks since I'd heard from him. The last thing I remembered, he'd had his hands threaded through my hair and his lips on mine, and he'd been whispering lyrics to my favorite song in my ear.

If I didn't have the secret special cell phone that he had given me, I would have thought it was all a dream. All of it.

"I want to give you this phone. I'll contact you. One, four, three, one is the code to unlock the phone." Then, he'd winked.

In some ways, I sensed he was paranoid. He didn't want anyone knowing his number. He would have his security check his car and room before he stepped in. I guessed I would be the same way, if I were über-famous and everyone wanted a piece of me.

He had said he'd reach me through the cell, and because I was who I was and because I was like every other stupid, hopeful girl in the world, I'd been waiting for him to call, but all I'd received were random texts.

I tried to read into the random texts he had sent because I was a woman. Women did that—read into things that weren't there. But they were just that—random.

Pictures of nuggets and fries.

A landmark of the city he was touring.

Pictures of the audience from the stage.

At least he was thinking of me, but what plagued my mind was the not knowing if this was all it was going to be—random texts till the end of time. I wondered if I'd ever see him again.

There was a slight ounce of hope still, that tiny spark that said, even though he had his rock-star status, he'd want to see me again, and maybe I wasn't just another girl to him.

The sane part of my brain knew that was not remotely possible, given his lifestyle and the amount of time he spent on tour. So, I tried to water down that spark of hope, push it down where I couldn't dig it up and feel disappointment.

Maybe I had imagined it—our connection.

It was a mindless fling. That was it.

When I placed the desserts on the serving station, Anne, one of the waitresses, turned in my direction. Her eyes were frantic. "Some customer is totally freaking out over the quality of his steak. Good Lord, we have a high-maintenance one on seven. Do you mind taking the crème brûlées to table thirteen? It's the cutie's birthday and he requested crème brûlée, not cake."

I glanced down at myself, sweating and probably smelly. My hair was pulled back, my face shiny from the grease. Sugar covered my station and half of my apron. I was not in decent form to be seen by customers.

"We're down two waiters today. Please, Sam," she pleaded, rushing to the back of the kitchen before I had a chance to say no.

Aggravated, I huffed and balanced three plates in my hands. This was why I was a sous pastry chef and not a waiter. I had problems with coordination and balance.

With my hip, I pushed the door open and entered the restaurant. The chatter of the patrons filled my ears, but I concentrated on one thing—not falling. I'd done it before in the kitchen, and it wasn't cute.

As I focused on the plates in my hands, my feet did the walking to table thirteen. I'd been working at the restaurant long enough to know where each table was. The plates jiggled in my hands, and I walked faster to my destination, wanting to put the plates down on a sturdy surface.

When I made it there, I smiled, glad I hadn't face-planted on the floor with three plates of dessert. "Crème brûlées?" I asked, placing the plates on the table.

"Samantha?"

I glanced up and blinked, shocked at the familiarity in Josh's voice, though I'd only heard him speak once before.

Staring back at me was the handsome shoe salesman, seated right by a woman about his age and an older male who could be his father.

He did a double take my way and widened his eyes. "Sam," he said my name softer this time, as though he were uttering it to himself, like a word he wanted to repeat just because.

I was surprised that he even remembered my name.

"Hi." I waved.

The younger woman's eyes ping-ponged between us.

"You work here." His voice was low, as though he couldn't believe it. It wasn't a question. It was stated as a fact.

I chuckled nervously. "No, I just like to deliver food to tables for no reason."

And that was when he smiled. I remembered his smile—the one with two dimples, the one that was boyishly cute, the one that was contagious and had me automatically responding with a smile back.

I shifted my weight, rocking back on my heels, the awkward silence building between us. Then, I broke the quiet. "Happy Birthday!" I said, averting my gaze from his to the table. "Well, you guys enjoy."

I turned to leave, but he stood, and his voice stopped me.

"Wait." His tone was quiet yet firm, the words a command but sounding like a plea.

He blinked a couple of times and we stared at each other for a few brief seconds. My breath caught.

"Uh, so this is my sister, Casey." He motioned to said sister with one hand and then to the older man. "And my father, Albert the 3rd."

I nodded, unsure of what to say, but I could see the resemblance now.

Josh and Casey shared the same wavy dark brown hair, but Casey's was longer. Casey's eyes were a steel gray, like her father's. Josh must've inherited his deep brown eyes from his mother. Albert had a full set of gray hair, his face handsomely young.

"It's nice to meet you." I wrung my hands together and rubbed them against my dirty apron to curb the uneasiness in my chest caused by their curious looks and the intensity of Josh's stare.

Casey smiled a cheeky grin, like she was amused by Josh's awkward exchange with me. "How do you know each other?"

That seemed to break some of the tension, and I laughed, recalling our encounter. "Josh sold me a pair of shoes at Nordstrom."

When Josh grimaced and his father's smile slowly left his face, I knew I'd said something wrong.

Albert's eyes narrowed. "Wait, you're still working at Nordstrom? I thought they gave you a raise at the law firm."

Josh let out a soft sigh. "Dad, not now, please. It's my birthday."

"Happy Birthday," I said again but this time directly addressing the celebrant.

"Are you going to sing?" Josh asked, his eyes dancing with hopeful humor.

"I'd have the whole restaurant fleeing if I belted out a note. I don't really sing."

He playfully narrowed his eyes. "For some reason, I think you'd have a beautiful voice."

"Seriously, you don't even know how terrible I am. Like, really,

really bad." My nose wrinkled at the thought.

His smile turned sweet. "At least sit and join us for a minute."

"Yeah. Come join us." Casey pushed out the empty seat next to her. It was as if she were Josh's wingman.

This guy was relentless, and now, he had his sister on his team, too.

"Uh . . ." I stammered. "I'm sort of on the clock."

He interlocked his fingers, like he was saying a prayer. "It's my birthday."

With his pout and his big chocolate-brown eyes, I was a goner.

I glanced around, searching for someone to save me, to send me back to the kitchen, or to give me another order to deliver. You just didn't sit with the customers when you were on the clock—at least, not at this restaurant.

"Five minutes," he offered, grinning. "Unless you'd like to sing instead."

I plopped down on the chair faster than a dog playing dead. There was no way I was going to sing.

When he passed a fork in my direction, I shook my head. Eating at the table with him would've taken the awkwardness to another level.

"So, you're a waitress here?" Casey asked with a mouthful of crème brûlée. "Oh my gosh. This is divine."

Her eyes widened at my masterpiece, and my insides leaped. The best reward for a chef was the praise given for their food.

"No, actually, I'm the pastry sous chef."

Josh's eyes appraised me. It was the same look he'd given me at the department store, as though he were studying my every feature.

"Wow. I'm impressed. This is amazing stuff. I doubt I could replicate this at home." Casey picked up her fork, tilted her head to examine the dessert, and then proceeded to chow down like it were her first meal of the day. She nodded toward Josh. "Try it."

Josh's eyes never left mine as he took his fork and placed it in his mouth. "You've got talent, Miss Sam."

"What do you think, Dad?" Casey asked.

"I think I don't like the fact that Josh is still working at Nordstrom." Albert's face turned sour, sour like his tone.

The mood shifted in the air, the comedy gone, sucked up into the vent as quickly as it had come.

Casey's face dropped, and Josh straightened in his seat, his jaw tightening.

"Please, Dad," Casey said, placing her free hand on her father's.

Albert's dessert sat on the table, untouched. It didn't seem like he cared that I was sitting right here, in the middle of their family discussion.

His eyes were intense. "Josh, if you need money to cover rent—"

"No, Dad." Josh's eyes cut to his dad in a way that said, *Stop.* "I don't. I'm doing just fine."

"If you're doing fine and your internship at Statford is paying you as much as you say they're paying you—"

"Dad," Casey cut him off, "it's Josh's birthday, and Sam here would just like for you to try her crème brûlée."

Albert's eyes darted between us, his face masked with annoyance. After a beat, he stood. "Excuse me. It was nice meeting you, Sam." He dropped his napkin on his chair and left the table, leaving a cold chill in his former spot.

Casey's apologetic eyes met mine. She excused herself and followed right after, leaving Josh and me alone.

Alone in the awkwardness.

"I'm sorry about that." His eyes were unreadable, fixed, staring where his father had walked off.

"No, I'm sorry. I didn't mean to say something I wasn't supposed to—about your job. And I ruined your birthday," I said, which forced his focus on me.

"Sam, you didn't do anything wrong."

I pushed out the chair, ready to stand, when Josh's words halted me.

"So, those hands, they make dessert?" His disappointed eyes brightened as he reached for my hand and flattened my palm against his. It was as if he just wanted to touch me, just like the first day I'd met him.

My breath caught at the tenderness of his palm. My hand tingled where our skin touched, and I pulled back, like I'd been shocked with electricity.

"So, you're a lawyer and a shoe salesman," I joked, but my voice quivered.

Men didn't usually make me nervous—unless they had ultimate rock-star status—but Josh . . . he made me nervous just by the intimacy of his stare.

"Studying to be a lawyer," he corrected. "And, yes, top salesman at Nordstrom." He winked. "I also have a paid internship at a big law firm downtown that I work for twice a week."

"But your father doesn't approve?"

He just shook his head, a bit of that sadness back in his eyes. He blew out a breath and looked back at the direction where his father had stormed off.

I frowned, hating his subdued demeanor. "Why not?"

"He doesn't want me working more than I have to. Long story." He waved his hand, done with that topic.

"What kind of law?" I asked, curious about the law student/ shoe salesman with the most adorable dimples.

"Adoption and child services. That's a long story, too."

One dimple appeared, not two, and it was my short-term mission to make both reappear.

"Lawyer by day, super shoe salesmen by night, saving women from their footwear emergencies, one shoe at a time. Wow, I'm the one impressed."

Both of his dimples appeared, and my inner champion raised

her trophy.

"I'm more impressed by this crème brûlée." He scooped another bite into his mouth. "I've always wanted to learn how to cook. Are you taking students?" he asked between chews. "Apprentice, by chance? I'd be willing to change majors if you were the professor." He smirked, his mouth full, looking super adorable.

"Nope." I chuckled. "Can't take students if I'm going to be a student myself. I'm applying to a culinary school at the end of the year."

"Another culinary school?"

"Yeah, I went to my community college for culinary arts. Now, I want to go to a cooking school that specializes in pastries."

"How did you decide on culinary school?" he asked, mid chew.

I shrugged, and using his own words, I said, "Long story. How about you? Why adoption services?"

"So, that's how it is going to be now, huh? Tit for tat?"

My chin dipped once. "Yep, pretty much."

"My mother was adopted. You?"

"Really?" I blinked, surprised.

He was so transparent. It had been a long time since I'd met a guy so forthcoming, even before my first night with Hawke.

"I think that's sweet. Where is she today?"

"Not here." Something flashed in his eyes, as though he were hiding something. He nodded toward me, diverting the attention off himself. "Your turn."

The change of subject was abrupt, but I answered anyway, "I've always been into baking, even when I was younger."

"Did anyone in your family like to bake?"

"My mother." My chest tingled by the thought of her. Memories of us filtered through my head—throwing flour at each other, our cream countertops covered in white dust, pans everywhere, the scent of cocoa and vanilla permeating the air. I rubbed the center of my chest at the memory.

"If she's anything like you in the baking department, she's got major skills. You should start your own bakeshop."

We were supposed to . . .

A pang hit my chest, like a dagger. Hard and painful. "Yeah, that was the plan . . ."

I'd been baking since I got my first Easy-Bake Oven on my fifth birthday. Our love for cookies and brownies had turned into bake sales at school, which had turned into a small made-to-order business in high school that occupied our kitchen. We'd had dreams and our future ahead of us.

We'd *had*. Past tense.

"Shit. Are you crying?" He leaned in and started to hand me his napkin.

The memory of us seemed so fresh, so real, that I didn't realize I had started crying. I swiped at my eyes and tried to play it off. At times, memories would trigger emotions that I kept locked deep inside. Deep inside where no one had the key.

"No, sorry." I scrambled from my seat. "I have to get back to work."

He reached for my hand again, and his apologetic eyes met mine. "Whatever I said, I'm so sorry."

"It's fine. You just . . . you just reminded me of something." I retrieved my hand from his and evened my tone to hide the hurt. "Josh, I have to get back to work."

"I'm sorry." He placed his hand on his heart and the sincerest look crossed his features. "I feel horrible."

"It's fine." I swallowed down the pain and gave him a weak smile. "Happy Birthday." Then, I rushed to the back of the kitchen to collect myself before I went back to work, not wanting to relive the past that continued to haunt me every day of my life.

chapter EIGHT

AT TEN O'CLOCK, I THREW my white apron in the hamper and sighed. I leaned against the narrow gray locker, letting my head rest against the metal.

What a night. I had served as half-waitress and half-pastry sous chef. I'd never seen the restaurant this busy on a regular weekend, packed like cats in the only litter box in the house. It was as if it were a holiday weekend.

Laughter erupted behind me, and when I turned my coworkers, Todd, Candice, and Jim were already in their street clothes.

"We're going out for drinks. Wanna come?" Jim called out, reaching into his back pocket for his phone.

My body was bone-tired, and my muscles hurt when I moved. "Thanks, but no. I'm beat."

Candice slipped her arm through mine. "Come on." Her pout was on full display and almost convincing. "Pretty please?"

If I wasn't so tired, I'd have been up for anything, but my body wanted a hot shower and my warm bed. I didn't have it in me. "I would, guys. You know I'm always down but not tonight."

It hadn't helped my mood when I pulled the secret phone from my purse during my break to see no missed texts.

Waiting for nothing totally blows.

"I'll just text you guys if I change my mind."

"You sure?" Jim called out before backing toward the exit. He pointed to me and grabbed Candice's arm. "Let's go, slowpoke."

"Bye, Sam," Todd called out. "If you change your mind, text us, and we'll let you know where we're at."

When they left, my whole body slumped against the locker. Numerous things were flying through my brain on fast-forward. Work, Hawke, thoughts of my mother, and the fact that I had to get my shit together and get the recommendations I needed to apply to culinary school.

That was the sole reason why I had left my small town to move to Chicago. To escape memories of my family, to start anew, and because Chicago was where Le Cordon Bleu College of Culinary Arts was.

I needed to get in. Not only because it was my dream to have my own kitchen someday, but because it had also been my mother's dream for me. And maybe, just maybe, I felt that, by fulfilling my dreams, I'd be fulfilling it for the both of us.

Stepping out of the restaurant and into the clear, cool night, a little bit of the tension from earlier oozed out of me. Something about the scent of the fresh air and the twinkle of stars against the dark sky calmed my insides. It reminded me of our small town in Carbarny. The stars brought back memories of when Chloe and I would have a midnight snack in my backyard. I would be dressed in my princess pajamas while Chloe would be dressed like she was going to some fancy-schmancy dinner party.

I laughed internally. Some things never changed.

Chloe and I would feign sleep, afraid to get in trouble for being up too late, but that was when Mom would join us, bringing us freshly baked cookies and never forgetting the milk.

I inhaled deeply. It had been years since her death, and I couldn't remember the last time I'd cried. I'd come to terms with that part of my life through counseling and talking it over with Chloe.

I didn't know what had happened earlier at the restaurant—how being around Josh had sparked those memories of her.

I pulled my hair into a high ponytail, reached for my CTA pass in my purse, and texted Chloe that I was coming home. It was our protocol when I worked a late night. Girl code, safety, and all.

After a beat, she texted back with an, *Okay.*

As I walked toward the subway, a couple of cars whizzed down the street. It wasn't the normal traffic because all the restaurants were closed for the evening. I clutched my CTA card in one hand while my other hand dug deep in my pocket, gripping my pepper spray. I'd come from a small town where nothing ever happened, but in Chicago, I knew anything could happen.

My feet padded faster to the subway when, in my periphery, I saw a car trailing slowly behind me. There was not another car in the vicinity, only the one a few feet behind me.

The streets were eerily vacant.

There was a chilly black silence in the air.

In two seconds, I was about to book it like a crazy woman. That, or empty my whole can of pepper spray onto the driver's face.

"Cut it out," someone called out.

When I heard the car door slam, I didn't wait for them to drag my body into the car and abduct me. I booked it, like a bull was chasing me and I had a target on my back.

"Wait!"

I ran faster.

Wait for what? Them to attack? Were they crazy?

I turned the corner, but I heard the stomp of heavy footsteps trailing close by. Whoever was behind me was gaining speed and closing the gap between us. Beads of sweat formed at the back of my neck, and my breaths heaved in and out in exertion.

In the next second, I staggered to a stop and held out my mace to protect myself. "Don't you—"

"Sam."

I squinted under the overhead light. "Josh? What the hell?"

"Whoa, don't spray," he said. Both of his hands were up, and he walked carefully toward me, his face cautious. "Sorry. My friends are idiots."

I panted and took a deep breath, pressing a hand to my racing heart to slow my breathing. "You scared the living crap out of me."

He laughed. "Drop the weapon, ma'am. I mean no harm." He inched toward me. "You have the right to remain silent." One step closer. "Anything you say can and will be used against you in a court of law." Another step. A flash of humor crossed his face.

It was hard to be mad at him when he was acting so goofy. We were a couple of steps apart when he stopped.

My heart was still racing. Racing like a car in the Indy 500. "What're you doing here, Josh?"

"I'm arresting you." Both dimples were on display. Under the overhead light, his chocolate-brown eyes lightened to an amber color.

I quirked an eyebrow. "And what did I do exactly?"

"You can plead the fifth if you want. I know it's not your fault."

"Uh-huh." And, now, I was smiling to match his smile.

"I really should blame your parents or the gods that be." He leaned in and took my hand in his, the one still clutching the pepper spray. "It's a crime to be this devastatingly beautiful."

I laughed. It was the worst overused line, but I couldn't help but feel flattered, especially by the way he was looking at me, like his cheesy line was the absolute truth.

"Whatever. You and your lines."

He grinned, his dimples deepening. "Really. It's not fair to the other women. And guys like me . . ." He placed his free hand on his chest. "We don't even have a chance."

His boyish good looks made my heartbeat pitter-patter and pick up in pace.

The honking in the background broke up our connection. My eyes took in the shiny black BMW that had pulled up next to the curb.

"Hey, hey, hey. Get in the car, birthday boy!"

Two guys were in the car. The driver had spiky yellow hair and the bluest eyes, and the guy in the passenger seat, halfway out his window, had a buzz cut so close to his head, I could see his scalp.

"Let's go!"

Rich, obnoxious boys with their fancy toys.

I shook my head and turned, ready to get home. If I wasn't home in ten minutes, I was sure Chloe would send out an APB on me.

"Josh, I'm going to go." I motioned my thumb toward the subway.

I didn't know why our paths had crossed again. Maybe it was a coincidence, or maybe it wasn't. My tired self at the moment didn't care.

"No, wait." He threw his friends a look. A look that said, *Beat it.* "Guys, go. I'll meet you at your place."

"Hell no, man," Josh's friend in the passenger seat argued from the car. "It's your birthday, and we're going to party."

The muscle in Josh's jaw jumped, his smile slowly fading.

"Josh, go with your friends."

"I want to be with you," he said softly, his words sounding like they meant more than they should. "I came here for a reason."

My jaw tensed because I didn't want to answer questions about earlier, on why I'd let the waterfall of tears flow.

"Josh!" The driver popped his head out the window. "Come on, man."

Annoyance replaced his normally happy demeanor. "Just fucking go. I'll get home."

His friends' eyes widened, and their mouths shut. Part of me believed that Josh didn't let the word *fuck* fly often.

"Your car?" the driver asked.

His car? Shoe salesmen could afford BMWs?

Josh threw them an aggravated look. "I'll just pick it up later."

"Just text us, 'kay?"

"Yeah," Josh called out, not bothering to look back, his eyes directly on me.

His black Beemer drove down the street and turned a corner.

"Nice ride," I said, gauging his reaction. "They must pay you a ton at Nordstrom."

"Long story." He took my hand in his, intertwining our fingers, as though it were natural for him to do so. "Let's go."

I let out an exaggerated sigh. "Josh, first of all, I don't know you. Second of all, what're you doing here? Third . . . I'm just tired." I retracted my hand from his, needing the space, needing to leave, needing my bed.

In one big swoop, he lifted me off my feet.

"Josh!" I yelped. My arms wrapped around his neck to steady myself. "Put me down."

"No." His voice was laced with humor. "First off, I want to get to know you. Second, I still feel like shit about earlier, and I want to make it up to you."

"It's not your—"

"Third, I just really want a drink for my birthday. One drink."

"Josh, please put me down," I insisted.

"I wasn't finished with my third point." He raised his finger for emphasis, a dimple emerging on his face. "You're tired, so I'm carrying you down the street to Jake's Bar."

"Josh . . ."

"Please, Sam," he pleaded with a pretend pout. "It's my birthday. I just got chewed out by my dad. My ex-girlfriend called me, crying. It's been a shitty day. I need a drink. Can you do that for me?"

His face turned tense, as though he were afraid of what I was going to say, and I decided, in his arms, that I didn't want to add to his shitty day.

"Only if you put me down."

"Okay." Without argument, he stopped and set me on my feet.

I peered up at him, noting how the moon highlighted the brown in his irises.

Stooping down, he pointed to his back and said, "Hop on."

I gave him a look. "Piggyback?"

"Unless you want to hop on my front."

I laughed. "Negative."

"You're tired. I want my drink. Hop on."

And I did.

My feet hurt, and he was offering.

He took off in a full-on sprint to Jake's Bar down the street. The neon lights were highlighted in blue against the red brick building. He gripped my thighs, and I linked my hands against his neck to keep from falling. We looked ridiculous, running down the street like we were children, but I didn't care.

The cool night air whipped against my face. My hair blew behind me. I angled closer, and the warmth of Josh's body radiated against mine, a contrast to the chilly night. Then, the tiredness dimmed, and I smiled, feeling carefree.

He slowed to a stop, and I hopped off his back. He wasn't winded at all, and I was impressed.

"Do you run marathons or something?"

He laughed and then leaned in. He brushed escaping strands of hair from my face, taming my flyaways. "Yeah, I run but not marathons."

"I'd be dying if I just ran two blocks, carrying a ton of bricks."

"Whatever, you weigh nothing." He opened the door, and I stepped into the bar. "I play ball a lot and swim. Typical boy stuff."

I had a feeling he was being modest.

I moved, and he led the way, holding my hand again.

The city bar was packed with patrons. Televisions lined the wall, music filled the air, and tables were topped with bar food.

We plopped down on stools against the bar, and the first thing I did before ordering was text Chloe, telling her not to wait up.

I ran my hands through my hair and readjusted my ponytail.

Josh pulled at a loose strand and tucked it behind my ear. "Stop, you're beautiful."

"Whatever."

"I only tell the truth." He tipped my chin with his fingertips. "So, what're you drinking?"

"Would it be lame if I just had water?"

He shook his head. "Nope. I'm not the peer-pressuring type. Have whatever you want."

He turned to the female bartender with a huge tat that trailed all the way up her arm. It appeared to be an image of a dragon's tail, and the rest of the dragon might have been hidden under her shirt.

"Can I have a Miller Lite? And this beautiful woman would like a bottled water."

He took out his wallet, but I stopped him, noting the glint of his Rolex watch on his wrist.

"It's your birthday, so I'm paying."

With a slow shake of his head, he said, "That's not how my mom raised me."

"Josh—" My voice was on the verge of whiny.

"Sam, it's water. You can just get me the next time we go out."

I quirked an eyebrow, looking at him with amused wonder. "Next time? You're pretty confident."

"That's what I'm hoping for."

When the bartender passed us our drinks, he threw down his black Amex to open a tab. Curiosity spiked within me.

First, the BMW, then the Rolex, and now, a credit card without a limit?

"What do you do for a living again?"

His eyebrows pulled together, as though he didn't get my question because he knew I already knew the answer. "I'm a full-time law student and part-time shoe salesmen?" he answered my question with a question.

"I mean . . ." My voice trailed off because it was none of my business, yet curiosity pushed to the surface.

"Go ahead. I'm an open book."

"Is that why you answer everything with 'long story'?"

"Touché, Princess." He lifted his beer bottle and tapped it with my water bottle.

My face scrunched up, nose wrinkled, eyebrows pulled together. "Are you going to keep calling me that?"

"Pretty much." He motioned one hand for me to continue.

"I know you're not struggling for money." I pointed to the watch on his wrist. "And that ride? Your Beemer?"

"Yeah . . . that." He shifted with unease, and his focus dropped to the table. "High school graduation bribe."

I cocked my head, but I was unsure if I should be nosy about a guy I didn't even know.

With one long exhale, he hesitated, measuring me for a moment. "Let's just say, my family has money."

"Is that all I'm getting?"

He nodded. "For now. I can't talk about it now 'cause it's my birthday, and it just brings up all these memories I'd like not to think about on the day I was born."

I threw him a pointed, unsatisfied look, and he flashed me a dimple.

"It's not first-date conversational stuff," he said.

"Date? I think you kind of kidnapped me."

He placed his hand on his chest, feigning offense. "Me?" he scoffed. "If I remember correctly, you're the one who jumped my bones."

"Whatever! I hopped on your back." I slapped his shoulder, and my mouth fell open. "You told me to."

"Tell that to a judge, and see if he believes you." He narrowed his eyes, challenging me.

I laughed, and when I did, he leaned in closer.

"Red or blue?"

"What?" I frowned, feeling the heat from his proximity.

He waved one hand in the air. "It's our first-date speed round."

"I'm sorry, what?"

He threw back his head and peered up at the ceiling and then back to meet my eyes. "It's like playing Twenty Questions on our first date but speedy fast."

"This is not a date!" I insisted.

"Fine, whatever." He tapped the bar. "Red or blue?"

"As in, which is my favorite color? Neither."

"Princess, just tell me which word pops up first in your head. No-brainer here."

"I just don't get the point."

He tapped the bar again. "The first thing that pops in your mind is your true answer."

And then I decided to humor him. "Okay, fine. Red."

"Brownie or cookies?"

"Cookies."

"Christmas or New Year's?"

"Duh!" I laughed. "Christmas."

He face split into a wide grin. "Sunset or sunrise?"

"Sunset."

"Money or happiness?"

"Happiness," I said softly. Because ultimate happiness was hard to obtain when life got in the way.

"Beer or wine?"

"Beer."

"Love or lust?" His cheeks reddened, his eyes getting intense.

"Love." My cheeks flushed at my honesty.

He paused and placed a finger against his lips, contemplating.

"And what was the point of that?" I asked.

"To see if we are compatible." He winked. "And we are."

Goodness gracious, was he corny, but weirdly enough, it added to his appeal.

"Please don't tell me you've used that before."

"I haven't." He leaned toward me, pulling the stool forward. "I don't know why either. That's a good pick-up line."

I shook my head, amused.

His eyes took in my face, his one look bringing warmth to the apples of my cheeks. And I took him in as well. His eyes were like the deep chocolate in the middle of a molten cake. He had the handsomest face, a face that would never change.

"You must look like your mom," I commented.

His father was good-looking, but they didn't look the same. They didn't have the same eyes or hold the same smile.

"Yeah." His voice dropped, his happy demeanor disappearing.

The chatter around us seemed to dull to a low buzz, and I wondered again where his mother had been for his birthday dinner. I remembered him simply saying she wasn't there.

A sudden dread washed over me as I asked the question, "Where was she tonight?"

"She's dead," he said quietly, confirming my fear.

He tipped back his beer bottle, taking a long swig, most likely to bring back the warmth to his chest.

The air escaped my lungs in a swift exhale because I knew about death. I knew how much it hurt. I knew how the burn never went away, even after years. I knew how much one would sacrifice just to have that person back on earth again, how one would spend their days differently. If I had my mother back, I'd never waste a moment, not a minute, not a second.

As though I knew it was what he needed, I angled closer and hugged his middle. "I'm sorry."

His somber look tore at my insides. His eyes glossed over, and if he was going to cry, I was about to lose it, too. "

It's okay." He turned back to his beer. "It's times like this, my birthday—because she used to make my birthday so grand—that I miss her. It's not the same without her. My dad can't deal. My sister forces us to go out for functions and shit. I just want to forget, but I can't."

I hugged him tighter, smelling the scent of his laundry detergent through his clothes. His strong arms encircled my waist, holding me, too. Though I was comforting him, he was comforting me also.

"She was my favorite person, full of life and positivity. You could never dim her light. Even when she was suffering at the end and cancer had spread throughout all her organs"—he winced—"she wasn't worried about herself. She was only concerned about whom she was leaving behind."

I choked back a sob as tears were about to let loose. I wished my mother had been that selfless. I wished she had thought of me first—how much I'd needed her, how much I couldn't live without her, how much I would miss her every single day.

"She was beautiful, kind. And she forced me to follow my dreams." He released a gut-wrenching shaky sigh. It took energy to breathe through his thoughts. "I just miss her, so damn much." His voice came out so heartbroken that my insides crumbled. "She died on December twenty-third, right before Christmas."

He opened my dam of tears again, and I hiccuped into his chest as thoughts of my mother rushed to the surface. Loss could relate to loss, as pain could relate to pain. I appreciated his honesty.

He pulled back and tenderly brushed the back of his hand down my cheek. "I'm sorry. That's two for two today."

And then I let it out because I wanted him to know that I felt his heartbreak, that I understood.

"Something about today, or you . . . reminds me of my own mother." I swiped at the bottom of my eyes and blinked, forcing my focus on the overhead light above us to prevent any more tears from falling. "She passed away my freshman year of culinary arts school."

"Sam . . . I'm so sorry." He pulled me tight against him, rubbing my back with his palm, gently yet firmly.

I had no desire to back out of his comforting embrace.

"How?" he asked.

And then it started. The familiar choking sensation crept up my throat, as if someone had their hand around my neck, gripping tighter, tighter, tighter until I couldn't breathe.

"She took her own life, overdosed on prescription drugs"—I squeezed my eyes shut and rushed out my next words—"when my father left us." The salt from my tears touched my lips.

My trembling limbs clung to him, and he held me until my whole body relaxed against his. Josh had unleashed memories of my mother. Something about him reminded me of her, but I couldn't put my finger on it. His embrace tightened until the chaos from the customers around me ceased, and all I heard was silence.

Time passed, and even though I was pretty sure the bar was about to close, I was afraid to lift my head. I was a tad embarrassed that I had cried a river on his shirt.

When I peeked up, Josh was looking at me. And he did the opposite of what I'd thought he'd do.

He smiled, two dimples and all. "I thought you fell asleep, and I didn't want to wake you. And I'm pretty sure my shirt is wet from your drool."

The patrons at the bar had disappeared. His drink was watered down and sweating on the bar top.

I gave a watery laugh, defusing the awkward moment.

"Whatever . . ." I averted my eyes and scanned the room.

The bartender was drying up glasses and wiping down the bar. The music softened to a quieter beat.

Josh's smile faltered, and he brushed the side of my cheek with his hand. "What do you want to do, pretty girl? Anything you want, we'll do."

I peered up to his gentle eyes and answered with hesitation. "I just want to go home."

He nodded and stood, extending his hand. I wrapped my fingers around his, and that comforting warmth spread up my arm. It was hard to believe I'd just met this guy mere weeks ago, and it was only our third encounter. The calmness in his demeanor and soft fierceness in his hold made me feel so safe with him.

When he kissed the back of my hand, I inhaled deeply.

"Then, let's take you home, Princess."

There was something so natural, so comfortable, about being around Josh. And I realized this night hadn't turned out how I'd thought it would.

chapter **NINE**

"HAPPY BIRTHDAY, PRINCESS!"

I pulled the covers over my head and turned over. "Five more minutes, Mom. Please!"

And then I heard it. I should have known.

I heard the struggle, the dragging of a heavy object against my wood floor, and Chloe's laughter.

BAM!

Ice-cold water. All over me.

The blue Rubbermaid bucket was tossed to the side.

I screamed and jumped out of bed, hopping up and down, as though that would warm me up. "You jerks!"

I chased Chloe around the room, my arms outstretched, my clothes dripping wet.

She cowered behind my mother. "It was your mom's idea! I swear!" Chloe pleaded.

One look at my mom's face, and I knew she was the mastermind.

My nose wrinkled right before I bum-rushed them into a group hug, my sopping wet clothes dampening their clothing.

My mother grabbed my face and kissed each of my cheeks. She reached for my hand, and with her signature smile, she recited her favorite made-up poem to me, "Happy Birthday, my favorite girl. / I wish for all your dreams to come true, / For all the good things will happen to you. / We'll bake a cake or two, and just know that I love you."

I jolted to a sitting position, my eyes searching the room.

My hands flew to my heart. My breathing turned erratic.

I wasn't back in my room in Carbarny.

And my mother wasn't here.

I flattened one hand against my chest, pressing down the ache, as I relived those happy times.

It was odd, but while I was awake, I only remembered the morbid times, the times toward the end when my once-hippie, happy-go-lucky mother had been so different. When, some mornings, she wouldn't get out of bed, wouldn't eat, wouldn't speak. I hated those days.

In my dreams, I'd see her as she had been—happy . . . free.

My phone buzzed beside my bed, and I bent down to reach for it. Josh's picture flashed on my phone with a caption.

Best. Crème brûlée ever. Best birthday ever. Thank you.

Even though I had insisted Josh didn't have to take me home, he had. And he'd used the 'birthday-boy-card' as an excuse from the bar to the subway and all the way until he walked me to my door.

Not once had he mentioned my mother. Maybe thinking of my pain only reminded him of his. We had exchanged numbers but only because I'd wanted to make sure he got home okay.

I smiled as I texted him back.

You're welcome. And thanks for making me cry the whole night.

No problem. When can I do it again?

This guy. He was relentless.

The silence is killing me. No date for that wedding yet?

I'm not the dating type.

I figured.

I widened my eyes at his candor.

I'm not the hooker type either.

I didn't mean that. You're the fall-in-love-and-hang-on type.

I smiled again.

You've got lines, bro. Boy, do you have them.

You've said that already. My question is, when will my lines finally work?

I was about to text him when something buzzed from the bottom of my purse. My breath stalled, and my heartbeat leaped into my throat, like a frog jumping on a lily pad. I stared, unblinking, at my black leather bag on the ground. My cell was in my hand, so it had to be the one Hawke had given me.

I slid off the bed and fell to my knees, dumping all my belongings in the process. I picked up on the third ring and steadied my voice though my pulse was racing. "Hello?"

"Sunshine?"

His voice made my heart flip like a cooked pancake. It was glorious and beautiful, as though he woke up, singing.

I flattened my bed head with one hand. It wasn't like he could see me, but hearing his voice made it seem like he was in the room.

"What're you doing?"

"Nothing as exciting as you." I willed my pulse to calm down; otherwise, Chloe might need to call 911.

"I've missed you."

The way he said those words with no inflection in his voice . . . I wondered how many girls had been fed this line. Still, my stomach did nonstop somersaults, and my heart soared.

"Sure you have." I laughed, stood, and paced the room. My body could not sit still. My pulse increased to call-the-ambulance tempo. I bit my thumbnail, trying to calm my nerves.

"I have missed you." His voice dropped, all cheeriness disappearing. "I need to see you." His voice held a degree of fierce emotion.

A low breath escaped me, and I fidgeted with the bottom of my shirt. "Come on over," I said bravely even though I knew it wasn't that easy.

I sat on the edge of the bed and pulled my duvet over my knees, reveling in the warmth of half of my body being under the covers. "Where are you anyway?"

"Vegas."

I bit my lip and played with the edge of the comforter. We were miles away from each other. Even if he wanted to see me, he couldn't.

"Sin City? Nice."

"We're playing at MGM Grand today," he said. "Have you ever been to Vegas before?"

"Not yet."

The only places I'd ever been outside of Carbarny were Chicago and Canada—to bury my dead grandmother when I was younger. That fact would dim a conversation real quick.

I heard him take a deep breath and blow it out.

"I'm going to ask you something, and before you think too much about it, I need you to agree to what I'm asking you before I ask it."

I laughed. "So, I have to agree to something without even knowing what I'm agreeing to?"

The smile was back in his voice. "That's exactly it, Sunshine. Because I know you."

No, he didn't. Not really. Romps in the sack didn't count, but I wanted to humor him, and moreover, I didn't want our conversation to end.

"Okay, ask me then."

"You'll overthink things. I'm sure you're overthinking us right now."

Us?

I couldn't control the lightness in my chest at his words. I didn't want to hope for more. I should be satisfied with what we had. Chloe would be. But I didn't work that way.

"It's been two weeks since you called me, Hawke. What *us* are you referring to?"

"I know. I just knew, if I called you, it'd be harder to stay away."

His words, the sincerity in his tone, and his admission that he had been struggling not to call me made my heart swell. But I had to gain control and keep a level head.

I'd been dumped two times before by two men who I'd been madly in love with. One had left me for a cheerleader, and the other couldn't handle me after my mother's death. I'd like to believe neither of those times were true love because, if they had been, we would've lasted. Either way, I didn't want to be the one hurt in the end, and judging by the differences between us, it was bound to happen. Me, with a stake in my heart.

"Don't," he whispered.

"What? Don't what?" My voice sounded shaky, even to my own ears.

"Don't overthink this. Do you have a passport?"

I tightly held the phone against my ear. "Yes. Why?"

"I'm sending the plane to come get you. I'm touring Europe for a couple of weeks. We leave tonight and . . . I want you to come."

I blinked and reeled back, glancing at the phone, as though I didn't believe what he had said.

"Sunshine?" A nervousness resonated in his tone.

"Are you crazy?"

"You have no idea." He laughed, his voice a bit unsteady. "But that's not the point. What do you say, sweetness?"

The intensity of his tone stilled me. But not my raging, reckless pulse.

It was insane and absurd and not responsible. I didn't have that many vacation days left at work.

But there was one question I needed to ask him. "Why?"

"Why what?" He seemed confused.

But I was more confused. "Why do you want me to come with you?"

He cleared his throat, and his next words rushed out. "Because I miss you."

I closed my eyes and exhaled a long silent sigh. His words made my chest ache because I missed him just as much or even more. Though I didn't want to listen to his sweet talk, I couldn't help it. "I doubt you are lacking company, Hawke."

"The only person I want to see is you. I need to see you. You, Sunshine." His voice sounded as though it were on the verge of desperation.

The way my nickname ran off his tongue made the inside of my palms sweat. Forget my palms. My whole body warmed.

I stared blankly at my comforter. Some of the down feathers had escaped from a little hole, and I pushed them back in.

"You're overthinking things again, Sunshine. Now, my one question."

I blinked. "What?"

"Do you want to see me?"

I scrunched my eyes, knowing that hearing him through the receiver was nothing compared to holding the real deal. "Yes, but—"

"No *buts*," he said, sounding anxious now. "Tilton will be there in three hours. Don't worry about packing. If you need clothes, we'll have my assistant grab you what you need. I've gotta run. I'll see you in a bit."

"Hawke—"

"I'll see you later Sunshine," he said, sounding a little excited.

And then the phone went dead.

I BLEW OUT A SERIES of soft, short breaths, and my stomach rolled with butterflies when Tilton opened the door to the limo that would take me to the private jet.

When he picked me up from my apartment, he didn't say a word other than, "Hi."

I tried to press him for more information, but I didn't get much other than, "Mr. Calvin will inform you upon your arrival."

Gah! The man was so frustrating!

Almost as frustrating as my relationship with Hawke.

Almost but not quite.

I'd never, in my whole twenty-three years of existence, ever done something this crazy. Up and leave the country? Spontaneity was not in my DNA.

When I had hung up with Hawke though, I'd called work to take a few days off, telling my boss it was a family emergency. It was the most believable excuse I'd had, and I couldn't tell him I was leaving the country.

When I'd told Chloe, her usual carefree self was nonexistent. She hadn't been all uppity-up on the idea of me leaving for an extended period of time with Hawke. She'd made valid points—one being, I didn't know him that well yet, and two being, he hadn't called me in weeks. Anyone else would have thought that Chloe was a little jealous, but I knew her. I could read the concern in her eyes.

I knew she was more worried about my attachment to him. Although I was more than concerned for the both of us, I'd lied and told her I knew what this was—a fling and nothing else. Except this wasn't a one-time fling. This was a three-time fling that was about to extend into Europe.

Nervous butterflies stirred in my belly with each step leading me to the airplane. I had stuffed shirts, jeans, and socks into my backpack for the short trip, so I hoped I had enough. Who knew what we were doing or where we were going to be at the end of the trip? All I knew was, I wanted to see him. So, I was here.

I wanted to act cool and collected and normal, but I was more like crazy chaotic. With each step up the stairs, my pulse sped up, like drums playing on the inside of my wrists.

I heard the chatter of laughter, and then I stopped and took everything in.

Cofi was sitting on one of the tan leather couches that spanned one side of the plane. Max and AJ were situated on the singular seats, facing forward. A couple of them were with women I didn't recognize, but it was seeing Hawke that shocked me. He was at the back end of the plane on a couch big enough for five.

I had imagined our reunion so many times over these last few hours. It was nothing like this. I hadn't expected him to have some half-naked girl on his lap. I hadn't expected him to be laughing at something she'd just said. I hadn't expected him to be with anyone but me.

"Sunshine." He tipped his chin in acknowledgment.

"Hawke." I clenched my jaw and kept my voice level, pretending that seeing him with another woman hadn't just hurt me like a hard shove against my chest.

Hawke extracted himself from the woman's grasp, slow and smooth, in his natural style, and he strolled forward. Irritation was written all over her face, whereas mine stayed still like a statue.

With one hand, he threaded his fingers through my hair and pulled my head back, placing his dominating mouth on top of mine. I anchored myself, pretending like he didn't affect me. At least I tried, but he kissed me long and hard until every one of my limbs felt weak, and it felt like my feet were floating on air.

God, I had missed him. This playboy, this domineering, spoiled rock star. I had missed every inch of him.

But I was pretty damn pissed.

Hollers came from around us, but he didn't break our connection, only deepening his kisses, sliding his tongue against mine.

I didn't know if he was kissing me for my benefit or to show the other woman that he was the boss.

Who knew what his motives were?

I was kissing the man who I was totally infatuated with. The hot male with the rock-hard abs. The one who had sung sweetly in my ear after we had sex. The one who was tearing down all my barriers and forcing me to live on the wild side. The one who I liked way too much for my own good.

When he released me, my eyes were unfocused. I was a little dazed, a lot breathless, and even more light-headed, but then I caught sight of the brunette with the big boobs who probably had the same reaction to his nearness.

I bit my tongue. Maybe, by feeling pain, I could snap back to Sensible Sam.

Staring into his green eyes that I'd dreamed about, I knew I couldn't do this. I couldn't share. I wasn't a girl who settled for less than what I deserved.

The cheering of our audience was enough to have me cowering in the corner from embarrassment. Cofi was the worst of them all, yelling obscenities.

When Hawke threw one arm around my neck, I moved away and turned toward the exit. "I can't do this. I-I have to go."

"What? Why?" He gripped my hand, stopping me mid stride.

The plane was about to take off, but the door was still open.

Before I left, I needed to know. "What are we?" Hope bloomed in my chest. The wrong answer, and I would be gone, down the stairs and out the door.

"You're my girl," he uttered the statement, like it was a known fact and as though I didn't have a choice in the matter.

But they were just words. I wanted more.

The brunette bombshell was on Cofi's lap, laughing at something he'd said. Awareness pushed to the surface. She was just a groupie to be shared by all, and I didn't want to be *that* girl.

I needed to know if I was just another groupie to him. I needed to know what I meant to him. I needed to know why he'd asked me to come here when he obviously had enough company.

"Does that mean you're exclusively with me?" I couldn't bite back the annoyance in my tone.

He tore his eyes away and ran one hand through his dirty-blond locks. His reaction was my answer, and my stomach dropped to the floor, slipping through the plane and falling onto the runway.

I'd made a mistake by coming here. I needed to leave but had to know the truth first. "Have you been sleeping with anyone else?"

"Yes." There was the answer, honest and without hesitation.

God, it hurt. Hurt hard.

I jerked away, adjusted my backpack on my shoulder, and stormed out the door and down the stairs.

I guessed it was too much to wish for the rock star to stay celibate in the two weeks we'd been apart.

In one swift movement, he stepped in front of me and drew me against him. I pushed at his chest, but he held me by linking his arms around my waist.

"When I'm with you, I'm only with you." He gripped my chin, but I jerked away. His answer knocked the wind out of my lungs, despite the pain I was already feeling. "Why can't you just live in the moment with me, Sunshine? I missed you. I invited you here."

Every word was like a slice to my skin. Another word out of his mouth, and he would slice me to the bone.

"No expectations. No regrets. Live in the moment." His eyes showed such certainty, as though that were the only way to live.

I gritted my teeth and stayed silent.

Easy for him to say. He wasn't getting emotionally attached.

He ducked his head, so we were eye-to-eye. "Ask me if I've ever invited a girl to come on tour with me. Don't believe me?" he insisted. "Ask the guys. While you're at it, ask them who I talk about nonstop. There's no other girl with my phone number. There's no other girl I'd drop anything for, except for you."

I blinked back angry tears. "Except you slept with another girl." Probably more than one. I wanted to ask him how many, but I bit my tongue instead.

"But I only like you," he said, gaze alert, jaw set.

An intensity showed in his eyes, making a tiny part of me believe him. The hopeful part of me wanted to believe him.

The corner of his mouth lifted into a smile, and there was a quiet desperation in his eyes.

That was the difference between men and women. With men, it was just a physical release, but with women, it was everything—emotional, physical, and spiritual.

"Why did you invite me here? If it's sex you want, you can have any girl. You've already proven that." I couldn't hide the bitterness in my tone or dim the quiver in my voice.

His fingertips grazed my back. "I don't want anyone but you, Sunshine. We don't have to have sex if you don't want to—though that would make things less exciting." His devilish smirk was on display. "I invited you here because I missed you." He released a breath. "And, if you must know, these last few weeks"—his smile faltered—"I've been lonely as fuck, and the last time I was less lonely was with you."

"You could've called me, Hawke." I wanted an explanation, an answer. I knew he'd been texting me, but if he'd truly missed me, he would've picked up the phone.

He tore his gaze away, his jaw clenched. "I wanted to forget you. I thought . . . maybe . . . I could."

I sucked in my bottom lip and stared at him. There was a vulnerability in his eyes that I hadn't noticed before. I doubted he let anybody see it—ever.

"I thought that, maybe if I scratched the itch, it would get better, and I'd forget you, but it only made it worse. I only wanted to see you more."

My breathing slowed as I took him in—his dark green eyes and his chin-length dirty-blond hair that brushed against his cheeks because of the wind.

"Stay with me, Sunshine," he whispered, his eyes pleading. "Be here in the present with me. I've missed you so much."

That was the difference between me and him. I'd been trying to commit every moment we'd spent together to memory because it had seemed like a dream, and he'd been trying to forget me.

Yet he couldn't.

My forehead fell against his, and I nodded. *"Okay, I'll stay."*

chapter TEN

SWEAT FORMED BEHIND MY NECK under all the heat, the chatter around us echoing through the cabin, while the blanket covered us in our own cocoon of bliss.

Hawke's stubble tickled my chin. "We're here."

He had thrown the blanket over our heads, so no one could see us making out like teenagers. Sometimes, it was too much to take, and I wanted to rip my clothes off and have him take me, but his hands never went under my clothing.

His words from earlier rang in my head—about how we didn't have to have sex on our European adventure. I was most definitely not on board with those plans.

"Where are we?" My voice was groggy and soft and horny as Hawke skittered tiny kisses across my jawline. My arms wrapped around his neck, and the heat of his body pressed against mine.

"Paris, Sunshine. The City of Love." He met my lips, but I turned, afraid that my morning breath would scare him away. He gripped my jaw to prevent me from moving and kissed me hard. "My lips," he said. "No one kisses these lips, except for me."

"Not even Chloe?"

He laughed. "Fine, but I'm going to be a little concerned if Chloe kisses you the same way I do."

"Hawke, we've landed. Quit fucking around until we get back to the hotel."

I recognized AJ, the bass guitarist's, voice.

Hawke kept me covered but peeked up from the blanket. "Shut

up. We're just taxiing in."

I removed the blanket off my head, flattened my bed head, and smiled at the guys.

"And there is Miss Sunshine herself," Cofi cooed.

The girl from last night was on his lap, and they reeked of weed. *Wasn't that illegal on a plane and highly dangerous?* It wasn't like they even cared.

He squinted and inhaled deeply, and then he extended the blunt toward my direction.

"No, thanks. I quit," I joked.

Everyone laughed at my sarcasm.

Hawke pulled me closer. "Listen to me. When we land, it's going to be crazy. Crazy like you've never seen. I need you to stick to Tilton at all times," he said, his gaze alert, eyebrows wrinkled.

The seriousness in his tone made my stomach clench with worry.

"Okay."

He gripped my chin and ran his thumb along my bottom lip. "I'm going to have to leave you with him and meet you at the hotel."

I reeled back and searched his face, unaware that we'd be making separate departures. "Where are you going when we land?"

His eyes flickered toward my lips, as though he were debating if he should kiss them again. "Back to the hotel. We can't leave together. This is how it always goes down because the photogs are nuts." He bit my chin. "Stick to Tilton. He has strict orders to watch over you."

The plane pulled to a stop, and when the doors opened, a broad male stepped in, wearing designer jeans, a gray button-down shirt, and sunglasses.

"How are my boys?" His tone was loud, menacing, and authoritative.

By the way he stood, I somehow assumed he was their manager. His eyes glazed over us women. No cares. No greeting. No acknowledgment. "All right, we need to go over our schedule today. I'll brief you in the limo on the ride to the hotel. We won't have a lot of time to get settled in. We'll need you guys to get changed, and then we'll be off to our first interview at the radio station. Then, we'll have press at the studio. Don't worry; they'll have translators. Chop-chop, kiddos. We've got a long-ass day ahead of us before the concert." He pointed to Cofi. "Let's try to keep this European tour out of the papers, okay, Cofi?"

"Yes, Daddy Alan." Irritation was heavy in his tone, like a teenager tired of getting reprimanded.

Yep, he was the manager. I'd heard the guys toss Alan's name around before.

The boys laughed, Hawke included, and then two burly men stepped into the plane, making the narrow fuselage feel even more cramped.

Alan pointed to their bags.

When Hawke stood, he laced our fingers, and with his free hand, he pointed to my backpack. "That one, too."

Alan's forehead wrinkled, and he rubbed one aggravated palm down his face. "No girls on the trip, Hawke." His jaw tensed, and his vision focused on our joined hands.

"Says who?" Hawke linked an arm around my neck and walked toward the exit, about to bypass Alan.

Alan gripped his forearm, jerking him to a stop. "What did you want me to do, Hawke?"

He shrugged Alan off, his eyes tight. "Quit fucking paying off the devil."

"So, she can run off her mouth to the press? Ruin your name?"

"She'll come back. She always does."

"And you make more than enough to keep her silent for years."

"That's not the fucking point."

Alan stepped in front of him and tipped his head in my direction. Through his flat, cold eyes, his thoughts were readable. He thought of me as cargo that needed to be dropped off in the dumpster or anywhere that wasn't on this tour.

Hawke only pulled me in tighter against his side. "She's not any girl. This is Sunshine." He walked out with me attached to his hip but not before I saw the muscles in Alan's jaw jump.

When his eyes widened, I knew he recognized my name. The most disgusted look crossed his features, but Hawke was no longer paying attention.

I pushed down the unsettling feeling in the pit of my stomach as we stepped outside. I was here with Hawke, not their manager.

Two Hummer limos and an SUV were waiting in the distance. Another private jet similar in size to ours was taxiing in.

Hawke drew me in and kissed the top of my forehead. "I'll see you soon."

He tipped his head toward Tilton and released me. I swore, they could communicate with only a tip of their chins and a squint of their eyes.

I watched Hawke's retreating back and gripped my stomach, already missing the warmth of his body next to mine. Cofi bumrushed Hawke and threw him a playful punch. AJ threw an arm over Hawke, the other holding his guitar in its case. The whole band reminded me of brothers. The sight of them walking toward their limo, strolling against the sun, was a picture-perfect poster.

"Ms. Clarke." Tilton motioned to the car with his hand.

"Oh, sorry." I'd forgotten that the big, bad bodyguard was behind me.

He opened the door, and I slipped in, bouncing onto the black leather cushion. The stickiness of the seat stuck to my jeans, but the first thing Tilton did was blast the air on high.

As soon as we were on the busy road, chaos erupted. Hawke hadn't been exaggerating. My pulse accelerated with fear, taking the scene in. Hundreds of girls with signs lined the entire street, all of them crying and yelling and trying to see inside the darkened windows. Cars were unable to get through even though multiple law enforcement vehicles with sirens were directing traffic.

I jumped back when the women pounded on our car, looking through the pitch-black windows. Even the cops couldn't stop rowdy women from jumping on the hood of our moving vehicle.

Through the crowd, I had lost the SUVs in front of us.

Tilton drove slowly through the chaos of people, and when there was a small path for the car to squeeze through, he pressed his foot to the pedal, taking off.

"Hawke wasn't kidding. That was crazy." My whole body turned, so I could get a glimpse of the women chasing after our car in a full-on sprint.

"You haven't seen crazy yet," Tilton mumbled in his deep monotone voice.

And I hadn't.

The closer we got to the hotel, the worse it got. I still couldn't see past the herd of people. The screaming and disorder caused me to pull my knees up and curl into myself. I closed my eyes to dim the noise. It was sensory overload—the air blasting, the hollers, and the pounding on the windows. I swore, the impact of their fists would smash through the glass.

And then . . . silence.

I opened my eyes, and pure darkness engulfed the car. Fear threatened to choke me.

"Til-Tilton?" I was unable to hide the quiver in my voice.

"We're in the garage of the hotel. You're fine now."

I wondered if anything shook him. Given his large stature and the steadiness in his eyes, probably not.

Once we were in the hotel and I was able to stretch my legs, my whole demeanor changed. I didn't realize how tense my body had become until I walked out of the car, needing the air and the space to move.

An elegant elevator took us up to the grand hotel lobby. Marble floors spanned the massive hotel lobby. In the center stood a tall bouquet of cream roses and orchids cascading over the porcelain vase. The scent of fresh flowers filled my nose, and the rush of the water in the fountain calmed me. I had never stepped into such an immaculate place before.

I tapped Tilton's shoulder. "Where are we?"

"Paris." The side of his mouth tipped up into an almost smile at his own wry joke.

Of course I knew I was in Paris, but my face brightened because I felt like I'd cracked a safe, chipping at his cold, hard demeanor. "Har-har," I replied. "No shit, Sherlock. What hotel are we in?"

"The Four Seasons." The hard lines in his face were back.

I shrugged. It was fun while it'd lasted.

My eyes scoured the area as Tilton moved double time in front of me.

"Stay put." His eyes meant business as he proceeded to the check-in counter.

I stared openly at the people around me, taking in my surroundings. It was fascinating to hear them speaking the beautiful French language, the language of love. I watched a couple and took in the cadence of their words and the inflection in their voices. The women seemed to hum in agreement.

In that moment, I wished I were worldly and knew other languages. In another life, at another time, where I was loaded and lived in luxury, I would've gone to school in France. France was the world-renowned place of cuisine, especially pastries. I had always dreamed of coming here, tasting the delicacies, immersing myself in the culture. It was surreal to finally be here.

Tilton tapped my shoulder, which broke me out of my trance. With some papers and key cards in his hands, he led us down the hall, past the normal elevators, and stopped in front of a pair of even more elegant-looking elevators at the end. Once inside, he inserted a key card and punched in a code, and then the elevator took us higher.

"Where are the guys?" My ears popped on our ascent. We must be going pretty high.

"They had to take a detour to lose the crowd."

After the elevators opened, I followed Tilton to another set of double doors where he punched in another code. When he opened the door, my mouth dropped to the ground, kept going, and stayed open.

Goodness gracious, the things money could buy, I swear.

It was as if I had stepped into some modern architecture magazine. The space was open and airy with a motif of cream and winter whites.

The beautiful cream-white marble floor was etched in gold and complemented the simple satin curtains against the walls. I inhaled deeply, filling my lungs with the scent of fresh flowers that accented every corner of the room on every glass table.

The door shut behind me, and when I turned, Tilton was gone. The only item left in his place was my backpack on the floor.

My fingers pressed against my plain lime-green T-shirt. I suddenly felt underdressed and overwhelmed by my situation.

I, Samantha Clarke—born in Carbarny, Illinois, population 2,300—was in Paris, staying at the Four Season's penthouse suite. And all I had brought were jeans and some brightly-colored shirts.

I fisted my hand against my mouth and silently screamed, and then I proceeded to jump up and down, like I'd won the lotto.

I had to share my excitement with someone who would get just as excited as I was, so I pulled out my phone from my back pocket and called Chloe.

"Hey. Did you make it?" Her voice oozed with concern, exactly like it had before I left.

"I did! I'm going to FaceTime you." When the picture came up, her face was caked with green goo, and I reeled back, not prepared. "Oh."

"Exfoliation." She shrugged. "It's a seaweed mask. Where are you?"

My frantic elation was back in full force. "In Paris." I turned the phone so she could see the room. "At the Four Seasons, in a penthouse suite!"

"Ah!" she yelled. "Omigodomigodomigod!"

And then we were both jumping until I started getting dizzy by the motion of her phone. God, I loved my best friend. It took a few seconds for both of us to calm down, and I made my way to the couch, plopping down, back-first into the billowy cushions.

"Where did you fly in?"

"I dunno. We were on Def Deception's private jet."

"Omigodomigodomigod!" she squealed again.

I melted against the cushion as I thought of Hawke. "Chloe, we made out like teenagers on the plane."

"Omigod!"

I flinched at her loudness.

When the door flew open, I sat up, feet planted on the ground, and composed myself freaky fast, my smile dimming from my face.

Maintain composure.

Two bellmen walked through the door with a cartload of luggage, followed by Hawke. The look on his face when his eyes met mine lit up my insides like a Christmas tree in the middle of Times Square.

I waved at him and whispered into the receiver, "Chloe, I have to go. I'll call you later."

But she must not have heard me because she kept going with her nonstop, "Omigod!"

"Chloe! I gotta run, babe."

"Take pictures. Lots of them. Text me often. But, most of all, be safe, baby girl!"

"But of course." I grinned at her. "Love you. Bye."

Hawke paid the attendants, but his eyes never left mine.

When I hung up the phone, he stalked toward me like a stealthy cat sneaking up on its prey. "How do you like the place?" His simple question brought goose bumps to my skin.

I straightened on the couch, ready for him in case he was going to pounce. "It's all right." My voice was oddly calm, opposite to my pulse beating irrationally against my wrists. Little did he know, just a few seconds ago, I'd been screaming at the top of my lungs.

"Just all right?" He dropped to his knees and got nose-to-nose with me. He leaned in and dropped a kiss on my lips. "I ordered room service. Fries and nuggets." His crooked smile made my heart pitter-patter pop. "Is that okay?"

He remembered that from our first night together. I wanted to grab him by the ears and pull him closer, but I maintained my composure.

"Yes, that's fine." *Gah!* I was a better actress than I had given myself credit for.

"I'm about to leave in a second. Make yourself at home, and walk around the hotel. I've started a tab for you. I have press to do, but I'll be back."

He pulled my thighs apart and cupped the side of my face, brushing his nose against my chin and stopping right below my ear. "I'm going to make up for those weeks I didn't get to see you."

He scented my neck, and then he bent down and bit the tender part, just before my neck met my shoulder. My body was hypersensitive to his touch, hypersensitive to his voice, hypersensitive to his advances.

When I pulled back, he went in for another kiss on my lips, deeper this time. He opened the seam of my mouth with his tongue. My breathing was labored as he laid me against the couch, flush against him.

But then the banging on the door had him slowly moving off of me.

"No," I whined, wrapping my legs around his waist.

"You don't know how bad I want to stay here with you."

"Then, do it." My big puppy-dog brown eyes begged him to stay.

"Duty calls, Sunshine. And Daddy's gotta bring in the dough." He kissed my chin. "I promise, we'll have tonight to spend time together."

With one last kiss, he jumped off me and walked out the door, not before throwing me one last crooked smile.

With a heavy sigh, I pouted and pushed myself up.

I guessed if he had work and I was on vacation, I needed to make the best of it. My feet padded through the plush carpet that led to the master bedroom. A California king-size bed was situated in the center of the massive room. The curtains matched the bedspread in cream-colored velvet with swirls of gold.

I walked past the sitting area, and for the second time since I'd entered, my jaw dropped to the ground and stayed there because there was a Jacuzzi the size of a tiny swimming pool in the master bathroom.

I lifted my head to the ceiling and thanked the heavens for this experience.

I needed to enjoy this alone time.

Grabbing a robe from behind the door, I grinned.

It was time to get acquainted with the Jacuzzi.

chapter **ELEVEN**

DARKNESS ENGULFED THE ROOM. THE curtains were drawn to prevent any city lights from filtering through. When a draft crept up my nakedness, I pulled the sheets closer, turning to see Hawke was not beside me.

Hawke had strolled into our penthouse after his rock-star obligations with flowers and duck confit, a famous Parisian meal. It had been the best night to start off my short European vacation, and I was missing the absence of his warm body next to mine.

Wrapping the satin sheet around my body, I swung my knees over the side of the bed. A tiny sliver of light was peeking through the bottom of the bathroom door. I knocked on the door before turning the knob and walking in.

When I approached, Hawke flipped around.

His eyes widened, surprised at my arrival. "What're you doing up?"

When I took a step forward, he brought a fist to his back, hiding something, and awareness prickled my skin. The ringing in my ears, coupled with the increase in my heart rate, had me feeling dizzy, but I pushed through it.

Doing drugs—any type of drugs—was a deal-breaker.

"What's in your hand?" My voice trembled, showing my fear. I'd been here before, years ago with my own mother. I didn't want another repeat—a repeat of my past.

"What?" he asked, blanching. "Nothing." His words matched his face, blank as a white canvas, unreadable.

"You asked me once"—I swallowed hard—"if you didn't write your songs, if that would've been a deal-breaker for me." I tipped my head toward his hand. "If you're doing drugs, I'm done. I don't care how much I like you." I had to step out of this situation before I got in too deep, before I liked him more—or worse, before I fell in love . . . before I could love him and then feel the need to save him.

The hardest part of retelling an agonizing story was the first few words. I bit my cheek and forced myself to start speaking, "You know about my disappearing father, but my mother . . . I watched her slowly kill herself with prescription drugs."

"It's Tylenol, Sunshine," he insisted.

My eyes narrowed, and disappointment flooded my insides. The red needle on my bullshit meter was teetering on the far end. "Show it to me then."

His eyes grew hard. "I've watched my mother battle her addiction with coke and heroin and prescription drugs for as long as I can remember. It's the reason she keeps coming back for money that she is not entitled to. Like I told you before, I'm not going to let anyone or anything control me. If you haven't figured it out, I am very much a control freak."

My eyes dropped to his fist. "What's in your hand?" Naturally, I was too trusting, but I wasn't naive enough to think that he didn't have everything at his disposal.

He stepped toward me, reached for my hand, opened my fist, and dropped a pill in my palm before storming out to the bedroom.

My stomach nosedived to the marble floor. *Shit!*

It was Tylenol.

Great. Just great.

I guessed my bullshit meter was broken.

Anxiety crept up my throat, and I entered the bedroom, ready to beg for forgiveness. He was slumped over on the couch, turning something over and over in his hand. When I stepped closer, I realized it was a guitar pick.

"I got hurt a while back. Fell off a stage."

I remembered. It'd happened two years ago, and it had made front-page news.

"So, yeah, sometimes, I feel lower back pain and take Tylenol with codeine for it. But I'm not addicted to meds, and I don't take hard-core drugs. That's not me."

His fingers dug into the guitar pick, and he blew out a breath. "I don't believe in blind trust." His voice was low and strained and hurt. "I don't trust very easily. My circle is small, intimate. I don't even trust all of the band members. I mean"—he shook his head—"not with anything real. Cofi, I do, and Tilton. Everyone else . . ." His voice trailed off.

"I'm sorry." I was a step away from him, but he still hadn't lifted his head.

When I ran my fingers through his hair, he lifted his head, his eyes tired, sad even.

"And you, Sunshine. I trust you. I don't know what it is. Maybe it's the fact that you haven't sold our story to the tabloids yet, or maybe it's because you don't push me about my mom. I don't know what it is, but I trust you, and I just wish you'd do the same for me."

I inhaled deeply. I'd hurt him, and I knew exactly why. It was the simple things that money couldn't buy that mattered to him, and trust was one of them.

Our eyes locked, and I swallowed the guilt down.

"Sunshine, I've never lied to you," he said, eyes intensely locking with mine.

"You can trust me," I promised him. "I'd never betray you. Ever."

From the look on his face, the way his eyes peered into mine, I knew he believed me. I sat down next to him, and our thighs touched.

"Want to hear the latest one?" He let out a sadistic laugh, one that felt like tiny spiders were nipping at my skin. "Alan paid her off again."

I'd gathered that much from what I heard on the plane, and I was curious, but I didn't want to pry.

I rested my chin on his shoulder while he stared blankly in front of himself. "She's suing me again. Nothing new."

"For what?"

He exhaled deeply. His exhale was frustrated, tired, defeated.

"Shit, she was so high on our first tour. I doubt she even remembers what went down. When she lashed out at the President of MCA Records, I thought we were toast. That's when Alan stepped up. He was part of MCA, assigned to us. He knew my mother was the one screwing up our gigs.

I'd emancipated myself from her when I was sixteen. What else was I supposed to do when she'd depleted our accounts to fund her lifestyle?

Now she suing us for unpaid wages because she had originally been our manager."

I snuggled closer, hating the coldness in his stare, the hate in his eyes, the bitterness in his tone. "What does she want now?"

"The same thing she always wants—money. Now, she's suing for emotional distress." He flexed his fingers, forming a fist.

"Maybe you should countersue for the same thing."

The side of his mouth lifted into his signature crooked smile. "I should, shouldn't I? But then she'd use the money I'd already paid her to pay me if I won the suit."

When he rested against the pillows, I followed and lay down. Facing each other, we were so close. I felt the warmness of his breath against my face. The vulnerability in his eyes were laid out for me to see.

"Alan paid her off last week," he said quietly "I only found out through Cofi. I know Alan keeps me in the dark sometimes, but all I want from him is the truth."

"Understandable."

"I mean, I know why he does it. I just hate paying the bitch off all the time."

Silence engulfed the room, and we stared at each other, his tormented eyes to my understanding ones.

I shifted with unease, needing to break the silence, to make him feel better. That was what I did. It was what I was good at—fixing things.

I unclenched my fists and noticed the tiny pill was still in my sweaty palm. "So, yeah . . . you still need this?"

After a soft chuckle escaped him, he plucked the pill from my hand and popped it into his mouth, swallowing without water. Then, his look turned serious. "Stay for the rest of the tour. It's only for the next few weeks."

If only the world worked like that, where I had no bills to pay and no school application process to worry about.

"You know I can't. They only gave me three days off."

He pinched my side, and I yelped.

"No, seriously, I can't. I have to fly back home the day after tomorrow to make it back to work in time."

He nodded, but it didn't lessen the unsettling feeling between us, this feeling that our short time together was already coming to an end.

chapter TWELVE

WHEN HAWKE PROMISED ME A good time, he fulfilled.

After his morning interviews, we hit the town, rock-star style.

We left the hotel incognito—hats, sunglasses, and total tourist wear. Even Tilton had his own getup—a Hawaiian shirt and straw hat. It was hard not to laugh at the way Tilton's hat fanned over his face.

I was sitting in the Suburban, windows down and summer wind blowing my hair in my face. Because of logistics and safety and because Daddy Alan wouldn't allow it, there were some things I could only see from the comfort of the leather seats of the Suburban, but it didn't matter because my smile could not be dimmed.

We saw the Louvre, the Eiffel Tower, Champs-Élysées—Clemenceau, and Notre Dame—drive-by-style. I stuck my head out the window, camera in hand, and snapped enough pics to fill two scrapbooks. I wanted to spend my vacation with Hawke, and that was what we were doing. Every time I turned his way, his crooked smile had lit up his face.

The sightseeing from the car was enough for me. Eating takeout in the car was enough for me. Spending time with Hawke was enough for me.

But he had planned so much more.

"Where are we going next?" I asked, shutting my window, as Notre Dame passed our view.

He shrugged. "Don't know."

I waved an accusatory pointy finger his way. "You're such a liar."

"I really don't." He shrugged again.

"And the worst thing is, you are so good at it. I wonder if I should believe anything you say at all."

He ran one hand through his wavy locks. "We're almost there, Sunshine. You'll just have to wait for your last surprise."

My eyes flew to my phone in my hand, searching for the time. It was two in the afternoon, and my stomach churned as the minutes ticked by. Our time together was dwindling down. It was like sitting on your favorite ride at a theme park, knowing that it was going to end. I didn't want our adventure to stop.

Hawke sensed my sadness because he said, "Don't worry. I'll bring you here again."

"Yeah, whatever," I said, joking with him. "Empty promises."

When would we have free time? When would he be on tour in Paris again? When would we have another opportunity to tour the City of Love?

Probably never.

He scooted over and pulled me into him, and my heartbeat picked up at his nearness. He gripped my chin to face him. "Next time, it'll be just you and me. No band. No bodyguards. Just the two of us."

Impossible, I thought to myself.

But, from the determined look in his eyes, I knew he meant it. He wanted it to be just the two of us as much as I did.

When the car stopped, I leaned over him and squinted through the tinted window to try to make out where we were. When Tilton held the door open to let us out, I took in the sign, and my eyes flew to Hawke's.

"No." *No way. No way. No way.* My voice shook with disbelief. "Cordon Bleu?"

Le Cordon Bleu was a well-known culinary school with branches worldwide. I planned to apply to the one in Chicago. But here, in Paris, the culinary capital of the world, this was where it'd all begun. The original school had been founded in Paris in 1895.

"Sunshine, did you want to admire the school from the car?"

"What?"

"Because I have a private tour scheduled with their head chef. He said you could use his kitchen."

My mouth fell open. A swarm of flies could've flown in and out. And then it happened.

I couldn't hold in my excitement. I bounced up and down in my seat like a total lunatic, clapping my hands like I was five, squeeing like I was a teenager. Usually, I was able to hold it together in front of the rock star and keep my cool, but not today. Not when this was the best day ever.

"Oh my God," was all I could say on repeat.

His crooked smile widened. "Relax, Sam."

And then I did.

I brushed my hair from my face, totally embarrassed that I had lost my calm and cool demeanor.

He reached for the door and extended his hand. "Let's go. We've got exactly an hour and a half until we're out of this place, and I have to get to the stadium for sound check."

I stepped out of the car, and before we walked in, I went up on my tiptoes and pulled back his baseball cap, tenderly pecking him on the lips. "Thank you," I said.

His signature smile slowly left his face, and lines on his normally smooth face creased his forehead. An unfocused gaze filled his vision, and with a light touch of his hand, he rested his palm on my cheek . . . but in the next second, the vulnerability I'd witnessed was gone.

He tipped his head toward the entranceway. "Let's go."

I let him take my hand as I half-skipped into the entrance of Le Cordon Bleu, hand in hand with Hawke Calvin, rock-star extraordinaire.

THE RIDE BACK TO THE hotel was filled with my nonstop chatter about Chef Alain Pepin and his gifted technique in making croquembouche, a traditional French wedding cake. In the US, we would call it a tower of cream puffs. The culinary master had instructed me on how to perfect the crème puffs decorated with caramel and spun sugar. We had filled half of the crème puffs with chocolate and half with vanilla. Then, we'd spun caramel and dipped the puffs in the caramel concoction. The chef had taught me how to stack the puffs in a circular motion and maintain balance and symmetry so that the tower would not fall.

Hawke sat back and listened as I rambled on about Chef Alain's technique and perfection in the kitchen until we were interrupted again by the ringing of his phone.

He held up a finger and began talking to someone, seemed like Cofi. I could tell Cofi was giving him the rundown, and Hawke said that we'd meet them at the concert.

When he hung up the phone, my happy-happy-joy-joy moment was gone.

Hawke immediately spit out directions, "Tilton, head straight to the stadium. Alan's shitting himself because I'm not there." He leaned back, unaffected, and then turned my way. "I'll have Tilton drop me off first, and then you can get ready and meet me there."

I glanced down at my stained shirt. Caramel had spilled on the middle of my white baby tee when I was decorating the crème puffs. I didn't want to part from him, but I looked like a slob next to his perfection, and I needed to change.

"Did you have fun?" he asked.

I nodded, but my smile from earlier was absent because the hourglass of sand that indicated our time together was quickly dwindling down. "I had a great time," I said, my tone sullen to match my mood.

When he pulled me onto his lap without warning, my heart jumped to the middle of my throat. His fingers pressed against my back, so lightly at first that I didn't feel it and then increasing with pressure until I felt it everywhere.

"I'm glad you had fun, Sunshine." A devilish smile graced his face. "I think I had more fun watching you in action."

I gasped when his velvety tongue outlined my lips.

"Can I hire these hands?" He put one said hand on the thickening bulge between us. "For cooking?"

I laughed because he was not talking about food. The privacy barrier began to lift from the middle of the limo, blocking my view of Tilton, causing my internal temperature to rise twenty notches.

"I think it's time for my midday snack," he said, his tone husky with desire.

His touch was hypnotizing, and my whole body tingled under his fingertips.

He guided me to my back while his fingers worked the button of my jeans. Everything with Hawke was a first. First one-night stand. First Paris experience. Now, the first time having sex in the back of a limo. Check, check, and check.

"Are you on birth control?"

"Yes." My arousal could be sensed through my voice, and my whole body flooded with warmth.

"Because I don't have any condoms," he breathed.

I wiggled beneath him, and my knees fell to the sides. I wanted him so badly, needed him with a passion so strong, I didn't care anymore.

A moan escaped my mouth when his fingers pierced me, and my wetness met where he touched, my desire for him increasing twofold. There was no doubt I would give him what I very much wanted myself.

"Are you clean?" I asked, unable to control my hunger for him any longer.

My hands moved to the buckle of his pants, unzipping him and reaching for his hard length. The feel of him against my fingertips had my mouth watering, and when my fingers wrapped around his cock, his loud intake of breath sent a thrill right through me.

"I get tested every month, and I've never been without one."

And I decided that I trusted him. Because I did and I couldn't wait any longer, I positioned him at my entrance, and in one swift movement, he filled me. I gasped at the fullness of him.

A fiery fever rushed within me as my fingers threaded through his hair. His eyes locked with mine before he kissed me deeply. Tongue against tongue. Skin against skin. The electrifying magnetism between us was palpable.

"You feel . . . you feel so good, Sunshine." His words came out in broken, husky puffs.

He moved above me with raw, animalistic passion that I had never experienced before—not like I had a lot to compare him to, but still. I wondered if he was like this with everyone or just me. I wanted to believe it. I wanted so badly to believe I couldn't compare to the rest of the women he'd been with.

When the car parked, his movements quickened, and his deep breathing accelerated. I knew he was close. Close to ecstasy, and I was, too.

The tingling started at the base of my spine, creeping up my legs and to my core. He gripped my ass tighter, indenting his fingers in my skin, as he drove deeper, deeper, deeper inside me.

"I love how you feel. I love you," he moaned as we both climaxed.

We came together in blissful rapture with me biting down hard enough on his lips to prevent myself from screaming.

And, just as I came down from my high, his words registered in my ears.

Did he just utter those words? Was he for real, or was it only in the heat of the moment?

I held on to him, arms around his neck, legs wrapped around his waist. And I decided I never wanted to let him go.

"Tell me, it's only ever going to be me." I couldn't help it. I couldn't stop the words from flying out. My grip tightened around him.

Sadly, a knock on the limo window had him pulling out of me so abruptly, I felt cold and empty. Our eyes locked, and he cupped the side of my face. I read an intensity in his eyes that was mirrored in mine.

"It's only ever going to be you."

I leaned into his touch, but then the knocking on the door heightened, and he straightened and tugged up his pants. After he pulled me up, I readjusted myself in my seat, and after one peck on the lips, he opened the door.

"I'll see you later. All right, Sunshine?"

And then he was gone.

I blinked at the door he'd slipped through and wrapped my arms around myself to bring back the warmth in my body.

With Hawke, when I was with him, I was on the highest of highs, but when we weren't together, I was in the lowest of lows.

I knew I had to take control of this situation. Put myself more in the driver's seat. I needed to take care of myself because no one else would.

THE NIGHT PASSED BY ME in a blur. In one moment, I had entered the stadium, and in what seemed like the next minute, I had left and was in the limo, heading back to the hotel after the concert.

I could feel the high of the boys as they chatted away. I assumed this was how it was when you went on tour—the excitement of being in a new country, the new material, the screaming fans.

Hawke stayed close beside me, his knee touching mine, but he seemed distant. Not to the rest of his band, but to me. He hadn't looked at me when he entered the room or touched me or kissed me on the lips.

He just bent down, and with his crooked smile, he asked, "Did you like the concert?"

I answered with pure honesty, "It was amazing!" Because it had been, and if my departure tomorrow hadn't been weighing on me, I would've been just as excited as all the fans who had filled the stadium.

That seemed to satisfy him, and he turned to Cofi and talked about their last song of the night, the closing of the concert.

I exhaled a shaky breath.

This was it. The end.

With Hawke, I never knew where I stood. He had said, when he was with me, he was with *only* me, but tomorrow, he wouldn't be with me.

So, it made me wonder, *Will he be with someone else?*

But he'd said . . . he'd said he loved me, and it was only me. Those were the words I wanted to believe.

My stomach churned, as though food were stuck in my intestines, but I shook my head, forcing the feeling away. There was nothing I could do. This was the nature of his life. This was how I had met him.

Hawke intertwined our fingers when we exited the limo and entered the hotel. That touch was all I craved. All I longed for. It was my last night with him, and I was determined to make every second matter. But I hadn't expected the whole band to follow us to our room.

A forced smile was stuck on my face. Funny how I'd mastered the fake face over the years—during my cooking final at culinary school when the chefs had to taste-test our food to the aftermath of my mother's death to now where our hotel room was filled to the corners packed with people.

When I stepped into the main living area, it was as if I were on the set of a music video.

The music blasted on high in the background, the bass of the song thumping against my skin. Half-naked women swayed around the room, like puppies in a crate.

Who let these people in?

The band dispersed, greeting the strangers in Hawke's penthouse. What I hadn't counted on was Hawke doing the same. He left me standing in the middle of the room, alone, while he walked across the living room area to greet a couple I didn't know. One guy had his hair slicked back into a short ponytail with a beautiful blonde pressed up against one side and a leggy brunette on the other. A group had formed around Hawke, waiting for their turn to greet the rock star.

After five minutes, I plopped my butt on the closest thing next to me, which was a low circular couch by the television. Over the next hour and a half, I experienced the true life of the rich and famous. The bar was covered in bottles of expensive hard liquor, while the center table of the room was loaded with joints and powder and pills. I was straight-up in my own theater, watching the scene unfold before my eyes.

I wanted to raise my hand, call a time-out, and retreat to my apartment in Chicago, but I couldn't. My only savior was Hawke, who had come over twice to ask if I was okay, but he was beyond inebriated. I'd been watching him closely. He hadn't taken anything, but he kept pounding back the drinks, as if it were water and there was going to be a drought.

After an hour of no Hawke, I stood. I'd had enough. My flight would be leaving at eight in the morning, meaning I needed to be at the airport at six, meaning I needed to get some sleep. I staggered into our bedroom and was shocked to see multiple people having their own personal party in the room.

Two girls in Daisy Dukes were on our bed—fully clothed, thank goodness—making out in front of a stranger who seemed to get a kick out of getting the two girls to kiss.

I rushed to retrieve my backpack from the closet and slipped one strap over my shoulder. My eyes searched for a safe haven, any-where, but there was nowhere to go.

Even our balcony was occupied, crammed with at least a dozen people in a space made for six. I padded across the plush carpet, my Converse indenting a path to my decided destination where I could get some peace and quiet—the bathroom.

I shut the door and locked it. Then, I chucked my backpack on the floor and threw some towels inside the massive tub. Once I had a good amount of cushion, I stepped into the cloud of towels and laid my head down. That was when the loneliness hit.

Highest of highs and lowest of lows—that was how I felt when I was with Hawke.

Heat formed behind my eyes. I wondered if he'd even remem-ber to wish me good-bye. My eyes shut, and I forced myself to sleep and dream of when I'd had the best time of my existence, just hours ago.

Numerous times during the night, people banged on the door, wanting to use the bathroom. I refused to answer. There were three other bathrooms in the penthouse; they could use one of those.

When the doorknob jiggled and the door unlocked and creaked open, I jumped up in the tub.

"Sunshine." Hawke had one arm slung over Tilton's beefy shoul-der. It was as though Tilton was keeping him upright.

I hopped out of the tub and rushed over to grab Hawke's other side.

"I think I partied way too hard, Sunshine. Not . . . feeling well."

He reeked of alcohol and smelled like cigarettes. I stripped him of his wet shirt—maybe from sweat or, more likely, someone had spilled something on him.

"You're going to take advantage of me now?" His crooked smile made my heart hurt, like pins being jabbed into a pincushion. Then, he passed out.

I stared up at Tilton, about to freak out. "Did he take anything?

I mean, is he on anything?" God, I knew nothing about hard-core illegal drugs. In that aspect, I was totally out of my element. There was a first time for everything, but I wasn't about to jump on board with this first.

Tilton shook his head, and my whole body relaxed.

"He just needs sleep."

"Hawke." I patted his cheek.

His head lolled from side to side.

"Hawke, do you want water?"

I glanced at the door behind me, hearing loud laughter, which only meant the party was still going on, full force.

Hawke was out cold, so I nodded to the tub where Tilton lifted his almost six-foot frame into the oversized basin.

When Tilton shut the door behind him, I ran over to make sure it was locked, and then I glanced down at my watch. Only three more hours until I had to head to the airport.

My feet shuffled against the cold marble floor, and I sat against the edge of the tub.

Hawke's chest lifted when soft breaths escaped him. He stirred in his sleep, and his eyes fluttered open and shut. "Sunshine?"

He extended his hand, and I intertwined our fingers. I decided, for the few hours that I could, I would lie next to him, so I slowly got into the tub filled with towels instead of bubbles and nestled against his warm skin.

"Mmm," he muttered, pulling me close.

His skin was clammy to the touch.

I pulled back and studied his face. "You okay?"

"Too much," he slurred.

I didn't know what he was talking about, but I doubted he did either. He seemed incoherent, and his words made no sense, even when they were strung together.

"Too much," he whispered.

"Too much what?" I brushed his blond hair away from his face.

Too much alcohol, work, life?

"Do you want water?" I asked.

He didn't respond.

"Stay, Sunshine." His facial features scrunched together. "Please."

He was dreaming. He had to be.

I put one finger on his lips. "I can't."

The lines in his face eased, and I snuggled close to his chest. It wasn't the most comfortable of poses, but I was determined, hugging him tightly.

"Stay," he said again, repeating the word he had said earlier.

"Why?" I whispered against his neck.

His forehead creased again, and my stomach clenched as I watched him.

"Lonely," he whispered. "Need you."

I held my breath at the intensity of his words. *He was adored by millions, could have anything with one word, yet he was lonely?*

And, finally, I understood.

He didn't trust the people around him, and in the brief amount of time I had spent with him, I realized why. He was the bank, bringing in money, fortune, and fame. Everyone around him received the same by association. Nothing was as it seemed; no one was genuine.

"I'm trying . . ." he said, his words muffled.

I threaded my fingers through his hair, feeling his silky blond locks slip through my fingertips.

"Trying to what?"

"Trying to stop . . . be better."

I strained my ears to listen. He was mumbling, and I couldn't make out what he was trying to say. But then I made out the words that caused my heart to swell.

"Better . . . better for you."

When his whole body relaxed, I knew he was out. I tried to

readjust his arm, so I could get into a more restful position, but he was dead weight, so I settled for uncomfortable so that I could stay near him. With one long exhale, I kissed him on the lips.

I fell asleep on a bed of clouds, nestled against the chest of a man I was falling for.

Who was I kidding?

I had already fallen. Hard.

THE BANGING ON THE DOOR woke me from my sleep. I rubbed my eyes and jumped to a sitting position.

My watch said ten o'clock. "Omigod!" I leaped from the tub and opened the door, surprised that I hadn't tripped over my own feet.

Tilton's seven-foot frame stared me down, his face stoic.

"I missed my flight," I said, my pulse beating in my throat.

By the look on his face, he already knew. His response? He turned around and walked out of the room. Typical Tilton move.

When a strangled-animal sound came from behind me, I turned. Hawke was hunched over and had his hands over his eyes. I approached at a slow pace.

With one eye open and the other one squinted, he stared up at me. "Morning, Sunshine." His crooked smile made an appearance, even through his hangover pain.

"I missed my flight."

He stood, still shirtless. The sunlight coming in through the window highlighted the black art against his toned tan chest. He stepped out of the tub, rubbed his face, and said, "I'll call in the jet."

"Aren't you guys leaving today?"

They were going to head on to their next leg of the tour—London.

"Another jet," he answered, reaching for his phone in the back of his pocket.

And, just like that, my crisis was averted. Money knew no limits.

The next hour moved like we were on fast-forward. Hawke had scheduled the jet to leave at the same time they would be leaving from Paris—Le Bourget, the private airport we had flown into. There was nothing for me to pack. Everything I had brought was in my one large backpack.

When I exited the bathroom and stepped into our suite, my eyes widened, taking in the scene. I had expected a trashed hotel room, given the amount of people partying and jumping on the bed last night, but no, the place was immaculate. In our room, the bed was made, and all the pillows were placed where they should be. Fresh flowers were back on the tables. The only remnants of last night were five large garbage bags in the foyer.

Chaos followed these boys everywhere, but I guessed there was damage control trailing right behind them.

Cofi strolled into the room, followed by AJ, the bass guitarist, and Max the lead guitarist.

"Sunshine, you ready for London?" Cofi asked.

"No, she's going home." Hawke shut him down quick as he bent down to zip up his suitcase. "She's leaving when we leave."

"Are you bored with Hawke already?" The guys laughed behind Cofi. "Because, if you need a change of scenery . . ."

Hawke jerked upright and shoved at Cofi's chest. "Quit it. Let's go."

The action was so sudden, I flinched.

Hawke grabbed my hand in a possessive manner—one that had my insides singing because, for a moment, I felt like I belonged to only him.

The boys trailed behind Hawke, and once we hopped back into the limo, the chaos of the crowd erupted again. I swore, these fans never took a day off. Police cars surrounded us and escorted the limo the rest of the way to the airport.

Alan was in the car this time, reciting the band's itinerary for when they landed in London. AJ seemed like the only guy paying attention while the rest of the men sat back, uninterested. When I tried to meet Hawke's eyes, they were fixed outside the window, as though he were thinking deeply.

When Tilton opened the door and it was time to say our final good-byes, my heart sank like an anchor in the ocean. This hurt. To look at him hurt. To breathe the same air hurt. Everything hurt.

Since we were not officially together, there was no guarantee that he was going to ever call me again. I could just ask him, but I was afraid of rejection, afraid to seem too needy, afraid to show him that he affected me in ways I didn't want to admit.

Laughter erupted from the band, including Alan. Cofi must have cracked a joke, but I hadn't heard it.

"All right, so . . ." I dug my feet into the gravel and inched toward my rock star. "I just want to thank you for yesterday and for bringing me to Paris." So much emotion leaked from my voice that I felt self-conscious, so I stared intently at the ground, unable to meet his eyes.

What Hawke did next surprised me. Without warning, he lifted my chin, wrapped one arm around my waist, and kissed me—mouths closed, no tongue. No words needed to be said as a strong emotion passed from him to me, one where I knew I would be missed.

All I could hear was the roar of the airplanes' engines in the background and the beating of my heart in my ears. And all I could smell was Hawke's scent, his musky, masculine cologne and his unique signature.

The kiss was long. He didn't release me until the guys started clapping.

And, when he did, he said, "I had the best time, Sunshine." Then, he stepped back, shoved his hands in his pockets, and walked away.

I didn't know if he was saying good-bye. He hadn't asked for his phone back, yet he hadn't said he was going to call this time. I waited and waited for him to turn around, but he didn't. I finally let out a low breath and turned toward my destination, my own private jet.

I had a lot to think about during my flight home. Putting my racing thoughts on pause, I fell into a deep sleep.

When I awoke, we were already pulling into Schaumburg Regional Airport, a private airport in a suburb about forty-five minutes outside of the city of Chicago. I'd had the craziest dream—one where I was in Hawke's arms, and it was just the two of us, sitting in the open at an outdoor café.

I sighed loudly. *Only in my dreams.*

chapter THIRTEEN

THE NEXT WEEK FLEW BY super quick. I immersed myself in work and television and everything non-rock-star related.

Hawke had texted at random times. No calls, just random texts since I'd last seen him a week before. I waited for those texts and hoped for some calls. Somehow, I believed that things between us would change because I thought we had shared something special in Paris, but it didn't.

As the September leaves covered the trees in a burnt red and deep orange, I thought of him nonstop, which only fueled my sullen mood. I told myself it would pass. That our love affair had been brief and without promises. There was no way to know what the future held for us, and that was something I couldn't change.

So, I decided to drown myself in work. I wiped the sweat from my brow and discarded my white apron into the hamper in the locker room. Being back to my normal life and routine had me wondering if my time in Paris had all been a dream.

"Shift's over. You're out of here, BFAW!" Candice patted my back and threw on her white apron.

"What?" I laughed, shaking my head at Candice and her acronyms that she would make up on the fly.

She playfully hit my shoulder. "Best Friend at Work, duh."

I smiled at her silliness. *How was I supposed to know that?*

When a phone rang in my purse, my breath hitched in my throat. For a few seconds, I stared at my black fold-over purse on the ground. It was Hawke. It had to be.

I dropped to my knees, my hands digging to the bottom, and I pressed the receiver to my ear. "Hello?"

"Sunshine?" Hawke's usually smooth voice sounded strained, maybe even agitated.

"Yeah? What's wrong?"

"Where are you right now? I've been trying to call you all day."

"I've been at work. I can't have my phone in the kitchen. Why?"

He huffed. "Someone must've been watching us in Paris because a photo was leaked."

My pulse raced at his words, but I tried to calm my fears and think the best. "So?"

"It was of us kissing." His tone dropped two octaves lower, and so did my stomach, plummeting to my toes.

I leaned against the lockers for support, letting my head bang against the metal.

"It's all over the Internet, and the media is swarming my hotel. In a matter of hours, they'll know where you live and that you came with us to Europe."

I'd never thought of the ramifications of being with Hawke or even contemplated that the paparazzi would be remotely interested in my life. And, now that it was here, I couldn't move, couldn't breathe, couldn't think of what to do next.

Candice, who had been fiddling with her phone while she waited for my conversation to finish, turned in my direction, her eyes wide. She stared hard at my face, at the phone in her hand, and back at my face. "Sam?"

She flipped her phone to show me the picture that was apparently trending on all social media sites. The photo had been taken outside the plane at the private airport. The band members were blurry figures in the background, but what was in clear view was me. They must've zoomed in because you could see my whole face before Hawke had grabbed my cheeks and kissed me hard on the lips.

I breathed in deeply through my nose and out through my mouth in one long, excruciating breath to prevent a full-on panic attack from taking over. "What am I going to do?"

"Sunshine, you're going to have to stay low for a while. Until . . . until I figure this out."

I grabbed my hair by the roots, my eyes searching the room for an answer, for divine intervention, for something. "I have to go to work every day this week." I couldn't have the paps disrupting my life and stalking me at the restaurant. The restaurant would never put up with that.

"Is there any way you can take off?" he asked. The normal calmness in his tone was not there, only replaced by a heightened worry. "You know what? I'm going to fly you somewhere secluded. Somewhere you can stay until this dies down."

My shoulders tensed, my thoughts a jumbled mess. "No, I took time off to be with you. There's no way my manager is going to give me more days off—unless he fires me. Then, I'll have plenty of time," I snapped with a bitter chuckle. I closed my eyes, praying to God I wouldn't be fired.

He huffed on the phone. "I need you to get home and stay there. Are you on social media?"

Who wasn't? I nodded, but he couldn't see.

"If you are, shut down all your accounts. I'll take care of this."

But how could he? He was all the way on the other side of the world.

"I have a great PR team, and we'll get this managed," he said, mostly talking to himself.

His voice lowered. "Sunshine?"

"Yeah?" I asked, trying not to hyperventilate.

"It's going to be fine," he said as though he were that sure.

I wished I'd felt as sure as he sounded.

"All right," I whispered, trying my best to believe him.

"Just get home as quickly as possible and stay there, okay?"

I nodded and clenched my eyes, not wanting our conversation to end. I pictured his crooked smile to keep myself calm. "Okay."

And then the line went dead.

When I opened my eyes, Candice's jaw was gaping so wide, I could see her tonsils. "Was that *him*?"

I pushed myself up and looked away. "Uh . . ."

"You weren't at a family emergency, you liar! You were in Paris, weren't you? Are you *with* him?" She bounced on the balls of her feet, excited, as though I had just told her Santa Claus was real.

I pressed a hand to my pounding heart. My heartbeat was racing like a ticking bomb ready to explode.

Where are the paps now? How long do I have before they find me?

My manager is going to find out that I lied to him.

Oh God. My heart is beating awfully fast. I hope I don't pass out.

"It's complicated. Yes, I was in Europe. I'm not sure what we are. Yes, that was him." I didn't want to elaborate on our non-relationship.

She immediately threw her arms around my waist and started to jump up and down, her large boobs pressing against my chest. "Oh my gosh! I cannot believe it." She pulled back, and a look of wonder came over her, her eyes sparkling. "I want an autograph! I want to meet him." She pressed her hands together, like she was in solemn prayer. "Please, please, please."

Oh, goodness. I never thought anyone would top Chloe. I guessed I was wrong.

"Okay," I said to placate her even though I didn't know the next time I'd see him.

"It's all over the Internet!" she squeed, fingers dancing over her phone.

I backed away and rubbed my sweaty hands on the front of my jeans. First things first, I needed to get out of here. Then, I'd figure out how the hell I was going to deal with all of this.

"I have to go. Before they find me here." I took her hands in mine. "Please, don't tell anyone. It's really important." I hoped that maybe, since the majority of my coworkers were men, they stayed away from the normal gossip and social media sites.

She nodded, her eyes serious. "Okay."

I pulled her into another hug, tighter, squeezing her, like I used to squeeze Teddy Belly when I was younger, pouring my anxiety into that one hug. "I've gotta go. Thanks, Candice."

She shook her head and cast me a glance, her eyes intently focused on mine.

A frown formed on my face at the starstruck look in her eye. "Stop looking at me like that."

She dimmed her smile and bit her lip to prevent her smile from widening. "Okay. It's just so surreal."

"I know, I know."

My whole escapade with Hawke—from meeting him to joining him on the start of his European tour to the whole world knowing our business now—was crazy surreal. I didn't regret our time together, but I was beginning to regret that I hadn't taken his warnings about the paps more seriously. Not to mention, I'd lied to my boss, and now, he'd soon find out. I just hoped I wouldn't get fired. My only saving grace was that I had taken my earned vacation days and not extra time I hadn't been entitled to have.

I waved one last time, slipped my purse over my shoulder, and made a beeline for the door. The hope that my coworkers and boss wouldn't find out fizzled in an instant as I screeched to a stop by the front door.

Satan's Posse—otherwise known as the paparazzi—was gathered outside.

I quickly pressed myself against the brick wall.

Damn vultures knew where I worked? Didn't they sleep? How fast had word spread?

I needed to get home. I needed the comfort of my apartment. I needed to leave.

From my back pocket, I pulled out my phone and dialed Chloe.

"You're trending on Twitter," she said, elated.

I groaned. "So, you know, too?"

She chuckled. "Girlfriend, by the looks of this, everyone in the world knows."

"No." My eyes zoned in on the group of people holding their cameras, just beyond the glass double doors. "They know where I work! Chloe, I'm freaking out here." My hand flew to the bottom of my high ponytail, and I twisted and twisted, wanting to tug my hair out.

"Calm down. You'll be fine. Have you left yet?"

A few shallow gasps escaped my lips. "No, they are literally outside the restaurant doors. There must be at least twenty photographers." I bit my thumbnail, contemplating my next move. "I can't leave; they'll recognize me. Help me, please." The cold knot in my stomach grew into a triple knot, Boy Scout-style.

"Shit, all right. You can't go through the back door because I bet someone is waiting for you out there, too. You have to pretend like you're a customer. Who's there right now?"

I swore, it seemed as though she'd done this before, but I trusted Chloe.

"The whole flipping staff. We've got a full crew today. Jim and Todd are here. Candice, and she knows."

"Sam, listen. You have to tell Jim that you need his clothes. Change into them. Then, you need to leave with Todd and Candice."

"I don't want Todd and Jim to know," I whined. Then, I'd get the starstruck look from them, too. Or worse, what would my boss say? I hoped I'd still have a job.

"They'll find out soon enough. Or do you want to sleep at the restaurant tonight?"

I debated my options. A frown etched on my face when I realized that I didn't have many. "Not really."

"Okay. Then, you need to get going." As always, it was Super Chloe to the rescue. She could defuse bombs if she wanted to.

"Fine."

I skittered quickly into the kitchen, and the whole staff started clapping, hooting, and hollering. I wanted to roll up into a ball and disappear. There went the secret. Kyle, my manager, gave me a pointed stare and then lifted an eyebrow. I fidgeted with the edge of my shirt. Anxiety threatened to choke me.

Just when I was positive I was fired, he began to clap with the rest of them.

I gulped, my face flushing. "Guys . . . please." I had never cared about what other people thought of my life, but now, I wanted to crawl into a hole and never come out.

"Jim." I crooked my finger toward the back corner.

He already had his apron on, ready to work the evening shift.

"Todd, Candice." I tilted my head toward the back of the kitchen.

They laughed as they trailed behind, following me to the rear.

"Guys . . ." I shifted from my heels to the balls of my feet and back. In my list of embarrassing moments, this was making the top three. "I need your help."

AFTER THROWING ON JIM'S BAGGY jeans and hoodie with my hair tucked under a beanie I'd borrowed from one of the busboys, I looked like a not-so-attractive skinny male trying way too hard to be cool. I strolled out with Todd and had my arm swung over Candice, who was acting as my pretend girlfriend.

We timed our exit with a bunch of people who were already done with their meals. The sun was beginning to set in front of us, but it was still shining even though I'd prayed for the cover of darkness.

I pulled the hoodie low over my eyes and practiced my male

swagger as my eyes took in the paparazzi. Some were taking random pictures of those walking outside, and the others were talking among themselves. They probably ran in the same circles.

I ducked my head low as we exited, any lower and I'd be kissing the ground. A few of them threw a cursory glance our way, but Candice buried herself into my side, playing the part.

We walked down the block and around the corner, away from the swarming photographers. The tension in my shoulders and neck began to ease as we moved farther away from the restaurant.

Around the corner, Todd turned toward me. "Dinner's on you soon." He smiled.

I high-fived him and hugged Candice one last time.

"Yes, dinner on me, for saving my ass."

After our short good-byes, they rushed back to work.

A calming breath released from my chest as I started walking toward the train station. Without thinking, I pushed back the hood and pulled off the beanie, picking up speed, the cool of the autumn air threading through my hair.

In the next second, I heard it—my name being loudly called out, like a ripple of thunder in a storm. My eyes took in two photogs behind me. Then, two more. Then, one more.

Anxiety ripped through my body, and adrenaline pumped through my veins. I took off in record speed, running like a target was on my back. Problem was, Jim's baggy pants made it difficult to get traction. My body shook with terror, terror like I'd never felt before. I catapulted away from the vultures, my feet pounding against the sidewalk. Then, when I turned, there were more of them, like hounds running after a fox.

I heard all their questions like echoes.

"Samantha!"

"Are you dating Hawke?"

"Are you exclusive?"

Their voices carried behind me, and my heart jumped into

my throat, but I kept running, blood pumping and feet thumping against the sidewalk. I could tell they were getting closer by the growing cacophony of voices, but I ran because my life depended on it. And because I didn't have answers to any of their questions.

My legs were burning, and my stomach churned, making me worry I was going to barf up the chicken Parmesan I'd eaten today. I was sure they'd like nothing more than to take pictures of that. The thought made me run faster down the block and toward my destination—the train. When I turned the corner, I face-planted into someone's chest and fell back onto my butt.

"Whoa . . . hey there." Hands slipped under my arms, pulling me off the ground.

I glanced up, dizzily taking in a white polo shirt before meeting a pair of familiar brown eyes. Then, I fell into his arms, already defeated.

Josh.

He peered behind me, quickly taking in the scene rushing toward us. Then, he went right into action, steering me into a narrow alley. He towered over my body, both hands against the bricks of the building, framing my head, ducking his head to hide my face.

He leaned in close, and I could smell the mint on his lips.

"Why are a bunch of people chasing you?" His warm breath brushed against my cheek, forming goose bumps that skittered across my skin and down my neck. "Did you just rob a bank or something?"

"No." I tried to catch my breath, my chest heaving in and out.

"Well, you look like you just robbed a bank."

I glanced down at my attire. He was right. "Long story."

My eyes peered over him, and I cowered when I saw two photographers rushing past the opening of the alleyway.

Josh must've sensed my anxiety because he looked behind himself and then angled closer, pressing his body against the building, fully blocking anyone's view of me. It was as if he were a heaven-sent angel. An angel with a crazy contagious smile. To any-body looking in, we were just a couple making out in the alleyway.

He cupped the side of my face and brushed his thumb against my cheek. I rested against his touch, craving the comfort, silence, and security.

"Hey . . ." More goose bumps formed where his fingers touched my skin. "Do something for me?"

I peered up at him. "Yeah?" I noted how the overhead sunlight caught the brown in his eyes. They were normally chocolate brown, but right now, his irises looked amber, just like a glass of cognac.

"Exhale," he said soothingly.

"What?"

"You seem as though you live your life always holding your breath, afraid of the next thing that might drop. You can't live like that. Sometimes . . . once in a while, you need to let it out. You need to relax. Breathe out for me. I've got you." He leaned closer. "Exhale."

I blew out a deep breath, letting the tension out of my shoulders. I'd needed that. Through the chaos, I felt oddly calm in his presence.

His hand lay perfectly still on the side of my face. "Feel better?" He dropped his hand from my cheek.

"Yeah, thank you." I smiled up at him.

He was cute. Almost too cute. Boyishly handsome, as though his face would never age.

"Now, can you do another thing for me?" he asked.

"Sure."

"Make sure you brush your teeth after this, all right?" His face held its composure while I felt my features fall.

A flush crept up my cheeks, and the tips of my ears became im-possibly hot. I tried to remember what I'd had for lunch. It was the damn Chicken Parm.

His lips quivered, and then a deep chuckle released from his throat. "I'm totally kidding."

I shoved at his chest. "Jerk."

His statue self didn't budge.

His eyes were sparkling with amusement, not apologetic at all. "You should've seen your face. It was epic."

I blew another long breath in his face. "There. Take my stank breath."

"Do it again."

I blew out another breath.

And closer.

A smaller breath escaped.

And closer.

We were mere millimeters apart.

His eyes flickered to my lips, and I exhaled a tiny breath.

Or maybe it was a sigh?

His lips by my lips.

His hand by my head.

Voices echoed in the background. "Do you think she went down this way?"

When they were in the alley, Josh closed the gap between us and pressed his lips against mine. He pushed me against the wall, his hard chest against my soft one.

He was just playing a part, saving me from the paparazzi.

I didn't want to kiss him, but when his lips met mine, it was as if our lips were meant to meet. Meet in the alleyway.

It felt wrong, but at the same time, I wanted to taste him. See if he tasted like mint. And he did but didn't. He was a mix of coffee and mint and lip balm, an oddly sexy combination that had my whole body zinging.

It started with a series of slow, shivery kisses—deliberate and drugging me in the most sensual way. It was as though I were kissing someone I'd known all my life and he'd had years of practicing the seduction of kisses only to satisfy my lips.

My hands gripped his shoulders, squeezing his biceps. My body fit against his like perfect puzzle pieces. The cold air combined with the heat of our bodies only fueled my arousal.

A couple of people strolled into the alleyway. We could hear them, but I had no clue what they were saying, and at the moment, I didn't care.

My hands crept underneath his shirt, feeling the span of his back, trailing to his stomach, caressing the tight muscles of his six-pack.

A moan escaped his mouth as my fingers pressed against his skin.

Then, a door flew open down the alley, and I jumped. Automatically, Josh pushed me behind himself and sheltered me with his body, his breathing labored, his eyes alert.

An older guy with gray hair was holding a black garbage bag.

In all the hoopla, we hadn't noticed we were right next to a restaurant exit and some dumpsters.

My eyes flew to the busy street at the end of the alleyway. There didn't seem to be anyone with cameras looming on the sidewalk.

I let out a thankful low sigh and looked up at Josh, my mouth still burning from his kisses.

His eyes were unreadable.

"You okay?" Josh asked.

Was I?

I didn't know. My life had been turned upside down and inside out.

My thoughts brought me to Hawke and this situation I was now in because of him, but I couldn't deny that unbelievable kiss from Josh. A kiss that had triggered a tingling from the baby hairs on the crown of my head down to the tips of my little pinkie toes.

This was crazy.

He intertwined his fingers with mine and placed our hands against his chest. The thumping of his heart matched the pulse in my wrist. "Crazy intense," he whispered. It was as if he could read my mind, his brown eyes penetrating mine.

Comfortable silence ticked by until I tore my gaze from his.

He glanced behind himself. "I think they're gone."

"Thanks." I didn't know what I was thanking him for—saving me from the photographers or that unbelievable kiss.

The insane part of me wanted him to kiss me again, but that would be a bad idea. Kisses with Josh would only lead to more, and right now, I had more than I could handle.

When he stepped away, a strong wind chilled the heat I'd felt moments ago. Up close, Josh provided an easy comfort. Now, awkwardness filled the air, and my gaze veered to the right at nothing in particular. I didn't know what to do next.

Acknowledge the kiss or not?

"Anytime you want me to do that again," he said, "you just let me know."

I laughed. And, just like that, the weirdness was gone. I fiddled with the edge of Jim's hoodie "I should be getting home."

"Not before you have dinner with me first."

I blinked up at him. "What?"

"Well, I think you owe me."

Shoot, because of today's fiasco, I owed quite a lot of people.

"I just let you feel me up, so I think you owe me," I joked back.

Amusement showed on his face. "Plus, those photographers you're running from might be lurking around. I say you wait a while unless you want them to know where you live."

I scrunched my nose. Too bad they probably already knew.

"All righty," I conceded. "Where to?"

He tightened his hold around my fingers, bringing that familiar sense of comforting warmth to the surface. I barely knew him, but it felt natural, walking with Josh's hand wrapped around mine.

"Anywhere but here," he said.

chapter FOURTEEN

EVEN IN MY BAGGY CLOTHES, I didn't want to risk being recognized, so we ended up walking along the lake on Lake Shore Drive until the sun set in front of us, and the moon's silver light was shining over the water.

Good thing I hadn't gone home because Chloe had texted to let me know that our street was flooded with paps just waiting for my arrival.

Great. Just Great.

We plopped down on the concrete, our chosen spot overlooking the city. The building lights shone brightly in front of us, and the cool autumn breeze brushed against my skin as our feet dangled only a few feet above the water of Lake Michigan.

I lifted my head and took a calming breath, trying to put the chaos of work, of Hawke, of all my worries behind me.

When I opened my eyes, Josh was staring at me with a look of curiosity. "I think I have a few theories."

I laughed and motioned with my hands for him to continue.

"So, you didn't rob a bank?"

I shook my head, grinning.

With his thumb and his forefinger, he rubbed at his chin, as though in deep thought. "I think you're a real-life princess."

"Uh-huh," I said, playing along and laughing at the seriousness in his tone.

"From the land of Princessovia. And you came to the United States to escape the madness and responsibilities of being the next heir." He tipped his head for confirmation. "Am I right?"

I offered a noncommittal shrug. "Is that why you tried to fit a glass slipper on my foot?"

He pointed to me. "Exactly."

I decided to let him in on my secret. "Nope. Wrong. But what if I told you that I was dating—or *had* dated—a rock star?" Saying it out loud sounded unbelievable, even to my own ears.

His smile faltered, only slightly. "Rock star, huh?"

I nodded.

"What's said rock star's name?"

I gulped, realizing I wanted to let it out, to let someone else in on my secret, besides Chloe. Not that the rest of the world didn't already know now. "Hawke."

Hawke didn't need an introduction or his last name to be said.

Josh's mouth slipped slightly ajar. "You're kidding . . ."

I focused on the city in front of me, the twinkling of the lights from the skyscrapers within my focus. "Nope."

The squawk of a bird flying above us filled my ears as it soared through the sky, and I wished it were me. I wished I could escape, like the bird disappearing above the clouds, unnoticeable to anyone, free to do whatever it wanted.

Josh was quiet for a moment and then cleared his throat. "Figures, a beautiful girl like you would be with the lead singer of a world-famous band."

I shook my head. "It's not like that."

Every time I thought of Hawke, my heart would be weighed down because of the unknown.

"Live in the moment," he'd said.

And the moments together were exciting, but they were also brief and fleeting.

"I mean, we were dating or something, and then we weren't." My forehead wrinkled, and I dropped my eyes, watching the ripples of the waves at my feet. "We weren't exclusive, and I'm not sure we're anything now." Saying it was like a punch in the gut. It wasn't like I was going to force him into a relationship if he didn't want to be. "I mean . . . it wasn't specifically said. I really did think it was over until he called me today."

Josh angled closer, his voice soft, his eyes sincere. "You know you're worth more than that."

I glanced up at him, my knee touching his. "I genuinely like him. And maybe it's wishful thinking or hope blooming in my chest because I believe in fairy tales and happily ever afters and all that stuff girls believe in, but I swear, he felt something for me, too. At least . . . I thought he did." I averted my gaze, feeling silly and a lot embarrassed that those words had slipped out.

I hadn't imagined it. Hawke had said he loved me; he'd said that it was only me. But, if I'd meant more to him, if I had been more than a random fling, then I was worth more than a few random texts.

"No doubt." His eyes narrowed, as though he were thinking deeply. "There is no doubt in my mind that he's head over heels for you, Sam."

"Shut up," I said, bumping my shoulder with his. Now was not the time for sarcasm.

"You think I'm kidding?" He shook his head and sighed.

Then, he reached for my hand again, and I peered down at our connection. It was as though my palm had been made to fit perfectly in his.

"And he'd better not screw up because I'm sure anyone would be happy to hold your heart." His eyes held such sincerity that a rush of pink stained my cheeks.

"Please," I scoffed. "You and your lines."

He shook our intertwined hands. "I'm for real."

The intensity of his gaze was so serene, so compelling, that I couldn't help but believe him. I focused on the water hitting the concrete beneath my feet, reveling in the calmness, because I knew that it would be temporary, and tomorrow would be even more cra-zy than today.

I worried about work, about if the paps would disrupt my job—the job I needed to pay the bills and put me through school. I hadn't applied to Cordon Bleu yet, and if I wanted to achieve my dreams, the clock was ticking. My thoughts were a jumbled mess.

The length of the stressful day had my shoulders sagging. Josh must have sensed my tiredness because he gathered me onto his lap. There was a tranquility that surrounded Josh that made me jealous.

In a continuous motion, he rubbed the center of my back. He held me in silence, and eventually, my breathing evened out.

We looked like an odd couple—me in my baggy clothes and Josh in his polo shirt and dress pants. I laughed and cowered into his shirt as I thought about it.

"What?" A glint of curiosity was heavy in his tone.

I peered up at him. "We're a funny-looking couple."

The vibrations of his laughter lightened my insides. "That we are, Princess. That we are."

Staring into his warm dark chocolate eyes, I wondered how he had become so peaceful. I wished I could find peace like that.

Suddenly, years ago seemed like yesterday as memories came back. The pain from my mother's death was the same; it never less-ened. I craved his calmness.

I slipped off his lap and sat up straighter. "Can you tell me more about her? About your mom?"

His lips pressed into a smile, no teeth, and he nodded.

With his free hand, he picked a rock off the ground and tossed it into the lake. "Kathy Stanton, mother extraordinaire. She was my favorite person in the universe. Her presence would light up a room; her smile could brighten anyone's bad mood." His eyes clouded with old memories. "She was stunningly beautiful, and my dad was constantly jealous at the looks she'd get from other men, but that was nothing compared to her inner beauty." His voice quieted at the end.

He tore his gaze from mine and lifted his eyes to the night sky. "She taught me more about life in the time that she was dying than I'd ever learned in my whole life. Toward the end, she lived for me and Casey. She told me there was no point in living life if you weren't happy." His stare grazed my face. "Words so simple, but they packed a punch. I realized, nothing else mattered."

He blew out a breath and faced me. "Do you know Stanton Steel?"

I shook my head.

"The largest steel corporation in the nation?"

It still didn't ring a bell. I shrugged.

He pointed to himself. "Josh Stanton, not of Stanton Steel." He cringed and made a face, as though he'd eaten something spoiled and rotten and corporate.

"This is your long story?" When he nodded, I continued, "You didn't want to go into the family business?"

"Nope. I knew I wanted to be a lawyer ever since I interned at a law firm my junior year in high school."

Everything seemed to make sense—a life puzzle fitting together like a game of Tetris.

"So, they disowned you?" I asked softly. "Because you didn't want to go into the family business? Is that why your father was mad at dinner?"

"Nope, more like I disowned them." He picked up another rock next to him and tossed it in the lake. "Taking money from my family is like blood money. I'd feel like I owed them something, and I don't want to owe them anything."

"So, your dad is pressuring you?" I bit my tongue, willing myself to stop with the interrogation. Curious Cat was taking no prisoners today.

The way he shifted with unease let me know this discussion wasn't his favorite topic.

He drew back, his eyes conflicted. "Nope, it's not even him. It's more my grandfather. What concerns my father is me working at Nordstrom to make ends meet when he could just hand me the money. The law firm I intern for now pays me close to peanuts." He smiled, looking genuinely proud of himself. "But the thing is . . . I like peanuts."

I stared at the person in front of me, the one who seemed so carefree but was also riddled with his own family problems.

I tilted my head, assessing the boyishly adorable male with the warmest brown eyes. "That says a lot about your character—that you'd give up making millions with your family business to do what you love." I angled closer and nodded. "And it's awe-inspiring."

"Thanks, Sam." For a brief second, his eyes became distant. "But, sometimes, when I see how it's tearing my family apart, I wonder if it's worth it."

I bumped my shoulder against his. "It will be worth it. I promise you that. You just have to follow your dreams, do what you want."

But I, of all people, knew that, without the resources, this was easier said than done. There were bills to pay and school loans to apply for.

"Follow your dreams." His jaw tightened, and he placed his hand on top of mine, his eyes never breaking contact. "That's what my mother always said. And, before she died, she made sure we were out of my grandfather's grasp. That's why we moved from New York, where Stanton Steel's headquarters are located, to Chicago."

I hadn't known his mother, but I admired her strength, and I was envious of the unconditional love that she had shown her children.

I nodded and squeezed his hand. "I could imagine that was hard, but you have to do what's right for you."

The only sound between us was the lake, the swish of the waves rippling back and forth.

He blinked and stared at the water in front of us before meeting my eyes. "Tell me about your mom."

I inhaled deeply as her face was pulled to the forefront of my mind. Memories of happier times played in my head like a movie. "We were attached at the hip." My breathing slowed as my thoughts brought me back to my childhood. "We shared everything. She wasn't just my mom. She was my best friend. I lived with a real-life hippie, high on life." I smiled as thoughts of my mom and her care-free personality pushed to the surface.

"She loved my father beyond reason." I inhaled deeply. "She told me stories about how they'd met, about falling in love within weeks, and marrying a month later."

I focused on the water beneath us, the aqua blue slapping against the dark rocks. "She loved him even though he wasn't right for her. Even though he made her feel worthless because he was insecure." I swallowed a lump in the back of my throat and forced my next words out. "He was her life, and when he left . . ." My voice quivered. "When he left . . . she didn't want to live anymore."

I cowered into myself, my hands pressing to my stomach. "She spiraled into a depression. It was weird, seeing her so high on life one minute and doped up on antidepressants the next. I'd never felt so alone, so helpless. I was the only one who knew."

I took a deep breath. "She was dependent. It was like she needed it, and when she broke her ankle, they put her on opiates. So it was her antidepressants mixed with Vicodin." A visible shudder left my body. "After that, she'd take anything and everything, so she wouldn't feel. Oxycontin, Percocet, Fluoxetine."

Josh's hands wrapped tightly around my shoulders, but I gently shook him off. His consoling touch would break me.

"So, I did what I thought would make her happy. I baked every day and forced her to do the same. It was our passion since she'd taught me how to bake. We continued to bring baked goods to the nursing homes and homeless shelter, as we'd done before. I thought I was breaking her out of her funk." My lips felt dry, and my stomach clenched with sadness as I remembered what happened next.

"Cold?" Josh asked, rubbing his hands up and down my arms.

I shook my head. I was cold on the inside, not the outside. "And then she received the divorce papers." My hands wrung together in my lap, chapped from the continual process. "And that's when things got worse."

I didn't realize that tears had escaped my eyes until Josh pulled me to his side, his lips pressing to my forehead, and this time, I didn't push him away because I needed the ice in my chest to thaw. I basked in the comfort of his embrace, that consoling touch.

I decided I needed it out. I hadn't talked about it in such a long time that I needed to be free of the thoughts that had been weighing me down.

I shivered as another round of painful memories bombarded my mind. "I knew she wasn't getting any better. The day I found her, an empty bottle of prescription drugs were by her bed along with a note telling me she was sorry." I swiped under my eyes, willing the tears to stop, but they wouldn't. They couldn't.

I hadn't cried for my mother in years, and now, I'd done it three times in front of a guy I barely knew.

"I'm sorry," Josh whispered. Gently, he pulled both of my hands into his lap and held them tightly in his own, brushing his thumb on the top of my fist. "You know it's not your fault."

"But it is . . ." I choked on the saliva coating the back of my throat as my mind was burned with the memory. "Because I saw the signs, and I didn't tell anyone. I sat in the room as she cried and didn't do anything about it. I baked her cookies for weeks, thinking that would break her from her funk. I was stupid. I should've known. I should've known. I should've . . . I should've done more." *More to help her, more to stop the out-of-control consumption of pills. If I had done more, she'd be here. She'd be alive.*

"Look at me, Sam," he coaxed softly.

I shook my head. I couldn't meet his eyes, couldn't see the pity and sorrow in them that was recognizable in everyone's eyes that knew my story.

He didn't give in. His voice was gentle but coercing. "Open your eyes, and look at me."

The tone of his voice had me blinking my eyes open. My vision filled with Josh's warm eyes staring back at me. No pity, no blame, just compassion.

"It wasn't your fault."

My finger swiped at the hot tear that had rolled down my cheek, but he pulled my hand down.

"She was not well," he said firmly. "Depression is a sickness, a disease. You did all you could. Deep down inside, you know this is true."

I tore my gaze from his and forced my tears to stop as I stared at the darkness in front of me. "I don't know . . ."

The memories of her were pure and clear and dreadful. I wished that I could have done something to help her.

He stood and extended his hand. "Let's go."

My glossy eyes met his small smile. "Where?"

"Somewhere we can stop dwelling on the dead and live for the living." He jerked his head to the side, urging me to stand. "Come on." His smile was so endearing, one of his best qualities.

I stood and dusted the dirt off my borrowed pants. He intertwined our fingers, and I followed him, hopeful that I would find the inner peace from my mother's death that he had found from his mother's passing.

HE KEYED INTO HIS APARTMENT, and I laughed, walking in and slipping off my shoes.

"Um, taking me to your apartment, so I can stop thinking about my dead mother is a real class act."

He touched the tip of my nose. "Guys will be guys." He shrugged, but there was no seriousness in his tone.

My feet padded over the dingy white carpet. His apartment was a decent size—a one-bedroom studio in the West Loop of Chicago. Pictures of his family and friends were mounted in black frames in the tiny hallway that led to the combination living room and kitchen area.

The upscale furnishing of his apartment did not fit the small space. It was like he had bought the furniture first, run out of money for the rent, and had to downgrade in space. And it was awfully girlie.

"So, what do we have planned, Casanova? Or shall I say, the guy with the lines?"

A cream couch decorated with a pink, red, and yellow floral pattern sat against the wall in front of a large flat screen TV. A sleek coffee table sat in the middle of the floor. There was a PlayStation on top of the table along with other gaming accessories, a contrast to its feminine stand.

Josh gestured toward the couch. "Sit down, Princess."

I stripped off Jim's hoodie, feeling a huge relief now that I was only in my short-sleeved black baby tee. I'd been sweating under all the layers I'd used to disguise myself from the photogs.

"I figured, since it doesn't look like you're going anywhere soon, you can do what makes you happy, and I can do what makes me happy."

I was unable to hide my grin. "What grand plan is this?"

"One second." He rushed to his bedroom and emerged wearing basketball shorts and a sleeveless cutoff tee.

"We're playing ball?"

He reeled back. "Pfft. Yeah, sure. I have the hoop hidden here in my massive abode." He swept one hand across his apartment in an exaggerated gesture.

I laughed.

"No." He jumped into the kitchen, hands spread wide. "We're baking cookies." His smile widened.

"You know, cooking"—he pointed to me—"makes you happy. And eating makes this man happy." He jabbed his thumb against his chest.

I rolled my eyes with an exaggerated sigh, as though he had asked me to kill his puppy. "Fine. If I must. Even though that's what I've been doing all day."

I staggered to the kitchen but almost tripped on Jim's mile-long jeans. I rolled them up at my waist.

Josh frowned at my predicament. "You need to change before you trip and get blood all over my clean carpet."

I quirked a brow at his idea of clean carpet. "Yes, well, too bad I left my jeans at the restaurant."

"Wait right there." He disappeared before returning a second later, chucking a Chicago Bulls shirt and a pair of shorts in my direction.

My lips pursed as I eyed the shirt. "Even though I've lived in Illinois my whole life, I'm not into the Bulls."

"So? Neither am I. I grew up in Manhattan."

I smiled. He'd mentioned New York earlier but not the part he'd grown up in. "You grew up in Manhattan?"

"Yeah." He shrugged.

I slipped quickly into his bathroom, shucked off the jeans, and pulled the shorts on. They were baggy, but I tightened the string at the waistband to keep them up.

"Like Manhattan, Manhattan?" I asked, walking out of the bathroom.

I had grown up in a small country town while the male in front of me had grown up in one of the biggest cities in the nation. Our childhoods couldn't have been more different.

He nodded. "Born and bred in the center of the Big Apple."

I stepped over to the stool against his kitchen bar that served as his kitchen table. "Okay, I need more." My curiosity trumped any cooking that was going to be done.

He smiled—one dimple, not two. "More what?"

I blinked and pointed to his belongings. "Your things . . . they look like they belong in a home and garden magazine, but it's like you squeezed them into this tiny, old apartment. Did you actually choose this furniture?"

He glanced down at the table. "It's my sister's furniture. When I took off, I didn't want a dime. After a while, sleeping on the floor hurt my back." He averted his eyes, looking sheepish. "She moved in with boyfriend Robert when things got serious, and I got her old furniture." He tilted his head. "What's up with the twenty questions?"

"You know practically everything about me, and I only know tidbits about you. Don't you think that's a little unfair?"

He pressed his elbows on the counter. "No offense, but I think half the world already knows about you now."

I scrunched my face. "You had to remind me, didn't you?"

His eyes flickered with amusement. "How did you get here, Sam?"

"In the world?" I asked, being a smart-ass. "Through my mother. Born at Carbarny Community Hospital." I smirked.

"No, beautiful girl. Here, in Chicago. How did you get to Chicago?"

"I went through the small culinary program at a community college back home but moved here for the real deal. I'm applying to Le Cordon Bleu. You know this."

It wasn't fair that he knew my whole life story. I wasn't done with my interrogation.

"I do know a lot about you. Is it selfish of me, wanting to know more?" he asked.

I adjusted myself on the stool, swiveling it from left to right. "Yes, it's totally uncool, Joshua Stanton. Now, I get a turn. What is your deal?"

"One more." He placed his hands together, as though he were

saying a prayer. "Who decided for you? Who chose that school?"

My eyebrows pulled together. "Is this a trick question?"

"Nope."

I tilted my head and narrowed my eyes at him, wondering where this conversation was leading. "Me, of course."

He focused on my bracelet. "Yeah. You see, I didn't get that choice." His head bowed as a heavy sigh escaped him.

I couldn't imagine having someone, anyone, tell me what I was going to do with the rest of my life.

"Josh Stanton, at the end of the day, it's your life and your choice in what you want to do with it."

"You're right." His eyes flickered toward my lips, the lips that had been pressed to his earlier.

My phone rang in my purse on the couch, and I welcomed the distraction. Rushing to the floral sofa, I plucked out my phone. "Hello?"

"Hey, where are you?" It was Chloe.

"Um . . ." I glanced behind myself to Josh. "A friend's house."

She sighed, relieved. "It's pretty bad here, Sam. Like, I-don't-think-you-can-come-home bad."

I groaned. It was no wonder Hawke had called them Satan's Posse. They were keeping me from my own home? This was ridiculous.

"I'm coming home." I refused to let them dictate what I did and did not do with my life.

"I highly suggest you don't," Chloe said. "You come home, and then they'll just follow you to work. Harass you."

I rubbed a throbbing spot on my temple. "How did you become the expert on the paparazzi?"

"Duh, Google!" she said, trying to lighten the mood. "Repeat after me, 'Google is our friend.' It says that all of this should blow over in a few days. Until then, I really think you should stay away. At least for tonight. Let's see if they get bored when you don't show up."

I ran one shaky hand through my hair, fiddling with my dead ends. "Fine, I guess I can go to Candice's."

But Candice's place was smaller than Josh's. It was a studio. The place was so small that she and her fiancé, Jerry, slept on a futon that also served as their couch.

"No," Chloe said. "Don't leave. It's safer that way. Whose house are you at?"

"Josh's."

"Who?"

Of course Chloe didn't know Josh. I barely knew Josh even though we had shared some intimate secrets about each other.

I tried to whisper into the phone, but I was sure Josh could hear me. "The Nordstrom guy." Yes, I'd talked about him. I told Chloe everything.

She let out a low laugh. "And the plot thickens."

"No plot," I said quietly. "And I can't stay here. I'm coming home."

Then, her tone tightened. "I wouldn't, Sam. Best friend advice. It's not good out there. Like, I don't even think it's safe."

"Fine, I'll figure something out." My shoulders dropped, as I felt defeated.

"Trust me, I've barely left my room. I'm afraid they can see through our windows with their supersonic lenses, and tomorrow, my uneven breasts will be plastered all over their magazines."

We both laughed before we said our good-byes.

I hated this feeling, like my life had been turned upside down and there was nothing I could do to flip it upright again.

When I turned, Josh's face lit up. "Sleepover?"

"No, I think I'll just brave it."

"No, you won't," he said, face serious. "You can take the bed, and I'll totally take the couch. See? Perfect gentleman." He spread his arms wide and grinned.

I teetered on the tips of my toes and back to the balls of my feet.

"I don't know." I didn't want to burden him.

"Scout's honor." He lifted three fingers in a solemn oath.

"You were in Boy Scouts, weren't you?"

A knock on the door froze us both in our tracks.

"Shit! Do you think . . ." I was ready to bolt and hide in the bathroom or under the table or in the fridge.

Josh shook his head. "No. It's probably Andy." He laughed. "Andy was a Boy Scout, too."

He opened the door, and I recognized his friend. He had been the guy hanging out of Josh's car on the night of his birthday, the guy with the buzz cut where I could see his scalp.

Andy was built like a football player, not lean like Josh. Stockier. His baseball cap was flipped backward on his head, and he and Josh looked like frat boys standing together. All they needed was a beer in their hands.

Andy stepped into the living room, pizza box in one hand and a twelve-pack of beer in his other. He staggered to a stop when he realized that Josh had company.

"Hey . . . Sam, right?"

I slapped my palm against my forehead. "You, too? Damn gossip sites."

He frowned at Josh, and I realized that he hadn't known my name from the tabloids or the Internet.

"You're Josh's . . . friend, right?" The way Andy smiled, I knew that Josh had spoken about me before.

"Yes, sorry. I'm Sam. I think I met you on Josh's birthday." He was the guy driving Josh's car that night.

Andy dropped the pizza on the center table in front of the TV and then strolled to the kitchen. "That's right. And guess whose birthday is next weekend?" He opened Josh's drawers, as though he owned the joint, opened the twelve pack, got out a bottle opener, and popped open three beers, handing one to Josh and one to me.

"Uh . . ." I turned to Josh.

If Andy was staying over, I'd be jumping into a cab and heading home.

"Princess over there is crashing here tonight." He gave Andy an unapologetic look. "I'm giving you two hours, tops, and you're out-ie, man."

"What?" He slung an arm over Josh's shoulders. "What about our bromance? The first pretty chick who walks into your life after Jenny, and I'm out the door?" He shook his head.

Josh's face turned sour. "That was years ago."

"That's right. I've been keeping you company for years, and this is how you treat me?" he asked, feigning offense.

Josh extracted himself from under Andy's arm. "You'd think he would have changed since elementary school."

The side of my mouth ticked up. "So, you've known each other since the playground?"

Andy nodded in a continuous motion, pointing a thumb into his chest. "Transfer, baby, just like my best bud over here." He threw back his beer, chugging it like there was going to be a drought. "So, you coming to my birthday party next weekend?"

I cocked my head. "What?"

He leaned in, resting his hip against the black countertop. "We're having my birthday party at The Seg, this swanky restaurant that I rented out."

Andy must have come from money, too. You could only get in The Seg with reservations. I knew the Chicago restaurant circuit like I knew how to make chocolate truffles.

"I know the place."

"Well, you're coming right?" He turned toward Josh. "Tell your girl she's going."

I cleared my throat. "I'm not his girl."

Andy waved his hand like I hadn't spoken. "Whatever. You're going, Josh's non-girlfriend." He strolled toward the couch and plopped down, dropping his bottle with a thump on the top of the table and reaching into the box for a slice of pizza. "Dinner?"

"I'm not hungry for pizza. I'm ready for dessert." Josh walked over, laced our fingers, and pulled me into the kitchen. "I offered my place, and all I ask is that you bake me something because I have a really, really bad sweet tooth."

My eyes flew down to our joined hands before meeting his chocolate-brown eyes. Andy was already flipping through the channels. Clearly, he'd been here countless times.

Josh smiled again—this time, with two dimples.

Then, I nodded. "That, I can do."

chapter FIFTEEN

A LIVE BAND PLAYED IN the background of the fancy restaurant, The Seg. Plush velvet couches outlined the restaurant while tables were set in the center of the room, complete with full place settings.

The heat had died down, and Hawke and I were already old news. But it had been a week since our lip-locked picture was made public. A week since he had said he'd fix everything. A week since I'd heard his voice. I'd like to believe that he was keeping his distance to protect me, but it still hurt that he hadn't once checked on me since then.

The hot summer sun of Paris seemed like eons before. Now, the leaves had begun to fall off the trees as we approached the middle of September.

It seemed to Hawke like we never existed, and to me, it was as if my world revolved around him. I googled Hawke constantly and watched every entertainment show to get a glimpse of him. I was irritated, but I couldn't get mad. He'd never treated me badly. He had never promised me anything. It was my own fault for wishing for something that could not be.

I wanted more. I wasn't this girl—a one-night random hook-up whenever he was in town. I was a relationship kind of girl. I needed stability. That was who I was in my core.

I stuffed the phone back to the bottom of my purse and promised myself I wouldn't look at it again. I was here with Josh for Andy's birthday party, and besides the two men, I didn't know anyone.

The posh restaurant was packed with people who reeked of wealth. I took in all the women in their makeup, fitted cocktail dresses, and four-inch designer heels along with the thousand-dollar handbags slung over each of their shoulders. Most of them were standing next to guys who were as equally good-looking. All the men exuded power in their semiformal wear—some in pinstriped button-down shirts and crisp pressed pants while others were in a full-on suit and tie.

My hands flattened against my mid-length black skirt that hit right above the knees. I'd borrowed it from Chloe's closet. She was a marketing exec and wore suits daily, so I had known I'd be able to find something appropriate to wear. The Seg was fancier than any floral summer dress in my closet, so I had outsourced for the occasion.

I glanced around, looking for Josh, but a tall blonde caught my eye. She was stunning with her Pantene-sleek hair that rested in the middle of her back and her scooped-neck cocktail dress that hugged her model frame.

Two men were vying for her attention, and I could understand why. She was beautiful.

Where my hair was a dull sandy-blonde, hers was a shiny platinum, almost white blonde, tucked behind her ears. She stood out from the rest, like the star actress on a movie set. Her black dress was accented with white pearls around her neck. Simple but elegant was how I'd describe her.

I straightened in my seat when Josh strolled back from the restroom.

He pulled out his chair and sat down. "Hey, thanks for coming. Did you see Andy's face when you came in? He totally thought you wouldn't show."

I shrugged. "No problem. Maybe I should have dressed up a little more. I feel so . . . I don't know."

He ducked his head and angled in closer. "Pfft. These women

have nothing on you. Trust me." His intimate stare did not waver, holding a sensuous flame. He'd been staring at me like this since he picked me up from my apartment.

Where I didn't fit in, Josh totally did. Hair slicked back, skinny tie and suit on. Whatever he did, you couldn't take the wealth out of his appearance.

"So, this is your crowd?" I asked.

He rested back in his chair. "Nope. My crowd is Andy and Will. Will was the other guy that was with me on my birthday. These guys are just their friends."

He pointed his beer bottle in my direction, and I clinked my wine glass against it.

"So, did Will come from Manhattan, too?"

"Nope. Andy and I went to prep school together. We met Willy while playing ball in Chicago." He glanced back at his friends, who were laughing against the bar.

Seeing the three of them reminded me of Chloe and me back in high school.

"They're good guys," Josh said. "They know the crap I go through with my family. They were there for me when I didn't know anyone here. When you met them on my birthday, they'd just had too much to drink, but at heart, they'd do anything for me."

"Good friends are irreplaceable," I said softly, fingering the thin white-gold necklace at my throat.

"That, they are." He tipped back his beer and took another swig.

"Josh?"

I heard an elegant voice from behind me.

I peered up and blinked at the beautiful blonde from earlier, standing right by our table. Her eyes flickered from me to Josh, almost hesitant to look back at me again.

"I haven't seen you in ages," she said. Even her smile was perfect with her Crest White teeth. Her eyes were almost angelic—the deepest blue I'd ever seen.

Josh openly blinked. "Jenny . . ." His voice visibly shook in a low-ered whisper.

I recognized her name. Most definitely his ex.

There was no doubt that he hadn't expected her to be here. He stood and jammed his hands into his pockets. Josh was always af-fectionate with his friends, so this closed-off version was a huge contrast.

"It's been a while." His eyes scanned the area, looking anywhere but at her. "How have you been?"

"Good. Really good." She wrung her hands together and shifted her weight on her four-inch black heels.

He glanced back at Andy, who raised his palms up, as if to say, *I had no idea.*

Josh's jaw tightened. Andy approached, but Josh turned, forcing his attention on the immaculate blonde.

"What're you doing in Chicago?"

"I was in town, visiting Jeanine, and she invited me. She didn't think it would be a problem since we all know each other. I'm sor-ry . . ." Her voice trailed off.

That was when Josh placed a hand on her shoulder.

"It's fine," he said, his tone turning apologetic. "I'm just sur-prised to see you; that's all. I'm sure the birthday boy is happy about our little high school reunion." He attempted a smile, but it still seemed forced.

She placed her hand over his, and her face relaxed into a huge smile, as though his touch were all she craved. And then I knew. I knew that she still loved him.

She released a lighthearted laugh and focused back on me. "Hi," she said, leaning over, "I'm Jenny."

The beautiful girl exuded kindness. It was in her sweet voice and in her delicate features and her kind demeanor. For the first time, I was kind of jealous that I didn't have the same appeal.

Josh hit the top of his forehead. "Sorry, my bad. Sam, this is Jenny."

When I stood, he crossed to my side and slung an arm around my shoulders, pulling me closer.

I cocked an eyebrow, gave him a side glance. "It's very nice to meet you. I'm Josh's friend."

When she extended her hand, I shook it.

As soon as the words left my mouth, Jenny's face brightened. "It's so great to meet you."

Jenny sidestepped when the waitress arrived with our plates. Josh sat down first, and I followed his lead. Jenny blew out a soft breath and gazed at Josh with longing, as though he were all that she ever wanted in the world.

"It was great seeing you, Jenny." Josh picked up his fork to speed up their interaction, and my chest ached for a girl I didn't even know.

"Yeah, it was great seeing you, too." She swallowed, false bravado in her tone. "And you, too, Sam. I hope you have a great time tonight. The band sounds amazing. And free drinks, right?"

"That's right." I raised my glass in her direction.

Her eyes dropped to the ground. "I guess . . . I guess I'll let you guys get to your meals."

Josh had already stuffed food in his mouth, and it seemed a little rude, so unlike his normal gentlemanly behavior. He was out of his element, and it shocked me.

Jenny turned and walked away, and then she straightened and walked back toward us. "Josh . . . uh . . . ."

He jammed his mouth full of pasta. I was afraid he was going to choke.

Jenny sucked in her bottom lip and placed a hand on his arm. "Can I please talk to you for a second?"

Josh's eyes darted around the room, looking anywhere but into Jenny's sweet face. I shifted with unease at the awkward silence that was building between them as she waited for his response.

Finally, he reached for his water and gulped it down. I swore, I saw the sweat forming on his brow.

Jenny's hand dropped from his arm to his wrist. "Please. I just want to talk." All her vulnerability was displayed in her clear blue eyes that were begging him to listen.

He blew out a breath and then closed his eyes. When he opened them, they were conflicted.

Finally, he nodded.

"This will take just a couple of minutes. I really hope it's okay if I steal him for a second," she said, her voice hesitant, her eyes hopeful.

I nonchalantly waved one hand. "Yeah, sure."

Josh stood, reached over, and squeezed my hand. "I'll be right back."

When he winked in plain view for Jenny to see, her smile faltered.

I wanted to ignore the stark difference in his reaction to her versus his playfulness with me. I also wanted to ignore the way her eyes flashed with hurt because she had noticed, too.

When they walked to the bar, I ducked my head into my soup, pretending to eat. I placed my phone on the table and focused on the screen, trying to look inconspicuous. I was not being a snoop. I was not studying their reactions. I was so not trying to strain my ears to hear their conversation.

It was as if I were watching a movie play out. No words needed to be heard to understand what was going on. At first, the conversation seemed light, and she said something to make the corners of his mouth lift. When she angled closer and touched his arm he flinched and jammed his hands in his pockets again, as if the last thing he wanted was for her to touch him.

He nodded while she spoke, but he dropped his focus to the

ground, unable to look her in the eye.

Things heated up quickly. When she placed both hands on her chest, my heart hurt for her. I could tell she was speaking with certainty and conviction. I could see it all over her face and in the way she leaned toward him, wanting to be heard.

When she reached for him, he backed away and placed both palms up.

I made out two words.

I can't.

That was when Jenny crumbled and cowered inwardly. She dropped her face into her hands and sobbed openly. Chaos erupted, and two girls rushed toward her side.

Josh looked visibly distraught.

He stormed my way and tilted his head toward the door. "Sorry, Sam, but we have to go." He was unable to look me in the eye. "I'll get you dinner somewhere else. I'll say bye to Andy and Will, but then we . . ."

Andy rushed toward Josh's side. "Yo, man, I'm sorry." He looked deflated. "I had no idea she would be here or that she was in town."

When I peered up, Jenny was gone, and the party had returned to partying. Who knew where she had disappeared to?

"I believe you, but . . . we just have to go," he said, voice rushed. His eyes darted around himself. "Happy Birthday, bud."

Andy slapped Josh's back and brought him into a half-hug.

In the next second, Josh intertwined our fingers and pulled us out of the restaurant and down the street. He seemed helpless for a second, not sure of where to go or what to do or what to say, so I took the lead and stepped up the curb.

"Hey, can we get tacos?" I asked, trying to smile. "I know a place."

"Yeah. Yeah, sure," he spoke. Yet he was not present; he was distant and upset.

As we waited for a cab, he tipped back his head, staring into the evening sky at the stars above us. He was quiet, his eyes lost in thought.

I placed one hand on his shoulder to try to get him back to the present. "Hey, you okay?"

When his eyes met mine, he let out an audible breath. "Yeah."

A cab pulled to the curb, and he opened the door to let me slide in. "I'll be better when we get out of here. Where's that taco place?"

"Oh, you're in for a treat, mister." I recited the address to the cab driver as Josh scooted in next to me.

I was rewarded with those two dimples I adored. The old Josh was back.

The cab driver drove us through the city, and Josh pulled me closer to his side. He rested his chin on the top of my head, and I relaxed in his hold as we watched the flicker of the car lights in front of us.

The small hole-in-the-wall taco place was packed, and the scent of grease and cumin permeated the air. I breathed in deeply, the smell only increasing the rumble in my stomach.

Josh reached for my hand and ushered us through the crowd.

I chuckled. "We totally fit in here, don't you think? You, in your designer shirt, and me, in my fancy dress."

He laughed. "Yeah."

My goal of the evening was to make Josh laugh every single minute. I didn't want a repeat of the unfamiliar Josh from earlier.

"What do you want?" he asked.

"The King Burrito with extra hot sauce."

"You like it hot, huh?" He winked. "I'll remember that."

He turned to the cashier and said, "Make that two."

"Hey, wait for the food. I'm going to seat-stalk those two over there." I motioned to two girls sitting in the corner. They looked like they were about ready to leave, so I needed to move quickly before someone else stole our seat.

"Okay." He held my eyes. So many emotions passed between us, some of them I didn't even understand. In the next beat, he pulled me into an embrace. "Thanks," he breathed.

My face was smooshed against his chest, and I wrapped both arms around his waist and squeezed. "You're the one who's paying for my dinner."

Against my cheek, his chest rumbled with his laughter, laughter that I'd missed.

I pulled away, and as I stared into his eyes, I knew, more than anything, that things between us were changing. We were getting closer with the intimacy of what we'd shared with each other. As I held his stare, I knew he felt it, too—the shift in our relationship. But, with my chaotic life, I wasn't ready to even think about being anything more than friends.

"I'd better get us those seats, or we'll be standing and eating."

Right as I turned away, I saw the girls get up and gather their belongings.

When they stood, I shoved myself into the small space in the corner of the restaurant. "Thanks," I said as they cleared out their belongings.

Josh plopped down on the bench opposite me, dropping the bulging brown paper bag. The bottom of the bag was darkened with oil, and my stomach cheered, pom-poms and all.

I rubbed my hands together and tore the brown paper bag open. "Ready?" My eyebrows danced.

"I was born ready." He loosened his tie, unbuttoned the top button of his shirt, and rolled up his sleeves.

As he relaxed in the chair, my curiosity about Jenny crept up to the surface. I wanted to know their deal. She was gorgeous and seemed sweet to boot. They were like a real-life Ken and Barbie couple.

"I didn't know you were such a heartbreaker."

When he shot me a look, I immediately regretted the words as soon as they'd slipped from my mouth.

He dropped his burrito midair, and he rubbed an aggravated palm against his forehead. "Sometimes, I feel like it would be better, being on the other side and having your heart broken instead."

"You're only saying that because you've probably never had your heart broken."

"I haven't," he admitted with a grimace.

It was visibly noticeable that it upset him to hurt her, and I didn't know what to do to help him. "I'm sorry. You don't have to talk about it."

"No, I need to. I want someone to tell me I'm not a monster because I totally feel like I'm the biggest douche in the world."

Trying to lighten the mood, I said, "And what if you are? What if you're the king douche bag of douche-bag central?"

"Sam . . ." His face contorted.

I gently shook his arm. "I'm totally kidding. Anyone who knows you knows that's far from the truth."

He stared blankly at the uneaten burrito in front of him. "I'm sure Jenny doesn't think so."

"So, what happened between you two?" I nodded toward his meal. "Eat and talk. You don't want to be a hungry douche. That's worse than being king douche, trust me."

His voice became distant. "It's fine, seeing her, but I didn't expect her to beg for me to come back when it's been years."

I pushed his food closer to his mouth. "Talk with your mouth full. I'll allow it for today." I pointed to his food. "Eat!"

He gave me a devastatingly sad smile and took a bite.

"Did she cheat on you?" That was the first thing that had crossed my mind, especially since she had been begging him to come back.

"I wish. Honestly, that would've been easier."

I pointed to his burrito, and he chomped down again.

"So, what happened? She has an extra toe or what?" I prompted.

He swallowed down the food and laughed. "No, but that

would've been an interesting story." His stare became distant. "She's beautiful and sweet and everything any guy could ever wish for." He met my eyes, unwavering. "But she just wasn't for me. I wasn't the guy for her."

I needed to know the reason she wasn't enough. "What do you mean?"

"We were together for most of high school. Did I love her? Yeah. But I wasn't *in love* with her." He shook his head. "I tried. I really did." He leaned back in his chair, his burrito totally abandoned now. "Imagine this beautiful girl begging you not to leave her and saying that she'd do anything . . . *anything* to make it work."

My facial features dropped, recalling my own memories. I'd been brokenhearted one too many times, and I could empathize.

"I don't get it." Because I didn't. She was sweet and drop-dead model beautiful.

"No one did." He rubbed the back of his neck with one hand and let out an exaggerated sigh. "I thought something was wrong with me. She could have any guy, and she picked me, but . . . she wasn't the one." He shrugged, as if in apology.

A soft exhale escaped me. Unrequited love stunk majorly. "That sucks balls."

"Pretty much." He averted his gaze, staring anywhere but into my face. "Did you know I cheated on her?"

Okay, wow. I reeled back, my response automatic.

He winced at my reaction. "Not my proudest moment, let me tell you." He narrowed his eyes, absently playing with his napkin on the table. "Not full-on cheating. But going on a date with some-one else is still cheating even though nothing physical went on. It happened a while ago, in high school, with this cheerleader named Chrissy." He scrubbed one hand over his face. "I don't know if I did it, so Jenny would leave me for good or because I wanted to see if something better was out there."

"So, which one was it?" I angled closer, waiting for his answer and needing to know.

"Both," he said. "And, after all of that . . . Jenny still wanted me back. She cried for days and blamed it on Chrissy. True, Chrissy was aggressive, but it takes two. I'd like to believe, if I was truly happy in our relationship, I never would've strayed. It's like I voodooed her or planted some sort of love potion."

"Or maybe you've just got the charm, Josh Stanton. Among other things," I said, trying to lighten the mood. I motioned to his body and scrunched my nose.

He let out a carefree laugh. "Sam, you're a genius. That has to be it. Now, if you're curious"—his eyebrows danced—"I can totally tame that curiosity."

"No"—I laughed, reaching for my burrito and bringing it up to my lips—"I think I'm good."

"I don't think you really are." He grinned, two dimples now.

When he ran his hands down his chest and suggestively touched himself, I busted out in full-blown laughter, some of the lettuce falling out of my mouth mid bite.

"Really? I don't know why that Jenny girl is so hung up on you."

"I don't either." He rested both hands on the table and leaned in, his face thoughtful. "You know that saying, *When you know, you know*?" The intimate look in his eyes warmed me from the inside out. "Well, I just knew Jenny wasn't the one. I knew *she* was out there somewhere, and I'd just know."

He took a savoring deep breath, his gaze riveted on my face. Something intense flared through his stare that made my heart jolt and pulse pound against the insides of my wrists.

I tore my eyes from him and took a bite of my burrito, a tingling sensation sweeping up the back of my neck and across my face. "So, you believe in fate and stuff?"

He shrugged. "I never thought of it that way, but yeah . . . I guess I do. Or maybe not even that. I'd say I believe in soul mates." He sucked in his bottom lip, his face thoughtful. "If you had seen my mom and dad together, you'd know. They were meant for each other." His voice choked with emotion. "When I tell my dad to date because I truly want him to be happy, he asks me, 'What's the point?' He says his better half is gone, that person isn't walking the earth anymore." He picked at the napkin on the table. "He says anybody else would just be a stand-in."

I placed my hand on his, lightly brushing my thumb over his fist.

Death sucked because it was the people who the dead had left behind that were the most affected.

"When she and my father met, he knew." His eyebrows knit together, and he focused on my hand on top of his. "For Mom, it was slow-moving. She didn't know it was him at first. She told me she wasn't into the rich-and-stuffy type." A chuckle left his lips. "But she'd tell you that fate was fate and that she stood no chance. He was meant for her. And I knew that Jenny wasn't meant for me and that's why I had to leave her."

He surprised me by placing his other hand on top of mine, sandwiching my hand in the middle. "It feels good to talk about my mom." Such sadness filled his eyes that I had to swallow back the lump in my throat. "I can't do this with many people. I always feel like I'm depressing them."

I exhaled a shaky breath. "It's because I know how you feel."

"I know you do. And Jenny's a great girl. I want her to be happy. Someday, some guy is going to swoop her up and treat her right." A whoosh of breath released from his mouth, and then he glanced in my direction, his eyes boring into mine. "Funny thing is . . . the day I finally cleaned out my old room and got rid of a box of stuff Jenny gave me from high school, is the same day I met you."

My heart beat loudly in my ears from his intensely unwavering stare. "Josh . . ." I tore my gaze away from his and clasped my hands together. "Your life is what you make it. It has nothing to do with me."

He smiled and touched the tip of my nose, forcing me to meet his eyes. "But what if you're wrong? What if things are destined?"

"I don't think so."

Drive and determination had brought me to Chicago. Yes, it was to escape the tragedy of my mother's death, but I was going to make a life for myself—by myself.

"I'm going to go to a top-notch culinary school, specialize in pastries and serve as head chef one day at a restaurant of my choice. That isn't fate, Josh. That's pure will."

"I don't doubt for one second that you'll head up a restaurant one day. But I believe in fate, Sam. I do. Especially when it comes to finding that one person."

"Josh, just like how you choose your profession, you choose the person you want to be with."

I'd watched my father choose a new woman and my mother choose her fate.

Fate didn't choose you; you chose it. Maybe I'd been tainted by my childhood, but that was all I'd ever known.

He stared at me for a second longer than was comfortable, and then he blinked. He seemed so sure of himself. "How about we see which theory wins?"

chapter SIXTEEN

MY HANDS DIPPED INTO THE large bag of chips as Josh continued to massage my feet through my thick wooly socks on my couch. Hanging out at his place had been used as an excuse to avoid the paps, but since my face had been blasted all over the Internet and every rag mag, hanging out and vegging on junk in front of my TV was our regular now.

The Fast & the Furious was playing in the background, a movie I hadn't seen yet. This had somehow become our norm as the colder weather moved in. While Chloe had been busy with her job and working overtime, Josh had been my constant, always there.

When Vin Diesel and Paul Walker stepped into the scene, I couldn't help but smile. One had to appreciate beautiful people at their finest.

"Look at that smirk."

"What?" I wiped the smile off my face and composed myself, popping a chip in my mouth.

Josh chuckled. "I'm used to women drooling over Paul Walker. My sister has him as her computer wallpaper, so yeah . . ."

He leaned over, and I popped a chip in his mouth as his hands continued to work on my sore feet. There was a comfort in being with Josh that relaxed me. Though I'd never admit it out loud, I was getting attached to him, our routine, and his cheerful, adorable self.

"I'm done eating chips for dinner. Let's get some real food," he said.

I pushed up into a sitting position. "Are you saying, Lays doesn't fulfill my daily nutritional requirement?" I quirked an eyebrow, curious as to what his real food entailed. "What kind of food are we talking about?"

"The kind that fills our daily requirements and then some." He smiled with both dimples. "Coozie's Pizza with extra onions and hot sauce."

We high-fived.

"Yes!" I lifted a fist to the ceiling. "Pizza and hot sauce," I singsonged.

Josh retrieved his keys from the counter. "Get ready, Sam. We're going to chow down."

"Five minutes." I jolted from the couch and into my room.

I was on a mission—a mission to fill my stomach to its max with Coozie's pizza. I rushed toward my dresser and pulled out a pair of jeans, shimmying out of my pajama pants. When I turned toward my bed and reached for the sweatshirt on my comforter, a familiar ringtone sounded on a phone I kept charged but no longer used.

For a second, I thought I was hearing things, and then my heart sped up in tempo. Before I could think of what I was doing, my feet moved, and I was digging to the bottom of my dresser where I pulled out the phone that Hawke had given me.

I waited. Seconds ticked by like minutes. Then, it rang again. The inside of my palms began to sweat as I picked up the call on the third ring.

"Sunshine?"

Hearing Hawke did things to me, irrational things to my body. My throat went dry as I just listened to the sound of his voice.

"H-hey," I croaked out.

Music was booming in the background. Wherever he was, he wasn't without company.

"It's so great to hear your voice, Sunshine!" he yelled over the noise. "I'm back stateside and in town."

My eyes fell shut. *Where is this going? What is he thinking?*

I couldn't see him.

Please don't ask.

"For a concert?" Of course not because I would've known. I'd stopped cyberstalking him, but I would've for sure known if he had a concert in Chicago. If anything, Chloe would've told me.

"Yes, for a last-minute charity concert. We're the surprise act. I want to see you."

There was no hesitation in his voice, and my rational side was screaming at me to think before I answered.

"Don't you miss me? Because, hell, all I've been thinking about is you."

Liar, liar, pants on fire. Then, why haven't you called me?

"Sunshine?"

"Yeah. Sorry, I'm just a little shocked to hear from you. You know, it's been a while." I rubbed the back of my neck and tried to slow my breathing.

"I wanted to call you." Sincerity leaked from his tone. "I just had to make sure that everything was clear, that the paps wouldn't hound you anymore. Who knows what they have access to or who's watching or listening?"

My mouth fell silent. I had no words. He should've checked on me, should have called or texted or something to find out if I was okay.

"I made it here. When Alan asked if we were up for this Chicago charity thing, I said hell yeah. I knew I had to see you again." His tone softened. "I'm going to send Tilton to come fetch you, yeah?"

I bit the edge of my thumbnail. *Say no. Say no!* "I don't know."

"I'm in town, and you don't want to see me?"

I did want to see him, but whatever was happening between us was teetering on unhealthy.

The door to my bedroom banged open. "You decent in here?" Josh's eyes were shut tightly as he waded into my room, arms straight in front of himself and palms out, walking like a blind man.

It was hilarious and endearing, and I shouldn't want Hawke when I had a man like Josh in my life.

My heart shouldn't beat faster when I talked to Hawke. But I couldn't control my heart. What the heart wanted was what the heart wanted.

I struggled with an internal debate. One where I debated even entertaining this call because, if I saw him, I'd be a puddle of mush again.

I wasn't this girl, unstable and weak. I prided myself on always making the right choices, concise decisions. But I was also never the girl who rock stars called. Things like this had never happened to me before Hawke.

"Who's that?" The change in Hawke's tone gave me whiplash.

Silence filled the air, and when I turned toward Josh, his eyes now open, his facial features dropped. A part of me sensed he knew who I was talking to.

"You've got a boyfriend now, Sunshine?"

"No, it's not that."

"So, are you going to come see me?" There was hope in his voice again, the same one that weakened my resolve.

I wanted to see him. Gosh, even though I knew, deep down, that was the worst possible idea, I knew I was going to see him. But I didn't want to go there on his terms.

I tore my eyes from Josh and focused on the carpet. "I'm going to dinner with a friend first, and then I'll meet you. Where are you at?"

"Keep your phone on you, Sunshine." His tone brightened. "Call me when you're done. I'll text you so you know where to find me."

I gripped both hands on the phone, feeling unsteady. "Okay."

"I can't wait to see you," he said.

"Thanks." *Thanks? God, I needed help.*

When I hung up the phone, the heat of Josh's questioning eyes was on me. He deserved an explanation, but I couldn't seem to find the words.

"We seeing a concert tonight?"

I peered up at him to see him smirking, as though everything were okay, but it wasn't. There was a twinge of sadness in his eyes.

"I'm assuming that was the rock star," he said, his voice taking a mocking tone.

I nodded, still trying to find my bearings. Thing was . . . I had fallen for a rock star and couldn't seem to find my way out of those murky waters.

"You're not ditching me for him, are you?" Josh's voice was light, but that was opposite to the disappointment in his tone.

"No. No, of course not." I straightened, giving him a shaky smile. "Let's go. I'm starving." The cold phone was stuck hard against my palm. With a sweaty hand, I stuffed it in my purse.

He shoved his hands into his pockets and rocked back on his heels. "I'm picking the pizza since you're ditching me later. So, I pick pepperoni."

"I'm not ditching you," I defended. "I just . . ." *Just what? Because I probably was ditching him.*

But it wasn't like Josh and I were dating. I was free to see whomever I wanted. *Still . . . why was my heart filled with so much guilt?*

There was intensity in his eyes, but he shrugged. "It's fine because I'm coming with you. I want to meet this rock star of yours."

I reeled back, trying to tell if he was serious. "Why?"

A muscle twitched in his jaw. "Because I want to see what he's got that I don't have."

"Josh . . ."

"I'm kidding, Sam." He chuckled, but I could tell it was forced. His irresistibly devastating grin was vacant. "I want to meet him. After all, right now, he's the biggest thing since electricity."

He wrapped an arm around my neck and escorted us out my apartment door in one swift movement. The restaurant was no more than fifteen minutes away.

Coozie's was the best Chicago pizzeria, hands down. The scent of cheese, meat, and spices infiltrated my senses.

Growing up, pizza had always been my comfort food. My mother and I had spent numerous hours in our kitchen making homemade pizza. The tastiness of Coozie's and their sauce reminded me of my childhood.

Josh tapped his fork against the table. "And here I thought, you were a smart woman, Princess." He adamantly shook his head. "New York pizza is miles better than Chicago pizza."

My head did a one-eighty, noting the packed-in Chicago patrons chowing down on their deep-dish pizza. "I think you're outnumbered here."

"If you need a fork to dig into it, then it's debatable that it's even pizza." His eyes taunted me for a comeback.

I dug my fork into my stuffed cheese and pepperoni pizza where I twirled the long, stringy cheese. The cheese strings hung from my fork like thick yarn from a needle. I stuffed it into my mouth, slowly pulling the silverware from my lips. "Mmm," I said, as though my mouth were experiencing a foodgasm.

His eyes flashed. "New York pizza is still the best," he said though his voice was less convincing. "I'm telling you, Princess, New York pizza all the way!" And then, just when I thought my ears weren't hot enough, he started chanting, "New York pizza! New York pizza!"

I pushed my chair back, stood, and covered his mouth with my hand. His voice was muffled against the inside of my palm, and we both started laughing.

He's a little crazy, I mouthed to the people in front of us.

Josh pulled me onto his lap and bit the inside of my palm. Something about him and his ability to make me laugh felt natural. It was his God-given talent.

I pressed my hand harder to his mouth, trying not to giggle.

"Young man, are you going to behave?" I gave him a stern motherly look.

When he nodded, I slowly lifted my hand from his lips.

"New York . . ." he started to say.

I pressed my palm against his mouth again.

"Josh!" I begged him with my eyes. "I'd really like to get back to eating. Okay, maybe New York pizza is the best, but in all honesty, I've never tried it. So, right now, the argument is over until I can give your pizza a fair chance, all right?"

He rapidly blinked, followed by a wide-eyed stare. "You've never tried New York pizza?"

"It's kind of hard when I've never been to New York."

"I'm going to take you one day. How about tonight?" He smirked like he was joking, but his eyes held such hope.

I swallowed, remembering Hawke.

Hawke was rough and sexy while Josh was stable and sweet. I couldn't help comparing the massive differences between them. I had a weakness for Hawke—a clearly irrational weakness that I couldn't shake. I'd like to blame it on Hawke's rock-star status, but it went deeper than that.

"Someday . . . but not tonight."

"Tell me something." Josh angled closer. His voice was thick and unsteady, but his hold was fierce, his hands tight around my waist. "Tell me why you're seeing him again."

I peered up into his gentle, beautiful eyes. With Josh, he was so transparent. I could see the curiosity and frustration and torment in his brown eyes staring back at me. I never had to wonder what he was thinking because I could just tell.

And, because he was so honest and up-front with me, I could only be the same with him. That was the nature of our relationship.

"If I could just turn it off and force myself not to want more, then I would. I like him. *Him*, not just the famous singer."

I thought of Paris and how sweet Hawke had been, taking me

on a mini tour and scheduling a session with the chef. It went be-yond his rock-star status and the physical attraction between us. It was his imperfect soul and creative, destructive mind.

"Josh, I don't want to lead you on."

If anything, his hold only tightened around me. "And you're not, Princess."

Before he released me, he kissed the inside of my palm, sending sparks flying up my arm.

Changes.

That was what was happening between us.

Chaotic changes.

AFTER DINNER, WE HAILED A cab.

Josh slipped in right beside me on the well-worn leather seat. Candy and gum wrappers were crumpled on the floor. The cab reeked of smoke and incense that had me holding my breath and debating on whether I should flag the next cab down.

I slapped Josh's hand when he tried to pay again. "No, dude. Not cool." I gave him a death stare.

He yanked his hand back and started to laugh. "Ridiculous Prin-cess," he said under his breath.

We stepped out of the car and into a crowd of hundreds stand-ing in front of the stadium.

"You'd think some rock star was in there or something," Josh said. It might've sounded sarcastic if he didn't look so endearing.

"Hold on." I pulled the special phone from my back pocket and placed it on my ear. "Tilton? It's me." I glanced up to the sign above me. "We're at the west exit. Okay, see you soon."

Between my fingertips, I twisted at my charm bracelet as the tension rode up my shoulders.

I hadn't seen Hawke in so long, and the thought of seeing him set me hot and cold, all at once. I didn't want to expect things from our relationship. Expectations led to disappointment. If I'd learned anything in life, it was that.

Yet I couldn't help but hope for something more. Something regular. Something real.

I snapped myself back to reality.

Just have fun, Sam. That's how this relationship started.

I want to see him, and that's why I'm here.

Josh snapped his fingers in front of my face. "Earth to Samantha. What's going on in that overanalyzing big brain of yours?" He tipped his head to the side. "You know you don't have to go. Right now, we can top that pizza with some dessert, if that's what you want." He squeezed my hand, his smile hopeful, and a spark of some indefinable emotion was in his eyes.

"Josh, I can't. It'll be good." I hoped. "You'll love watching them play live." I forced enthusiasm in my voice, for both of our benefits.

Whereas Josh calmed me, Hawke sent my nerves into a frenzy. Simply holding Josh's hand kept me centered while just talking to Hawke threw off my whole equilibrium. I had never been a wild child before. I'd lived my life functioning as a mother to my own mother. When I'd made that leap that first night with Hawke, I'd promised myself that I'd live out of my comfort zone, which was what I was doing.

Tilton erupted from the door, his almost seven-foot frame practically having to duck. I smiled big, and I swore, I saw the corners of his mouth twitch. Of course, I'd never seen him smile, but I had come to know him so well that I recognized the little changes in his facial features.

"Miss Clarke." When he approached and Josh stepped closer to me, Tilton's vein by his temple throbbed, a small indication that he wasn't happy.

I suddenly doubted my decision to bring Josh. A second later though, a new resolve settled in my skin. Who knew what Hawke and I were? But I didn't owe him an explanation of my friendship with Josh.

"Josh, this is Tilton. Tilton, Josh." I waved my hand between them.

Josh tilted his head all the way back to take in Tilton's height and he extended his hand. "Hey, buddy. I'm figuring I should stay on your good side." He flashed him a cool Josh grin, one that would have been contagious if Tilton were halfway normal.

Instead of taking Josh's hand, he turned and went toward the back of the arena. "Let's get inside before it gets crazy," he said in his monotone voice.

Josh scanned the area. "And this isn't crazy?" His eyes darted to the thousands entering the stadium, mostly women squealing as they tugged at each other's hands.

I pulled at the edge of his shirt and nodded for him to follow Tilton through the doors.

Once inside the private entrance, the chaos of the crowd dimmed.

"So, how are you, Tilton? How's it been on tour?"

"Good."

"Is Hawke doing okay? I was actually surprised to hear from him."

"He's well." Tilton had never been one for words. Sometimes, he would stay mute. At least today he was talking. Maybe he was warming up to me.

Josh laughed silently beside me, and I shot him a look. A shut-up-if-you-want-to-live look. It was good that Tilton couldn't see because I didn't think I could protect my friend from his almost three hundred pounds of lean muscle.

When we turned the corner, I took in a whole new level of chaos even though it seemed to be organized chaos. Everyone backstage had special badges around their necks. People were in every corner, moving like ants with a mission on an ant farm. No one was staying idle. Some were carrying boxes or clipboards; others were speaking frantically into their headphones.

My fingers fell to my parted lips when I saw a familiar face out of the corner of my eye. "Holy heck . . . is that Taylor Swift?" I almost lost my footing mid step. "Channing Tatum . . ."

Josh was unfazed as he reached for my elbow to steady me. It seemed like we were losing Tilton in my starstruck-ogling stage.

"Let's go, Princess. We're losing ground."

I guessed he wasn't the starstruck type.

I scurried forward, keeping my eyes on our target, the mean, lean bodyguard machine in a suit.

When he turned a corner, we followed him into a set of dressing rooms.

I chewed on the inside of my cheek, any semblance of control now slipping away, when Tilton opened the door that clearly said *Def Deception.*

When I stepped in, everyone's eyes flew to us. Everyone's, except for Hawke's. His stare—an arctic-cold death glare—was on Josh.

I inhaled deeply, wondering what was going to happen next. I hadn't thought this far. I had anticipated some sort of greeting, a kiss, a *hi*, or something, anything, but silence.

I saw pure murder in Hawke's eyes. Eyes that blazed with fire.

He was wearing his signature fitted torn jeans and a tight black tee, the sleeves rolled up at his shoulders. His tats adorned both arms.

I had to ignore that as a slew of emotions tore through me. My nerves were a jumbled mess. I knew I'd missed him, but for some reason, it felt like I was meeting a stranger. We were at level zero.

At first, I didn't know what to do. And I wasn't his, so I didn't need to explain why Josh was here. *But why did I feel like I was cheating on Hawke somehow?*

I released a deep breath when Cofi stood, breaking the tension. His smile was so big, I swore, I saw his molars.

"Sunshine!" He rushed toward me, reached for my waist, picked me up, and swung me around like a rag doll. "You're in trouble. It's pretty brave of you to bring another guy here," he whispered in my ear before letting me go.

He extended his hand toward Josh. "Hey, man. I'm Cofi."

"Hey," Josh said warmly, taking his hand.

I appreciated Cofi's friendly gesture.

My eyes flickered between Josh and Hawke's staring contest, and every muscle in my body tensed.

Josh stepped forward, the first to break the silence. "Hey, I'm Josh."

If I'd thought Hawke would be as friendly as Cofi, I was wrong.

Hawke's glare didn't change, didn't move, and didn't waver. He tipped back his head in his typical greeting, but he didn't say a word.

I cringed, hating the awkwardness in the room, hating that I'd brought Josh into this situation, hating that I hadn't even thought this through.

Even the band members could feel the strain because their eyes ping-ponged between Hawke, Josh, and me. No one uttered a word, which was so unlike the usual preconcert rowdiness.

Josh cleared his throat. "You know what? I'm going to get going." He reached for my hand and turned me to face him.

In a hushed voice, I asked, "I thought you wanted to watch the concert?"

"Yeah, that." He shrugged. "I realized, I'm not really into rock. I'm more of an R and B and rap kinda guy." He winked and then gave my hand a squeeze.

There was negative chatter in the air, but either Josh ignored it or didn't care.

He tilted his head toward the door. *Let's go,* he mouthed. "We can still get out of here. Last chance." He raised an eyebrow, his gaze questioning. "I know this awesome place for dessert." His smile seemed hopeful, but one look from me, and he knew I wasn't going to go anywhere.

He blew out an audible breath and then pulled me to the side, blocking everyone's view. "All right, so I'll just get going. I'll catch you later, Princess."

"Are you sure?" I angled toward him. "I want you to stay." Because I honestly did.

Josh provided a comfort that I craved, and I wanted him to enjoy the show. I could never have guessed Hawke's reaction to Josh. I hadn't expected him to be so cold, so rude, so brazen.

"No, it's cool. I'll just see you later." He went in for a hug, and I wrapped my arms around his waist. Then, he pulled back and gave me a sad smile that made my heart physically ache. "I'll catch you after the show."

Just when I thought he was about to turn toward the door, he seemed to think better of it. There was a fervor in his eyes that I'd never seen before, as though he were thinking something through in his head. His eyebrows pulled together, and just when I thought he was going to pull away, he did the opposite. He bent down and kissed me, hard, without hesitation, never breaking our connection, knowing full well that everyone was watching, that the band was watching, that Hawke was watching. My heart raced, and my belly filled with such warmth from his familiar lips.

My hands moved up from his waist to push at his chest, but he wouldn't budge. He placed his hand at the back of my neck and kept me in place for everyone to see.

Right before I was about to bite his lower lip to get him to release me, he backed away. "All right, bye." He smiled like this was normal between us, as though his kiss were like a high-five departure and not a bucket of gasoline being thrown onto a smoldering flame.

He threw Hawke a conniving little smile, and then he nodded to the guys and sauntered out the door. Josh played hard ball. No doubt.

And, when I turned, everyone's attention was on me. My ears

burned. My palms sweated. My pulse skyrocketed.

Hawke's eyes held pure jealousy, his jaw tight and his fists clenched.

A moment later, he stood and stalked toward me in his sleek, predatory way. Heaven forbid, he walk at a normal speed. Even if the President were standing before him, I doubted that he'd hurry.

He stepped into me and held my chin in a possessive manner, and I breathed him in—his musky cologne and one hundred percent male scent.

"Everyone, out," he barked.

"We don't have time," someone muttered.

"We're not leaving, so you can get some action."

I recognized Cofi's voice, but my eyes were strictly on Hawke.

His free hand dropped to my arm, pulling me into him, his grip greedy. There were questions in his eyes that I knew I'd be answering soon.

"Now." His voice was quiet yet firm. He meant business.

When everyone left, his hands dropped to my waist. Our breaths mingled into one. Lust, want, and greed could be read in the piercing green eyes staring down at me.

"Sunshine . . ." That one word made my whole body tingle. "Who was that?"

"Are you jealous?" My lips parted at his proximity, my pulse ticking up in tempo. I was baiting him, but God, did it turn me on.

"Yes." All honesty with no hesitation. "Who, Sunshine?" He bit my chin and pressed my body flush against his, his hands gripping my ass and pushing me against his hardness. "Are you trying to make me jealous?" he growled. "Because it's working."

He peppered kisses along my jawline, causing my breathing to hitch

"No." One word flew out of my mouth because I doubted my ability to form a complete sentence when his hands were on me.

"Who is he?"

"A friend."

He nipped at my neck. "Try again."

"A friend who feels more for me than I do for him."

It was the truth. It hurt to say it out loud. Josh did feel for me, and if I were to describe my own feelings for him in one word, it would be *ambivalent*.

Hawke lifted my legs and wrapped them around his waist. Our lips collided, and he dropped me onto the couch. My head bounced against the cushions, and I sucked in a breath, staring into his green irises.

With one hand, he lifted the back of his shirt over his head and flung it across the room. "Who am I to you?"

"Someone who feels for me but less than I feel for him."

"Not true." The intensity in his eyes stilled me. He pressed into me, his chest against mine, his fingers threading through my hair, his thighs trapping me underneath him. "Let me show you how much you mean to me." Kisses covered my neck, and teeth nipped lightly at my breast through my shirt.

I let out a shaky breath.

And, just when I'd thought I was in control of the situation because it was my choice to jump on the wild side, to live out of my comfort zone, I realized I couldn't have been more wrong.

Because when his hand undid the button of my jeans, I lifted my bottom. When he slipped my panties off, I didn't protest. When he entered me hard and fast, I didn't deny him.

And that was when I knew that the control I'd thought I had was slipping to where I couldn't see myself anymore. All I knew was that I was falling deep, losing myself in all that was Hawke Calvin.

chapter SEVENTEEN

WHEN YOU WERE WITH SOMEONE you enjoyed and you knew that you only had a limited amount of time together, hours seemed like minutes, and minutes seemed like seconds.

I blinked, and the concert was over.

Hawke's arm snaked around my neck when we entered their penthouse suite at The Palmer House Hilton. I held the bag of McDonald's nuggets, the scent of grease filling my nostrils, as it swung against my hip. Getting McDonald's seemed to be our after-concert tradition, one that I looked forward to.

The music rang loudly in my ears, the bass bumping against my skin. The rest of the band, friends, and groupies were already situated in the massive space—all over the couch, half-leaning on the counters, and spanning every inch of the immense room. The party was in full swing as everyone held a drink in their hand.

A pool table sat in the middle of the room. AJ and Carl were playing a round of pool with other people I didn't recognize.

"Sunshine. Hawke!" someone called in greeting.

Hawke saluted them with his free hand as he dragged me down the hall.

We passed the group of girls sitting on Cofi's lap. "Where are you going, Hawkeye?"

Hawke ignored him and continued to usher me behind him.

I heard one of the girls mutter, "He's such an ass when *Sunshine* is around."

I didn't miss her sarcastic tone either when she said Hawke's nickname for me.

Clearly, he didn't care. Hawke closed the door behind him and took the food from my hand, dropping the bag on the center table in front of the TV. The food was forgotten and abandoned. The city skyline was our backdrop, beautiful and clear, while the lights of the skyscrapers lit up the night sky.

He took my face in his hands, framing my cheeks. "I've missed you, Sunshine." His lips encompassed mine, sparking a fire in my belly, as he walked us backward to his bed.

"I'm pretty sure we were just reacquainted in your dressing room."

I felt his smile against my lips while his fingertips dug into my waist.

"That was a quick hello."

The warmth of his tongue against the crook of my neck set my body aflame.

"This will be the slow"—his hands caressed my ass, pressing me against his erection—"and forever-lasting greeting."

Boom, boom, boom.

The loud pounding at the door made me jump.

Hawke stilled, eyes hard on the door. "What the fuck do you want, Cofi?"

"It's not Cofi. It's Alan."

He let out an exaggerated sigh. The veins in his forearms pushed to the surface as he squeezed my ass. "One second." He placed one chaste kiss on my lips before he charged to the door and pulled it open.

"We need to talk, man." Def Deception's manager walked in with his usual cocky swagger. When he saw me, his lips pressed together, and his eyes narrowed, never breaking eye contact with me. "Alone."

I sat up straighter on the bed and stared him down. I had done nothing wrong.

Hawke exhaled heavily. "What is it now?"

"Why is it that you're always in a bad mood when she's in the room?" He tipped his head in my direction.

Hawke stepped in his line of sight, blocking Alan's view of me. "Because you're always butting into the little time we have together."

The little things he said in other people's vicinity only justified the reason I was continuing to fall for him. I crossed my arms and smirked for Alan's benefit.

Alan pinned me with his eyes. "You might not want an audience for this."

"I don't fucking care." Hawke's voice was void of emotion. "Spill it, or leave. Whatever you have to say can be said in front of Sunshine."

Alan cleared his throat. "*Starx Magazine* called me today."

Hawke threw up his hands. "What the hell does my mother want now? We fucking paid her enough to buy us another five years. Damn it!"

"It's not your mother this time. It's another girl."

Alan's eyes flickered toward mine, and my stomach clenched into a knot.

Another girl?

My arms wrapped around my center. I wanted to stick my fingers in my ears, so I wouldn't have to hear what Alan had to say next because, in my gut, I knew it wouldn't be good.

"So the fuck what?" He ran one hand threw his dirty-blond locks. "What are the allegations now? Rape? I hit her?"

Alan's lips pursed as he turned an eye my way, and then he said, "She's pregnant."

I blew out a breath like I'd just been punched in the gut, and the knot in my stomach tightened. It took a few seconds to get air back into my lungs.

Hawke jabbed his finger in Alan's direction. "That's some

bullshit right there 'cause I've never fucked any girl without a con-dom, besides Sunshine over there."

Alan reeled back. "You're not supposed to be screwing anybody without a condom, regardless of who it is!"

Hawke laughed. "You don't know how it feels to be inside her."

I cringed, wishing I could disappear, not enjoying the fact that my sex life was out for open discussion and hating hearing the de-tails of another woman he'd been with. I wasn't surprised, but it still hurt to hear it.

"Alan, that girl is lying. Print it. I'll take a paternity test. It's not mine."

"You don't remember a Jenelle Fabson?"

"Really? The only name I remember is mine because that's all they scream." He threw his hands up. "You know these women. You know they're only after their two seconds of fame and quick money that some magazine is going to give them."

"Think long and hard, Hawke. You've always used protection, even when you've been as high as a kite?"

My eyes scanned Hawke's face, but I couldn't read his eyes. His focus was on Alan.

I clenched my jaw and watched for Hawke's reaction.

Samantha, what are you doing here?

Pregnant woman? High as a kite?

Those words rang loudly in my ears over and over again, like a skipping record. My heart and mind were like magnets being forced apart. My heart wanted him and his free spirit, but my mind was screaming for me to end this now before I suffered undeniable heartbreak.

"That baby . . . is not mine," he said firmly. "Let them print her interview, and then I can have my lawyers so far up their asses, they'll be paying me for their lies." He walked toward the door and opened it. "Is that it?"

Alan's unmoving stance indicated he wasn't ready to leave, So,

Hawke lifted his eyebrows as if to say, *What are you waiting for?* After a few seconds of uncomfortable silence, Alan nodded and glanced at me one last time before walking out.

After the door shut, I gritted my teeth and staggered to the couch to get my purse. I needed time to think things through and to gain back any semblance of control I'd once had. I couldn't think with a clear mind when I was in Hawke's vicinity.

When our fling had begun, I'd convinced myself that it was what I needed, a little fun. Now, I was in too deep. This was too much drama for this small-town girl.

When he approached, I kept my gaze on the splash of art on the wall. It was an array of primary colors against a white canvas. The painting reminded me of my insides, the strings of red like my heart being torn to shreds.

His fingertips grazed my chin and forced me to face him. "It's not mine," he swore. "What's the matter?"

And maybe it wasn't his baby. But he certainly wasn't denying that he'd slept with her.

I was falling for a whore. Good God, I was never this girl. There was fun, but there was my integrity and my pride, and I needed both.

I pushed my foot into the Persian carpet and fiddled with the edge of my purse. "I thought I could share, but . . . I can't."

He reached for my waist, but I stepped back. If Hawke touched me, I would be a goner and give in. Give in to the magic of his touch.

With one large step forward, he closed the gap between us, tugging me in by the waist, his hold fierce and uncompromising.

He pressed the softest of kisses to my temple. "I haven't been with anyone since you. That was before, and this is now."

I closed my eyes. I hadn't expected him to say that. It had been weeks since I'd seen him.

But how did I know if he was telling the truth?

"I'm serious. I only want you, Sunshine." He pulled back, and his green eyes bore into mine. "This charity concert? This was a last-minute thing, and I pushed to come here because of you."

My hands gripped the sides of his shirt, needing something to hold on to. "I like you. A lot." Heat formed behind my eyes as deep emotions rushed to the surface. "Maybe more than I should because of who you are, but . . ."

I couldn't be with him without losing myself completely. I wanted more than what we were right now, more than a regular hookup or a random fling. Because I was a relationship type of girl. I'd thought I could do the temporary fun-with-the-rock-star thing, but I couldn't.

Hawke's one hand made its way up to the nape of my neck. "None of that fucking matters. All that matters is me and you."

"I'm afraid of getting hurt." I chewed on the inside of my cheek and tried to keep it together.

"You're the only one I've been with since the last time we were together. You're the only one I want to be with." His eyes never wavered from mine, revealing the intensity of his words. "Ignore Alan and the rest of them. I haven't touched drugs in years, and I don't even know that woman. That baby is not mine. All that matters is me and you, right now."

When I didn't answer, he spoke more fiercely, "Me and you, Sunshine. Okay?"

I peered up into his eyes. I wanted to believe him. I wanted to ignore the noise around me and pretend like we could work even though doubt plagued my mind. It was more than the other women; it was his whole rock-star lifestyle. It was the fact that there would be weeks where he wouldn't call me. Weeks where I wouldn't hear his voice. Weeks where I'd wait and wonder if our time together even mattered to him at all.

But, when he bent down to meet my lips, I let him have me, and all my sanity flew out the door.

This time, my heart won the battle against my mind.

WE IGNORED EVERYONE ELSE FOR the rest of the night and lay in bed. The city lights filtered through the floor-to-ceiling windows. *Who knew what time it was?*

Naked and in utter bliss, I turned over to find Hawke staring at me. I released a long sigh, knowing this was our only night together until our next night together—whenever that would be.

He brushed an escaping strand of hair from my face and intently stared at me. His eyes held a seriousness that I'd never seen before.

"Come with me," he whispered.

"Where?"

"Wherever I go. Just come with me." He smiled his carefree smile. It was the kind of smile that showed he didn't have to think about how he would make rent next month, the kind of smile that showed he had access to all of life's desires. "Come with me on tour."

I stared deep into his eyes. Rich, famous, and no cares in the world. But I had cares. I had a career and friends and a life. *Could I leave all of that behind for something that might not even work?*

"I can't."

"Yes, you can." His fingers trailed to my stomach, teasing me.

"No, Hawke." Oh, how badly I wanted to give him a different answer. But it was true. I'd been wondering how I'd feel when he finally asked me to stay, to come with him, to be with the band, to live this life. But . . . now that it was staring me in the face, I couldn't. "I have work, and I'm applying to Cordon Bleu soon, along with some other schools in case I don't get accepted."

His fingers inched lower. "How about I employ you?"

When his fingers pierced my insides, a low moan escaped me.

"I'll take that as a yes." He dropped his head against my neck and chuckled. Wetness met his touch as his length hardened against my leg. "I already booked you a one-way ticket."

I gripped his hand and stilled him before my brain turned to mush, and my words were incomprehensible.

He lifted his eyes to mine. Vulnerability showed through the green irises staring back at me.

"Even if I wanted to, I couldn't." I had to still get all my recommendations together and apply for school. I had goals, dreams, and ambitions that went above and beyond the rock star. Goals set in motion when my mother had been alive and goals that I would accomplish now that she wasn't here—for the both of us.

He wasn't giving up, his panty-dropping smile heavy on his face. It was as if I were talking to the Devil himself, and he hadn't heard a word I'd said.

Want, want, want. Take, take, take. That was what he was used to.

"You should do whatever you want to," he mumbled around kisses against my stomach.

"I have a job," I choked out, already falling under his spell again, caused by his soft, warm kisses.

"So what? You need money? I have all the money in the world. I'll add you to the payroll."

I didn't respond, but I started to pull away from him.

He sat up and sighed. "You're serious, aren't you?"

For some reason, I didn't think many people said no to Hawke.

"Very serious. I have obligations, Hawke. A job. I want to be a chef someday, have a career. I have aspirations beyond being your . . . whatever it is that I am to you." I jutted out my chin, my determination strengthening.

He needed to understand that I was serious.

His facial features fell, and the mood shifted when my stare didn't waver from his. He was the first to break eye contact.

He let out an audible sigh and narrowed his eyes. "Is that what you really want? To leave?"

And, like that, he shut down and turned away.

I reached for his face, trying to erase the disconnected look in his eyes. I didn't want to hurt him any more than I wanted to be hurt by him. "You're accomplishing your dreams, and I still want to accomplish mine."

I lifted my lips to kiss him and lighten the tension in the air, but he stiffened on contact. After a moment, he gave in, deepening the kiss, leaving me breathless and unable to speak.

He whispered against my lips, "What do you want?"

I angled away from him to read his eyes.

"Sunshine, what do you want?" he repeated. The fierceness in the span of green staring back at me tightened my chest.

Everything. "Nothing."

He huffed, dropped his head against the pillow, and faced the ceiling. With one hand, he pulled his long, wavy strands to the top of his head. "There's always a price. Everyone wants something. My mother, management, the band, the fans . . ." He blew out a hard breath. "And the thing is"—he leaned into me—"this is the first time I feel the need to give a woman everything she wants. So, tell me what you want." His eyes searched mine for answers. "Whatever it is, it's yours."

"Hawke . . ." *What could I tell him that wouldn't leave me defenseless?*

I wanted the happily-ever-after, the American dream. To do that, I needed to stabilize myself, get a secure job—my dream job. I wanted more than my mother had had, more than she'd wanted for herself. I wanted more from him. I wanted exclusivity even though I didn't know how that would work between us.

My breathing slowed as flashes of the past few months rushed back. "This whole thing with you has been amazing. I wouldn't have been able to go to Europe and experience everything without you . . ." My voice trailed off because it sounded like I was breaking it off with him.

"Shit, you're saying no." He rubbed at his brow, disbelief

crossing his features. "This is a first for me."

"Did you think I would just drop everything and go on tour with you forever? Stick around until you got sick of me?" I wrinkled my nose.

"That would never happen." His fingers brushed against my cheek, sending warmth down my neck. "What do you want?" he asked again. "A relationship?"

I'd seen his lifestyle, the women throwing themselves at him and the band on a daily basis. I hadn't even contemplated a relationship. I wasn't sure it was a viable option.

"Sunshine," he said his nickname for me, sounding tortured.

Say yes, my heart was begging me. *Yes!*

But I had my doubts. *Could this even work?*

"I can't go with you," I groaned.

"That's not what I'm asking." His eyebrow furrowed, thinking deeply, before scanning my face. "I don't do relationships. They're for pussies. But . . ." His face turned serious, as though he were turning something over in his head. "I want to try it with you." His face became hopeful, his green eyes shining. He wiggled both eyebrows in a non-Hawke-like playful way. "They have smartphones and Internet everywhere. We can video chat. Phone sex every day?" He sucked on his bottom lip and gripped my hip. "Come on, will you be my girlfriend?" The intensity of his stare seared through me.

I pulled back, searching his face for any doubt, but there was none that I could see. Only resolution. He was willing.

Shouldn't I be as well?

Butterflies stirred in the pit of my belly, the kind that made me giddy, but I forced my face to stay even. "Okay."

"Okay?" An impish grin spread across his features. "Don't seem too enthused about it."

There was no way I could go on tour with him, so we would have to do this long distance.

I stared into his hope-filled eyes, took a deep breath, and decided to take this leap—not only because of my want for adventure, but also because I genuinely cared for him and wanted to make this work.

I pushed gusto into my voice, yelling, as though I were experiencing an orgasm, "Yes! Yes! Yes, I'll be your girlfriend!"

A crooked smile touched his face. "That's better, Sunshine. Much better."

Then, he closed the gap between us, and I met the lips of my boyfriend, the biggest rock star in the world.

No big deal.

chapter EIGHTEEN

OUR GOOD-BYE WAS BRIEF AMID chaos. I eavesdropped on the logistics to get them to the airport—all the while, thinking of the distance that would soon be between us.

Hawke kissed me with reckless abandon until I was out of breath, and my feet felt wobbly, as though I were floating on air.

And I truly felt like I was flying.

That was, until he left.

When I hopped in the limo, thoughts raced through my head. I should be happy. Hawke was my boyfriend. I officially belonged to him now, and he belonged to me.

I tried to wrap my head around the enormity of it all. What it meant, where it would lead us, when we'd see each other again. But thinking of it only made my head and heart and stomach hurt, all at the same time.

When my five-story red-brick apartment building came into view, my whole body relaxed.

After I stepped into my apartment, Chloe's eyes met mine from the couch.

"How was the concert?" There was no inflection in her voice or light in her eyes. At one time, she would've jumped with glee at the mention of anything and everything Def Deception.

"Good." I dropped my backpack and purse on the floor and joined her on the couch, dipping my hand into her chip bag.

"You don't sound like you had a good time." She quirked an eyebrow, opened her mouth, and then shut it. But keeping her thoughts to herself lasted about a nanosecond. She threw both hands up and then said, "He's not good enough for you. Period. He can't mosey into Chicago whenever he wants and call you just to have sex. You're worth more than that, damn it! And where was he when you were stuck in that paparazzi debacle? Huh? Not even a call?" She flipped to face the TV again and stuffed more chips into her mouth. "I'm done, and I feel better. Thanks."

She'd been playing mama bear since my mama was no longer here.

"I know." I rested my head on her shoulder. The intimate gesture eased the tension in the air. "It's all messed up, Chloe."

She kept stuffing her face with more chips and shifting in her seat. "I know I'm the one who told you to have fun. Dude, I would've slept with his ass in a heartbeat, gone to Europe without batting an eyelash." She took my hands in hers. "But I'm me, and you're you. And you're in too deep. I can tell by the way you carry that damn phone everywhere. I can tell from the disappointment in your eyes when you reach for it and don't see a missed call. And, when you come back after seeing him, that look on your face breaks my heart." She stuffed more chips in her mouth, as though she were stress-eating. "Sam, even though I wouldn't have done things differently, we're totally different people. I can enjoy myself in the moment and not get emotionally attached."

"I'm fine," I said, totally lying.

"You're fine, my ass," she grumbled. "It's written all over your face, and even though I'd warned you time and time again, you still fell for him because you're you, Sam. I lost my virginity in my boyfriend's convertible. You had a candlelit meal after junior prom. I shouldn't have pushed you."

"You didn't have to push very hard." And it was the truth. I had made the decision to sleep with Hawke all by my horny-for-Hawkey self. No one else had decided that for me.

Her lips tipped up into a reluctant smile. "No, I didn't, but now, this shit has to stop. He can't just call you to hook up whenever he's in Chicago. That's not the kind of relationship you deserve, and that's not the kind you're used to."

I waited until she was finished and then said quietly, "We're together, Chloe." It sounded weird to even admit it out loud, like I was talking about another person and not myself.

She reeled back, her face cautious. "What does that mean?"

"We're exclusive. He's my . . . boyfriend." My mouth contorted into a forced smile, one that hurt my cheekbones.

"Really?" she scoffed, her eyebrows flying to her hairline. She opened her mouth to speak but shut it at the sullen look I gave her.

"I guess it didn't help that Josh gave me a more-than-friendly kiss on the mouth in front of him. I think Hawke was a little jealous."

She let out a belly laugh. "I knew I liked that guy."

"I do, too." *But not as much as he wants me to like him.*

"Well then"—she brushed the crumbs from her lap—"I think you should drop the rock star and give Josh a chance. He's more your type."

I rolled my eyes as exasperation hit. "Chloe, it's complicated." More than I could even figure out at the moment.

All I knew was, my heart wanted Hawke. And he wanted me, so I couldn't say no.

She leaned back, and her nose wrinkled. "I smell trouble. I mean, if this is what you want, what's with the sad face? You should've stormed in here, yelling at the top of your lungs. Instead, you trudged in here like someone had died."

"I just miss him." I wrung my hands together in my lap. "And, with Hawke being who he is and me being who I am, I don't see how this is going to work. I can't exactly quit my job to go on tour with him and expect to get into Cordon Bleu this spring. And I'm not letting anything get in the way of that."

Chloe's lips pursed together. "Maybe it can work." Her voice didn't sound very convincing. "Look at those celebrities married to regular people."

I looked at her through incredulous eyes. "Yeah, the majority of those people are divorced."

Her one shoulder shrugged, as if to say, *I tried.* "Samantha Clarke, you will live one day at a time and see what happens." She reached for one of my hands and squeezed. "I can't believe I'm holding the hand of Hawke Calvin's girlfriend." It was as if she were forcing enthusiasm into her voice.

"Shut up."

She picked up the newspaper in front of us. "Can you sign this?" She tried to say it with a straight face, but her lips quivered with laughter.

"Whatever." I snatched the newspaper from her, stood, and hit her on the head. "You're such a loser."

"But you love me anyway?" she called out as I strolled to pick up my belongings on the floor.

"Yes, I do," I replied, walking to my bedroom.

I dropped my oversize purse on my bed. When the buzzing sound from the bottom of it registered in my ears, I dumped all the belongings on my purple-and-pink comforter.

"Hello?" My voice was breathless and hurried and excited.

"Hey, Sunshine," Hawke cooed in his sexy, hoarse voice that fans would pay to hear.

We hadn't set any rules besides exclusivity, so I hadn't been expecting a call this soon.

"Hawke."

"No *babe*, baby? We're officially an item, and I don't even get a nickname?"

I dropped against my comforter as my heart did nonstop flips, like a gymnast on a floor mat. "Is *The Rock Star* not a worthy enough nickname? I'll have to think of one."

"Wait. Never mind. I remember one . . . though it'd be a little weird if you started calling me that in public."

I laughed. "What is it?"

"*Oh God. Please, God. Oh my God.*"

His seductive deep voice made my stomach clench. Memories of our sexcapade pushed through.

"Stop." I laughed.

"Stop? I don't recall you stopping me last night," he growled. "If anything, you were screaming for me *not* to stop."

"Hawke!"

"I'm joking, Sunshine." He chuckled. "You know I like to tease you."

"Yeah, you do." I pulled a lock of hair to my side. "Where are you now?"

"New York. I'm about to hop in the car to head over to an interview."

And so the distance began.

"I'll call you later?" he said, his voice sounding sexy and adorable.

I gripped the phone, pretending he was right beside me, not ready to let him go. "Okay."

"Bye, sweetness."

I miss you already.

"Bye."

I hung up the phone and exhaled a heavy sigh.

This was what I wanted, but why did I feel dread in every one of my bones?

MY PHONE BUZZED ON MY desk. I had brushed my teeth, washed my face, and changed into my pajamas. The pink hearts on my cotton pants were on full display. I rushed to the phone to see Josh's happy face on the screen, a picture he'd taken of himself when I wasn't looking.

"Hello?"

It had been two days since I'd heard from him, and I missed him.

I hadn't expected to miss Josh, but I did.

The last time I had seen him, his face had been connected to mine, lips on lips and hands on my hips. Part of me had thought our friendship was over. I had debated on calling him but hadn't wanted to lead him on.

"The Princess is awake." Josh's voice came out cheery and bright, his normal Josh self.

My whole body relaxed. Everything was once again right in the world.

"Yes, but I'm so tired. I have work early in the morning."

"It's eight o'clock," he countered.

"Yeah, but I just got home from a twelve-hour shift."

Candice had a wedding tasting at her reception hall, and I had volunteered to work for her.

"So, I guess a late-night taco can't tempt you?" The hope in his voice was endearing and tempting and so sweet.

Tacos? I sat up straighter on my bed. My stomach grumbled at the thought of warm corn tortillas, steak, and cheese melting in my mouth, sliding down my throat, and satisfying my belly.

"I really shouldn't." Though I hadn't eaten dinner. Somehow, the reality that I didn't know when I'd see my boyfriend again had been bringing me down.

"Oh, but you should," Josh said enticingly. "And, since I'm down the street at Los Compadres I'll get you some extra cheese on those tacos. I know how cheesy you like it."

I laughed. "Because you know I'm all about the cheese. That cheese. No lettuce," I singsonged Meghan Trainor-style.

He laughed. "Only for you, Princess," he said.

I chewed on the inside of my cheek. "Okay, come over, but I'm kicking you out at midnight."

"I know the princess turns back into Sam, the pastry sous chef, after midnight."

"Can you get me churros, too?"

"And I would do anything for love. And I can do that. I can get churros," he sang back, Meat Loaf-style.

"You're so silly."

After he hung up, I pushed the comforter off my legs and strolled to the kitchen. Chloe had left for the evening to hang out with her coworkers, so I got out the cutlery and plates.

Ten minutes later, I heard my door buzzing. I pressed the intercom button.

"Yo, yo, yo, I've got tacos." Josh's cheery voice echoed through the speaker attached to the wall.

I pressed the buzzer to let him up.

When I opened the door, the scent of grease and cheese had my mouth watering. Watering and wanting some food.

"I swear, they need to have taco delivery," he said, strolling in.

I took the drinks and the bag from his hands. "I'm pretty sure they have that."

"No, I mean, everyone knows about pizza delivery. It's a popular thing. There are eight hundred numbers and songs about pizza. I'm just saying, they need to do the same for tacos."

I dropped the bag on the kitchen counter and sat down, and Josh followed suit right next to me.

"Yeah, you should start a trend or set up your own delivery business," I said, noting how natural it felt to be in his presence.

"I think I shall do that, Princess." He tore the white paper bag in half and opened the foil to my taco and then his. Then, he wrapped his hands over his taco and took half of it in his mouth. "What are you waiting for?"

I scrunched my face at him as he talked with his mouth full, and he smiled, showing his teeth full of lettuce. Only with Josh was it super cute.

I laughed and then wrapped my fingers around the corn tortilla filled with goodness. When I took a bite, grease inched down my chin. "Mmm . . ." The taco was delicious. Hot, greasy, and oh-so yummy.

"Good?" Josh's face lit up.

I took another bite, puffing out my cheeks and nodding. "Like an orgasm in my mouth."

The side of his mouth tipped up, and his eyes dropped to my lips.

I stopped breathing.

He stopped breathing.

His tongue swiped over his full bottom lip, and I inhaled deeply.

I blinked, swallowed, and dropped my head back into my taco. A shyness bubbled up inside me, and my cheeks warmed. "I'm sorry." I didn't know what I was apologizing for.

I hadn't meant for those words to slip out. It was so effortless, being around Josh, that a part of me forgot sometimes that he wanted more from me than I was willing to give him.

He nudged his shoulder against mine. "Don't be. I like how I caused the orgasm." He winked. "Even if it's just in your mouth."

When I didn't laugh at first, he pinched my side until I started to.

I slapped his shoulder, thankful for his humor and his ability to make me smile so easily. "You're horrible."

"You're beautiful."

When he said these things along with the intense look in his eyes, I couldn't help but blush. I shifted, feeling guilty for enjoying his attention when I was committed to someone else.

I grabbed my horchata from the table and slurped it down through the straw to deter the attention from his words.

"So, I guess the rock star is gone?"

"Yeah, back on tour."

"Do you know when he's coming back?"

"No." I tried to shake the disappointment in my heart, but it was there, clear and inevitable.

"So, did he like that friendly kiss I gave you?" A devilish glint sparked in his eyes, humor heavy in his voice.

My eyes widened, my taco held midair. "What the heck was that?"

His eyes twinkled with mischief. "So, did he?"

"Yeah, so much so that he's my boyfriend now."

The spark instantly dulled, and his smile faded. "Oh." He blinked and focused on my face. "The kiss was that good, huh?" There was a lightness in his words, but it didn't resonate in his tone.

My chest tightened. *Why did I say that?*

"Why did you do that?" I asked, dipping my head back into my taco.

He shrugged. "Just a friendly kiss. It's not like our lips had never met before. Actually"—he pointed a finger for emphasis—"I believe you like my lips on you. They saved you. Me and my powerful lips."

"Uh-huh." I took another bite of my taco.

He let out a low breath. "I didn't think he was the settling-down type," he said quietly, mostly to himself.

He turned to face me, his knees hitting mine. "Why are you with him, Sam? You're beautiful and talented and sweet, and you can have any guy." His eyes searched my face, trying to look for an answer.

I paused before speaking, gathering all my thoughts, and I answered him the best I could, "Because the rock-star persona is not who he really is."

I knew Hawke's flaws and the depth of his character, and I still wanted to be with him. This wasn't going to be an easy relationship. If anything, it was going to be a long trek to keep us together, given the distance between us, but all of me wanted to at least try.

Josh bit his lip and nodded, turning away. I hated that I was hurting him, hated that this was ruining our evening and possibly our friendship. I didn't want to lose him.

"I don't want to hurt you, Josh," I finally said after a long moment of silence.

He picked up his taco, looking resolute, like he had figured something out. "Being your friend and having you in my life is enough for me." His eyes perused my face, and then he added, "For now."

We stared at each other for several long seconds. I was going to ask him to clarify when his phone buzzed in his pocket, and he picked it up.

"Casey?" he answered.

It was his sister.

"Yeah." With one hand, he rubbed the back of his neck, and by the drop in his tone, I knew something was up. "When did he fly in?"

He stood and paced the room, continually rubbing at his neck. "No, he's our grandfather. It wouldn't be right if I'm not there. I'm with Sam." He glanced over at me and laughed. "Nope. Not yet but soon." His walked back to me, picked up a piece of steak from my taco and stuffed it into his mouth.

"Hey!" I playfully slapped at his shoulder, but that didn't stop him from picking up another piece.

"Yeah, maybe I will. I'll ask her. Thanks, Casey. Love you, too." After he hung up, he grimaced. "Guess who came to visit?"

"Who?"

"My grandfather." The tightness in his eyes and the shift in his demeanor showed me how he felt about his dear old grandpa.

My fingers automatically reached for him, resting on his shoulder. "Just for a visit?"

He scoffed and dropped to the seat next to me. "Albert Stanton the 2nd coming to visit for no reason at all other than to see his family? Of course!" Sarcasm was etched in every word. "He's here to convince me to change my mind." He huffed and ran one hand through his hair, making it fan out in the front. "I guess he figured, since I'd been ignoring his calls, he'd just hop on the jet and stop on by."

"I'm sorry." That was all I could say.

My mother had been supportive since the day I was born. I hadn't known how to disappoint her because everything I did was perfect even though I was far from it. It was only after the end of her life that I had wondered why I hadn't been good enough for her to decide to stay.

"Maybe you can come with me?" His tone softened, and his eyes begged me to agree to his request. "We're all getting together for dinner tomorrow night. I mean, my sister suggested it. She thought maybe having someone there that he didn't know would make him think twice about laying it on thick about the company. Maybe it wouldn't get as heated." He stared blankly at the countertop, his fingers twitching at the edge of a napkin. "I just hate this guilty feeling I get every time I see him."

I inched closer, hoping my sincerity came across in my words. "What do you want, Josh? Not your grandfather, not your father, just you?"

One side of his mouth lifted into a sad smile. "I'll be fine. Don't worry about me."

I shook my head. "That's what you don't understand. I'll always worry about you, Josh. I want you to be happy."

He swallowed hard and pulled my hands onto his lap, examining my palms, lightly tracing the lines with his pointer finger. "This is your life line. Your head line." His touch brought tingles that traveled up my arm. "You're a highly creative individual, headstrong, determined." His voice lowered, sounding distant. "This is your heart line. You love fully, unconditionally." He swallowed hard, getting emotional.

I hated his withdrawn tone, the vacant look in his eyes.

I ducked my head to get into his line of sight. "You need to be happy. You can't live life making others happy because, at the end of the day, you're only accountable to yourself."

"Life's a box of shit sometimes," he murmured. "Seriously. It's like my grandfather wants me to be this big power exec and make millions. Do you know he threatened to take away my trust fund?" He stood from his seat and clenched his fists, like he wanted to punch something. "Like I care about my trust fund. Shit, I've been selling shoes, so I can pay my own way." He gripped the top of his head, looking like he wanted to pull his hair by the roots. "What I care about is what it's doing to our family. More importantly, what it's doing to my dad."

I stood and approached him, and when I extended my hand, he pulled me into him. I wrapped my arms around his waist and rested my head against his chest, the place that comforted me but the same place I was now comforting him.

"Josh, be happy," I begged him. "Whatever gets you there, make it happen."

He rested his chin on top of my head and wrapped his arms around my waist. A slow exhale escaped him, and he dropped his shoulders, sagging into me.

"What will make you happy?" I asked.

"Whatever I choose, it won't make everyone happy. Maybe that's just how life works." He blew out a breath. "I see myself as a lawyer. I don't want to make millions. We have millions. That didn't save my mother. That's not going to save me."

"Then, do it," I said passionately.

We held each other in silence for a few seconds, and then he pulled back and asked, "Will you go with me to tell him?"

His hopeful eyes met mine. I was unsure of what to do. I wanted to be there for my friend, but I didn't want to give him the wrong idea.

In the end, I decided that this was what friends did. Josh had been there for me in the alley. He had been there for me when I wanted to talk about my mother. I needed to do this for him.

I nodded. "Okay."

The exuberance on his face was uncontainable. In the next second, his arms were squeezing me again. The inhale and exhale of his breaths pressed against my cheek.

"Thanks, Princess," he whispered.

My whole body relaxed into him, and my arms pulled tighter at his waist because, although it shouldn't have, it felt so natural to be in his arms.

AFTER USHERING JOSH OUT, I went straight to the bathroom to get ready for bed again. After brushing my teeth, I slipped under my comforter.

Given the anxiety that Josh exuded just by uttering his grandfather's name, I wondered what would happen when they were in the same room.

He seemed so carefree, but I knew his family problems plagued his life.

They were family, of course, and from when I was younger, my mother had instilled in me that family was important. To my mother, I could do no wrong. I walked above water and most likely shit gold. She'd loved me beyond words, maybe overcompensating for my father, but I had known no different and only felt love.

That was one of the main reasons I couldn't understand for a long time why my mother had taken her own life. She had been a lover of life. And a lover of everything that was me until she hadn't been anymore.

The glint of my secret phone flashed on my side table, and I reached for the cell.

I bit my bottom lip and wondered where Hawke was. He hadn't called me all day, and I'd already left him multiple messages. I pushed in my pouty lip. This was his life, the lifestyle of going nonstop. It was how I'd met him, as a rock star, and to be with him, I had to accept this aspect of his life.

Should I call him again?

I decided I would, and if he didn't answer, I'd hang up and not leave another message.

Hawke answered on the first ring, which was a surprise for me. What wasn't a surprise was the noise of a party going on in the background.

"Sunshine." The way he uttered my name screamed everything sexual.

Having him on the phone had me sporting a smile that could not be contained. Cheesy smile was an understatement.

"Where are you now?"

I loved hearing the sound of his voice, even knowing the distance between us. His voice was what I hung on to.

"We're on the party bus. Guys, say hi to my girlfriend."

Girlfriend. Gah!

I sighed at those words falling from his lips, and my heart soared to unbelievable heights, higher than a helium balloon in an endless sky. I was Hawke Calvin's girlfriend. I belonged to him, and he was mine. I still couldn't wrap my head around the thought.

Coos of, "Hey, Sunshine," echoed through the receiver.

"I miss you, baby. I especially miss your wet—"

"Hawke!"

I wasn't a prude. Hell, last time he had been in town, I'd ridden his dick, as though he were my own personal bull, and we'd had numerous phone-sex rendezvous since then, but I didn't appreciate his whole band knowing about our sex life.

"What, baby? You miss me, too?"

"I do," I said, a lot breathless. "Did you figure out when you can sneak away, so we can choose what you're going to wear for Candice's wedding?" My chest bubbled with excitement.

Hawke had promised he'd come to Chicago when he was free to look for a suit for Candice's wedding. I'd decided that since he was officially mine, it would be wrong to take anyone else. Now, I was counting down the days.

Most likely, some high-end department store would be closing just for us to peruse. That was the only way he would be able to get out without getting mobbed.

"Yeah, I think I have some time in October. A little break for a couple of days."

I gripped the phone closer to my ear, like a deprived woman needing to get closer to her man.

"If you come tomorrow, I'll make it worth your while." Yes, I was using my body as persuasion to see him sooner. Bribes for my Hawke. I wasn't ashamed.

He groaned. "Give me a peek, sweetness. I've been a good boy on tour, like I should. My hand has had its workout lately. But it's nothing like the real thing."

I shifted with unease, knowing he was in a tour bus full of people who could hear him. "Hawke, the band is right there."

The chatter of the guys echoed loudly through the receiver, and then it stopped. When a door slammed shut, I knew he was alone.

"They're gone." The sound of his zipper being pulled down shot a shiver right to my core. "Don't make me beg for it baby 'cause I will. Give me what I want."

"I thought no one made Hawke Calvin beg?" I whispered, my voice seductively low. My hand slipped to the waistband of my PJs as a deep hunger took over, and heat spread throughout my limbs.

"You're the exception."

I tried to shimmy off the cotton pants, but they got stuck above my hips. The drawstring was tied into a triple knot that made me unable to chuck the pants off. I huffed as my fingers worked at the knot.

Way to ruin the moment.

"What are you doing?"

"Trying to be sexy and get out of my pajamas but totally failing."

He chuckled, his tone thick and husky and unbelievably horny.

"Why are you with me again?"

"Because you're you, and I love my Sunshine," he uttered the words without hesitation and not in the throes of passion but also with no inflection of emotion in his voice either. It was as if he were saying, *I love chocolate.*

I wondered if he meant it.

He hadn't asked me how I felt about him, but it was too soon for me. Saying the *love* word out loud would only make me susceptible to heartache.

"I want to see you, Sunshine. All of you."

When I finally was able to undo the knot, I released an exaggerated sigh of accomplishment. My underwear was horrendous, but I wasn't planning on giving my boyfriend a show.

"One second." After I pushed myself to my knees and chucked off my pajamas and underwear. I fell against the mattress in a big thud and picked up the phone.

"You all right there?"

"Yes," I said breathlessly even though I was breathless for a whole other reason. "Are you sure no one is watching?"

"Do you think I want anyone to see my girlfriend?"

I should have slipped off my shirt in the process, but now that I was comfortable against my pillows, I got lazy.

"Turn on your camera, so I can watch you." His tone was gruff and on the verge of desperation.

I shifted with unease. It felt forbidden in a way that made me uncomfortable.

When I positioned the camera at the right angle above my lips, his breath hitched.

"Open up for me, baby." His breathing labored as I did what I had been told. "Wider."

I guessed I could follow directions after all.

"Now, touch yourself."

My fingers went between the apex of my legs, and he groaned louder.

"Shit, one second." I placed the phone on the bed, anchoring it against the comforter so he could still watch.

"That doesn't mean I want you to stop. I'm harder than a diamond right now."

I tried to relax and let all inhibitions go. I'd never done this with anyone before—have a boyfriend watch me while I got off. There was a different level of intimacy involved.

"Touch yourself, Sunshine. I want to see you."

And I did while he stroked himself.

Loud guttural sounds escaped his mouth. If there was any doubt about what we were doing or what he was doing in the bathroom, it was obvious now for the whole bus to hear.

I closed my eyes, picturing it was Hawke inside me, his lean body on top of mine, his warm lips against my lips. And that was when the first of the tingling in the base of my spine initiated.

"Let go, sweetness. Pretend it's me right inside you and let go." Hawke's breathing increased over the phone, and I heard the loud thud of the cell hitting the floor. "I'm coming."

The sensation spread through my legs, building up and peaking, until I screamed his name, gripping my comforter to keep me steady as I entered blissful nirvana. Limbs shaking, breathing labored, my whole body quivered with sensation, and stars formed behind my closed eyes as we'd obtained the level of ecstasy together.

When my breathing slowed, I cleaned myself up and curled to my side, all of a sudden feeling empty and cold and alone.

I missed him so badly that the familiar ache in my chest intensified.

I brought the phone to my ear and rested it against my pillow. Hawke's beautiful face was in plain view, which only made that ache increase.

The sound of water coming from the sink echoed through the

receiver. "What's the sad tone for?"

This wasn't enough.

I blew out a breath. "I just miss the real thing. Miss you." My heart constricted at the distance between us, at the reality of our relationship. This was going to be our norm now.

"Soon, I'll be right there beside you."

"Okay," I said, trying to let his words lift my spirits. I hugged the pillow closer against me, forcing warmth back into my body and wishing I were holding my boyfriend instead.

The next few weeks couldn't speed up fast enough.

chapter NINETEEN

THE NEXT DAY, RIGHT AFTER work, I rushed home to get ready for dinner with Josh's family. After a sweep of gloss on my lips and a dab of blush on my cheeks, I changed into a floral dress and cardigan.

When I finished, I reached for Hawke's phone in the bottom of my purse to check if he had called, but he hadn't. I'd received a few random texts from him, telling me where he was, and in return, I'd texted him about parts of my day, taking pictures of what I had been baking.

The door buzzer broke me from my thoughts. I slipped on my jean jacket and checked my hair in the mirror hanging behind the door one last time, and then I opened the door.

"Hey," Josh said. A nervous smile played on his lips.

I pressed my back flush against the wall to let him in, my eyes taking in his attire. He looked business casual in a cream polo shirt and slacks. His hair was parted to the side, which only accentuated his young features. He was Gap, J.Crew, Banana Republic. All of the above. You couldn't take the yuppie out of the shoe salesman.

I tugged self-consciously at my skirt. "Am I underdressed?"

A dimple emerged on his cheek, subtle but noticeably there. "No. You look"—he paused, as though he were searching for the right word—"perfect."

My ears warmed from the compliment and from the way his eyes scoured my face. "Thanks." I slugged his shoulder in a friendly way. It was my go-to when Josh had me all flustered.

When we walked out of my apartment building, his newly waxed BMW was sitting against the curb. I could practically see my reflection; it was so shiny.

"Oh, you're so fancy. I see we're taking the Beemer today."

He automatically reached for my hand and intertwined our fingers, our hands drawn together like bagels and cream cheese. After he opened the door, I slid into the car.

"If we could take public transportation to where I used to live, I would. It's better than taking the car they bought me when I graduated. Another bribe gift."

When we were on the highway, I started to sense his anxiety from the way he rubbed the back of his neck, the crease between his eyes, and the way he chewed on the corner of his mouth, as though it were his snack.

"Josh?"

He didn't answer, seeming lost in thought, his eyes blankly staring at the cars in front of us.

"Josh," I said louder.

He turned and blinked, finally breaking out of his daze. "Sorry."

"It's okay." I offered my hand, palm up, and he didn't hesitate as he linked our fingers.

The strain in his shoulders relaxed at my touch. Funny how that worked—how a gentle touch calmed us both.

"You'll be fine," I soothed.

His eyes focused back on the road. "I only believe it because it's coming from your mouth."

The rest of the ride was silent, and my eyes widened, the farther we drove from the city. The houses seemed to morph into bigger and badder residences. I lowered my window, taking in the sights of the manicured lawns and the scent of the fresh air mixed with the newly cut grass.

Josh pulled down the long drive way and stopped at the front security station. Out of the miniature house by the gate came a guard, tall in stature and dressed in all black. He walked to our car and smiled. His teeth were the whitest teeth I'd ever seen, a contrast to his dark suit and bronze skin.

"Josh." The guard's eyes squinted, lighting up.

"My man, Stan."

They did a unique handshake, and I couldn't help but laugh at their interaction.

"You haven't been home in months."

Josh nodded, seeming a little sheepish. "Yeah, I've been busy."

The guard peered into the car and gave me a small wave. "I see that. Is this your woman?"

"Nope." Josh cupped one hand by his mouth and coughed out, "Not yet."

I shook my head, but again, I laughed. Josh couldn't help his charm. It was embedded in his DNA.

Stan placed his hand on Josh's shoulder. "One of the most real and genuine guys you'll ever meet." Stan, the man—aka Josh's wingman—stepped away and tapped the top of the car. "Josh, don't be a stranger. Nice meeting you, young lady."

The iron gate swung open, and my eyes took in the rolling meadows, green lawn, and the massive mansion in the horizon.

Josh's eyes flickered toward my direction. I couldn't do anything but blink, press my nose to the window, and take in the curved driveway bordered with lilies and roses. The flowers seemed to separate Josh's parents' house from the glitz and glam of the others. The driveway widened out and circled to a front entrance, an expansive entryway with dark wood double doors.

A sheepish grin touched his face. "This is actually a downgrade from our house in Manhattan."

My eyebrows flew to the roof of the car.

"But I won't let what I had frame who I want to be." He let out a long breath. "Ready?" He shifted the car into park, stepped out, and opened my door.

He was so focused on the entrance, like the boogeyman was inside, that it made my stomach churn.

"It's fine." I bumped my shoulder against his. "They haven't met Sammy, the Softy. She turns mean, grumpy old grandfathers into big, huggable teddy bears." I smiled to ease the tension in the air, and it worked when I saw the corner of his mouth tick up.

"Sammy, the Softy? Really?"

It had been the first thing to pop into my mind. I shrugged. "Let's go."

At the door, he entered a code, and we stepped into the foyer. I heard laughter coming from somewhere inside.

I lifted my head, noting the high ceilings, chandelier, and crown molding that accented the room. A double staircase fanned in the front, leading to the second floor.

"Homies, I'm home," Josh cooed playfully.

If it weren't for the light sweat from his palm clasped against mine, I wouldn't have even thought he was nervous.

I plastered a smile on my face, ready for the evil man. This situation had pushed out my protective side. Hardly anything rattled Josh, so the little that did had me on edge and ready to rumble. *I mean, how bad could Grandpa be?*

Josh's dad, Albert Stanton III, entered the room. His friendly demeanor was that of what I remembered when I had seen him at the restaurant for Josh's birthday. Casey and her boyfriend strolled in right next to Albert Stanton II, the grandfather.

His grayish hair was parted neatly to the side and had a little wave, just like Josh's. But that was where the similarities ceased.

His grandfather's stern eyes scanned me from the top of my head to the bottom of my non-designer shoes. The chill in his stare froze the blood pumping through my veins.

"Joshua."

If you listened hard enough, you could hear the disappointment in his tone, as though Josh's name should have been Albert Stanton IV.

"Grandfather." Josh released my hand, approached him, and pulled him into a genuine Josh hug.

I tried to ignore the way his grandfather's whole body stiffened, as though he weren't accustomed to the physical contact.

Josh motioned for me to come over. "I'd like for you to meet Sam."

"It's great to meet you. I'm Al." His firm hand took mine in a friendly shake, a contrast to his judgmental eyes. Then, he turned to Josh, dropping my hand. "Where's Jennifer?"

Josh's face blanched, his jaw tightened. His voice was tense as he said, "We broke up. You know this." The chill in the air dropped to arctic cold.

If Josh had thought me coming along for this family dinner would lighten the mood, he'd been wrong. From Al's face, I could tell I was subpar compared to Jennifer.

"Well, who's hungry?" Casey slipped her arm through mine. "Sam, it's great seeing you again. Let's go to the dining area."

I smiled graciously. She had a knack for shifting the awkwardness in the air.

She squeezed my arm and discreetly said, "Old G looks a bit hard at first, but deep down, he's a big, fluffy panda."

I glanced back at the older male, who had a permanent frown etched on his face. Panda? More likely a grizzly bear that would maul you when you turned your back.

"Robert, dear, have you met Josh's Sam?" Casey motioned to the taller male.

Robert was the only one wearing a suit jacket, and I wondered if he had just strolled in from a work event. The crease in his pants only accented his height. His slicked-back hair and dark green eyes reminded me of a banker.

"Hi, I'm Josh's friend." I took his hand in mine and gave him a firm handshake.

Robert quirked an eyebrow and shared a knowing glance with Casey. "It's nice to meet you."

It was obvious that Josh had mentioned me to his sister. Taking in her secret smile, I wondered if he had divulged my life story.

"Friend, eh?" His face broke out into a smile. "That's a first. In high school, girls fell at his feet."

I frowned. "Oh, I thought he was with Jenny all through high school."

"That didn't stop other girls from trying." Casey laughed as we entered the dining room.

A long chestnut dining table spanned the center of the room, surrounded by twelve chairs with exquisite carvings along the edges. The fine china plates on the table were outlined with a trim of gold and set with what looked like sterling silver flatware.

"Do you want a drink, Sam?" Casey tipped her head toward her brother and called out, "Hey, Joshy, take Sam with you to the wine cellar."

When Josh's eyes met mine, he threw me a thankful smile, all teeth. He held up a finger and excused himself from his father and grandfather. "I'm going to take Sam on a tour. I'll be back."

Al's disapproving eyes were like laser beams focused on the middle of my forehead, but I ignored him.

Josh gestured with his chin toward the kitchen door, and I followed. After entering the kitchen through the double doors, my nose was bombarded with a glorious whiff of basil and paprika and also the scent of something sweet. I scanned the area, appreciating the stainless steel professional oven. An older woman was setting the food on the kitchen island. She had a head of gray hair that hung below her chin and a grin so wide, I could see all her teeth.

"Joshy!" She practically bum-rushed him.

He picked up the tiny lady and swung her around. "Nora, my favorite person in the world."

She grabbed his face with her wrinkled hands, looking comically shorter than him as she held him. "Look at you. You're getting handsomer every day."

She pinched his cheeks, and Josh winced.

"Was there any doubt?" he said with a laugh.

When she released him, her eyes became fixed on mine, suddenly all-knowing. "So, you must be Sam."

"I am." I threw *Joshy* a sideways glance, wondering what he'd told this woman.

"I'm Nora." She took my hand in hers, and the warmth radiated up my arm. She exuded peace and kindness and warmth. "She's beautiful, Josh. Your description of her didn't do her justice."

I placed my hands on my hips. "So, what did Josh say about me?" I asked, my tone pinched and playful.

"Only the bad stuff," he joked.

Her eyes crinkled at the sides. "He told me a few things. About how he met the most beautiful, sassiest girl by selling her shoes and how she's the best cook in the world. At one time, I was the best cook in the world. Cooked for this boy since he was an infant. Now, he seems to have moved on." Her eyes lit up with an inner glow.

Josh motioned between us. "It's really a close tie."

"Boy, don't lie to your Nora." She shook Josh's arm. "This man right here is one of a kind. You'll never find another like him." She patted his heart. "Right here—this is what good men are made of."

It was Josh's turn to blush, and I laughed. It was fun, seeing him in the hot seat. We were a lot alike in where we didn't take compliments well.

"I should know," Nora said. "I raised this boy."

He pulled her in and kissed the top of her head. Internally, I swooned at the sweet gesture.

"Yes, Mom and Nora were the best of friends. I'm sure she can tell you stories of when I wasn't much of an angel, but we must get wine." He pointed to the cellar in an exaggerated motion and slung

an arm around my neck. "I only take the special girls to the cellar."
He winked. "Sometimes, they never make their way back."

"Nice meeting you, Nora!" I yelled behind me as Josh tugged me
toward the stairs.

The dark gray walls narrowed, the farther we descended.

Even though I knew Josh had been joking about not making my
way back, my skin chilled at the drop in temperature. "Um, should
I be afraid?"

His hand squeezed mine. "Remember? I'm your Prince Charming, white horse and all. I won't let the boogeyman get you."

We walked down a narrow hall and entered a massive wine cellar that would rival any restaurant. The soft purr of the cooling machine filled my ears, and I angled closer to Josh, feeling the cold in
the cellar. Smooth racks of cherry wood were situated on the wall,
holding endless bottles of wine. The low light overhead shone on
the labels.

Jaw opened and in awe, I took in row upon row of bottles organized by date.

"So, what're you thinking?" Josh asked, spreading his arms wide
for me to pick.

"I'm not a wine connoisseur or anything. I'm sure you know
more than me."

"No, you're the chef," he encouraged.

"A pastry chef," I corrected. "I know dessert wine, like what goes
with cheesecake, custard fruit tarts, and apple pie. Other than that,
I know nothing."

Josh peered over my shoulder and pulled one out, holding the
brown tag attached to the neck of the bottle. "Each one is sorted by
the name of the wine, the vineyard it came from, its type, and the
vintage."

Impressive though I was clueless. "I don't know what you're
talking about."

He chuckled. "It's all right. Just pick one, so I can drink the whole bottle to drown out the disappointment in my grandfather's voice. He's like a broken record." His light expression suddenly slackened, and he ran a hand through his short dark hair.

It wasn't fair. Life wasn't fair. His grandfather wasn't fair. Josh should be able to do what he wanted with his own life and future without feeling guilty about it.

"Pick one," he said again, tapping his foot and giving me his impatient face.

"No."

"Do it," he insisted. He poked at my side. "Do it!"

I scrunched my nose before shutting my eyes. Josh was relentless when he wanted to be. One day, he'd make a brilliant lawyer, one that would make a difference.

"I never give in to peer pressure, but since you're being a brat . . . eeny, meeny, miny, moe." I plucked a bottle out. The tag said *Monthélie 1er. cru Les Clous 2013*, whatever that meant.

"Dinner is ready." We heard from the top of the stairs. It was Casey.

I placed the bottle of wine in Josh's hand. "If it sucks, you picked it."

He shrugged. "I probably won't remember a lot from this night. Not if I can help it." He went silent for a moment. "Can we just hide out in here?"

I reached for his hand. "You brought me here as a buffer, so just know I'll be buff-buff-buffing away. I won't let him get another word in."

He nodded, his eyes almost hopeful, and he swung our hands between us, leading us up the stairs.

It was like Thanksgiving dinner. Nora had prepared a feast with turkey, stuffing, and potatoes. It was as if I were at a five-star restaurant, being interviewed to see if I was good enough to hang out with a Stanton.

At the table, Josh was to the right of Al while Albert, Josh's father, sat to the left.

Casey brought me into the conversation by asking about my career as a pastry chef.

"So, what restaurant do you work for?" Al asked.

I smiled. The judgmental look on his face could not be ignored, but it didn't matter. I was proud of what I did. I loved what I did. And, if anything, I could say that I did it for myself and paid my own bills.

"I work at Sheldon's Italia downtown."

"Her crème brûlée is to die for," Casey sighed. "Like, so good."

"You haven't tried her chocolate soufflé," Josh added, his eyes brightening.

"So, do you plan on working there forever?" Al asked.

The lightness in the atmosphere evaporated like an industrialized vacuum had drawn in the cheerful atmosphere and expelled an awkwardness that had the mood shifting. When Josh's jaw tensed, I placed my hand on his lap and squeezed his leg to placate him.

"No, sir, I don't."

"What's your next step? Head chef?"

I gave him a gracious smile. "I'm currently applying to Le Cordon Bleu in Chicago, and, yes, I want to be the head pastry chef one day. Maybe head up my own restaurant."

"Oh," was all the old man could say.

But, from that one word, I could tell what he thought of my grand layout for my future.

"That's my plan."

"Isn't Jennifer pre-med?" he asked, turning to Josh, as though I hadn't even spoken.

Josh stood, making his chair fly back. The movement was so abrupt that I flinched, and so did Casey. The air thickened with discomfort, but being Samantha Clarke, I clenched my teeth through it.

"Dad, Casey"—Josh gave them each a curt nod—"I'll see you

next weekend."

Al glanced around the room and gave a cynical laugh. "Did I say something wrong?" he asked, playing innocent though there was no innocence in his eyes. His comment was meant to demean me.

I tugged at Josh's shirt, hating the torment in his eyes and wanting him to sit. I'd come here to be the buffer, and I begged him with one look to calm down.

Josh's jaw was set in stone, his eyes fixed with fury. "If you want to degrade me and what I want to do for a living, go ahead, but don't be rude to my friend. She loves what she does, and by the way, she's very talented. Most of all, she's happy, but that's something you don't care about."

"Josh," I whispered, still tugging at the end of his shirt.

He extended his hand. "We're leaving, Sam."

One look in his eyes, and I knew he had already made up his mind.

I pushed my chair back as I stood. "Thanks for having me."

As we headed to the door, Casey chased us, pleading with Josh to stay. Albert started arguing with Al. Robert tried to play the mediator between them. It didn't sound cordial, more like a full-on war was happening.

Without releasing his hold on me, Josh kissed the top of Casey's head. "Love you."

"Josh, please." Her eyes were pained and pleading and tired.

"I can't." He shook his head. "He's just said too much. I tried, Case, but he's a broken record. Nothing ever changes. I can't take it anymore."

She hugged him and kissed his cheek, understanding seeping into her eyes. "Okay." Then, she turned and pulled me in. "I hope to see you again, Sam."

"Joshua!"

Every part of Josh's body stiffened.

When he didn't turn, the tone in Al's voice softened. "I just want to talk."

Josh held my hand so tightly, I thought my fingers would break, but I squeezed his back just as firmly, letting him know I was right beside him and had his back. His eyes were hard when he turned to his grandfather.

"Joshua, I flew all this way to see you," Al said gruffly. There it was again—the shameful undertone in Al's words, as though Josh owed him something, anything, most likely everything.

Josh stayed silent, his eyes still troubled, mouth shut, shoulders tense.

"Ten minutes. You're not even going to give your grandfather ten minutes of your time?"

The silence and their stare-down ticked on forever until Josh tipped his head in a curt nod.

I touched Josh's arm with my free hand. "I'll be in the foyer," I whispered. "Go talk to him."

His strained eyes met mine, the cold a contrast to his normally warm demeanor. I gave his hand one final squeeze before stepping away. I could still see them both down the hall.

Nora was at the front door with my jacket, her eyes down-turned. "Never did like that grouchy old man." She winked.

I was pretty sure Al and Nora were about the same age.

Then, I heard it.

Al's infuriated voice boomed in the background. "What do you mean, no? What kind of money will you be making as a lawyer? I can guarantee, you will make a hundred times more at Stanton."

Nora's light hand touched my shoulder, her eyes squinting in anger. "Robert has already quit his job and is working for Stanton."

Great. Now, Casey's boyfriend was working for the family business? No wonder there was more pressure on Josh.

"Are they moving to New York?" From what I understood, Stanton Steel was headquartered in New York.

"Robert works out of their Chicago office. That's where Albert works. But he has to travel to New York at least once a month. Who knows what will happen when the old man retires?"

The rumble in Al's voice brought us to silence.

"This is our legacy. We built this from the ground up, and what? You're going to let this company be led by a bunch of investors? Tell me why."

"Because that's not his passion," Nora said, answering for Josh but only loud enough for me to hear. "Because Josh is like his mother and lets his passion lead his life, not money or power."

When Josh remained quiet, his grandfather shouted, "This is bullshit!"

Josh remained still, taking it like the man that he was, but I cringed. I couldn't stand watching this. I wanted to help him, but I knew getting in between them would only make things worse.

"You're only taking this route, the lawyer route, because you know you'll have access to your trust fund in a couple of years. Well, guess what? It's not going to happen." Al's nostrils flared. "You're going to walk out on this family when we need you? I'm retiring in less than five years. It takes years to groom the CEO. Your father has been in this business for longer than you've been born. You need to start now, but you're telling me no. You're telling me we put you through Yale for business, only for you to go to law school? You're a disgrace to this family. A disappointment, damn it!"

Albert stepped between Al and his son, but it didn't stop the nasty tone of the old man.

I gripped my stomach. Every word that put Josh down was like a punch to my gut. Harder and harder, until one more word would have me on the ground.

Nora's eyes narrowed. Though she was short and a little round, I believed this woman could throw down, regardless of her age.

"I'm sorry," Josh finally said, his voice strangled. "Grandfather, safe travels home."

He turned and approached me, followed by his whole family. I hated the agony and anger and disconnect in his eyes.

His jacket was already in my arms, ready for him. I wanted out of here, but more than that, I wanted him out of here.

But his grandfather kept talking and talking and blabbing like his words mattered. "You walk out that door, boy, you have no more trust fund to depend on because that's for the Stantons, which you are not! You hear me? You're not getting a dime."

Albert blocked Al's path from moving forward. "Just go, Josh!" he said.

Josh couldn't get out of the house fast enough, and I trailed behind him, down to the curved driveway, past his car, and away from the house, away from the chaos, away from the crazy old man.

"Josh!" I called out.

But he kept going and going until I rushed toward him and placed a consoling hand on his back.

"The worst part is"—a heavy sigh escaped him—"I hate being a disappointment to this family. Fuck . . ." He blew out a slow, jagged breath, one where it sounded like it hurt to breathe. "Fuck!" He kicked a planter on the edge of the driveway and knocked it over. After staring at it for a moment, he seemed to think better of it and began to pick up the dirt with his hands.

I reached down for him. "Stop, Josh. What are you doing?"

I tried to pull him up, but he wouldn't budge.

"I'm cleaning up my mess." His voice quivered with pain and underlying anger.

My heart cracked at his sullen tone.

Sighing, I dropped to my knees and joined him, scooping up the dirt in my palms and dumping it back into the pot.

"Sam . . . what the hell?"

"I'm helping. We help clean up each other's messes, right?" I smiled sweetly, as though picking up dirt in the middle of the night in front of this palatial mansion was the norm.

He swiped his eyes with the sleeve of his shirt, sat cross-legged on the driveway and pulled me onto his lap, dirt and all. His head dropped to the crook of my neck where I felt his soft breaths leave his lips and touch my skin.

"I appreciate you so much. You know that, right?"

My fingers threaded through his soft dark brown locks as I held him against me, needing to comfort him, needing him to cheer up. "I'm pretty damn wonderful," I said with a chuckle.

But then something wet touched my neck. I didn't know if it was from leftover or fresh tears, but it sucker-punched me in the chest, and the crack in my heart broke into pieces, like shards of glass scattered on the floor. Heat formed behind my own eyes.

"I just want to hold you until this passes. Until I calm down." He let out a few breaths, in and out. "I feel like the biggest jerk right now."

When his body shook with tremors of guilt, I knew it was my mission to make the guilt go away because that was what I did. "Living your life doesn't make you a jerk."

He nodded against my neck, his warm breath blowing kisses against my skin.

"I know it doesn't feel like that right now." I rested my chin against his shoulder. "It will. In time, you'll realize it was the right decision."

I glanced out at the silent night and the twinkle of the stars above us. They were so calm and quiet, in opposition to the chaos happening in the house and in Josh's life.

After five minutes, his breaths evened out, and he pulled back to search my face. "So, I'm officially broke now. You still want to be my friend?" There was a hint of humor behind his tone, despite the seriousness in his words.

I smiled because my joking Josh was slowly making an appearance. I'd missed that dude.

"I guess," I said, feigning disappointment.

"Would now be a bad time to ask you if I could move in?"

I laughed. "Sure. You can sleep in Chloe's room."

He laughed, too.

Sitting on his lap felt so wrong and right at the same time. I loved consoling him, and the comfort of his touch brought a familiar warmth to the center of my chest. But we were just friends.

We stared at each other for a moment, and then I kissed him on the cheek. And, for the first time tonight, he smiled . . . this time for real.

chapter TWENTY

THE SWEET AROMA OF MY devil's food cake batter wafted up my nose. With one finger, I swiped the frosting at the edge of the bowl and brought it to my lips. "Mmm-mmm good," I said, throwing a smile at Josh.

It had been a few days since the awful meeting with his grandfather, and besides a few texts back and forth, I still hadn't spoken to Hawke. I had sent the last text, and he hadn't responded. That was the thing with wanting more. It never stopped. I'd wanted more than a hook-up-when-in-town relationship, and now that I had it, I wanted more of Hawke, too—more texts, more calls and communication, and more of his time.

I was starting to seriously wonder why I was putting myself through all this torture. Then, I'd backtrack and realize that this was his lifestyle, busy with interviews and promo. I wanted this, so I needed to understand and make this work.

"Yo, yo, yo, Earth to Princess." Josh waved his arms in front of me, pulling me from my daze.

I smiled and brushed some flour from Josh's cheek. I was teaching Josh how to bake because, the two times he'd brought over brownies for me to try, I'd nearly choked on one of them, and the other had the consistency of oatmeal.

He needed some major help in the kitchen. Our mission tonight was to bake a successful chocolate cake.

Before I dropped my hand from his cheek, he reached for it, pulled it down between us, and gave it a little tug. "Give me some sugar, woman! Powdered sugar."

His smile was like sprinkles on top of a cupcake and, a cherry on top of a hot fudge sundae. It was adorably cute and signature to Josh.

It was hard to swallow that Josh's grandfather didn't adore his grandson. It was hard not to be drawn to him because of his cheerful self and big heart.

"It's in the overhead cabinet." Sidestepping him, I reached behind him and pulled it out. My baking ingredients were all stored in white ceramic containers, each with the ingredient written in white chalk on a black label. "It says, *Powdered Sugar.*" I pointed to the sign and smirked.

He pinched my side as he passed me. "You think you're so smart, don't you?"

"Brilliant," I sassed.

It was our scheduled movie night, and this time, Josh had chosen the movie, but first I'd decided we'd bake a cake. Also, I knew it would distract me from my impatience with Hawke.

"How do I work this contraption anyway?" He took out my old KitchenAid that I had bought from a pawn shop.

The mixer was rusty and ridiculously old. It hadn't worked in years, but I kept it because it was my very first mixer. Call me Sentimental Sam because I kept everything.

"That old thing doesn't work. There's a hand mixer in the bottom cabinet."

He pulled at the handle of the KitchenAid, and it tilted.

"See?" I laughed. "It's a piece of crap. Use the hand mixer."

He angled his head, examining said piece of crap. The handle was brown, as it was an older style. "Why don't you have a better one?"

"Because they're like five hundred dollars." I moved past him and bent down to reach in the cabinet for the mixer. "Here."

"You're a pastry chef." He frowned. "You need a real mixer."

"When I make real money, I'll buy a real mixer." I pointed to his unmixed ingredients. "Get going. I need frosting." I slapped my hand against the counter to prove a point. "Chop-chop."

Josh saluted and then plugged in the hand mixer to stir the blend of powdered sugar with a few drops of milk. The white of the icing glistened from the light above me. With my wooden spoon, I was mixing the cake batter in my glass bowl when my phone buzzed on the counter.

When Josh glanced at the picture of Hawke and me on the screen, his grin slowly dimmed. I had taken the picture after a concert as proof because I swore, we'd never see each other again. Never in a million years had I imagined that we would be an official couple—me as his girlfriend.

I picked up the phone, placing the receiver by my ear.

"Sunshine . . ." Hawke's voice shocked me, sounding shaky and sad.

I stepped away from the kitchen, trying not to panic at his down-turned tone.

"What's the matter?" I turned to Josh, raised a finger, and walked straight into my room, shutting the door behind me.

Then, I heard it—soft sobs from my normally cheerful, self-confident boyfriend.

My hand pressed to my abdomen, my butt dropping to the edge of my bed. "Hawke, tell me what's wrong." I gripped the comforter, bracing for whatever he was about to tell me. I was certain he wouldn't cry for nothing.

"I fucked up, baby."

My stomach dropped at his words. "Are you drunk?"

"Yeah."

Flickers of cocaine and heroin and packets of other drugs spread across the table filtered through my mind as dread filled my veins. But I shook it off. He'd told me he wasn't into that.

"What happened?" I asked, holding my breath.

"She called me."

"Who?"

"My mom." A jagged breath escaped him. "I don't even know how she got my number. I don't talk to anyone she talks to."

"What did she want?" My gaze dropped down to my cream carpet, noticing the speckles of gray and brown. I had to focus on anything to keep me steady because just hearing him sound so broken had my chest slicing open, my insides slowly tearing apart.

"It's not even about the money. Sunshine, she wants to see me." His voice cracked with emotion. "She told me she's sick, and she was crying on the phone. She . . . she has cancer," he choked out. "She's dying."

I closed my eyes and let out a low breath.

Cancer? Could she possibly be lying about something this serious?

"Do you think she's telling the truth?" I could only imagine the psychological number she'd done on him while he was growing up, and now, the one woman he'd cut out of his life wanted back in. I wanted to jump through the phone and give him a consoling hug—of course, after transporting myself to his mother's house and giving her a good beatdown.

"Hell if I know," he said bitterly.

My fingers tightened against the edge of the bed.

Maybe his mother was sick. Maybe she wasn't messing with him this time. Death and sickness made people want to reconcile with their past. I understood that.

"What am I going to do, Sunshine?" he begged. "Just tell me what to do."

"Where are you?"

Did it matter where he was? Hawke was in the worst place right now, and all I knew was that I had to be there for him.

"I want to see you," I added.

He ignored my statement but continued to mumble under his breath, "I can't take this shit. I don't know if she's playing or scheming for another big payout, or if she's telling the truth."

"Hawke, can you come get me?"

That seemed to break him from his thoughts.

He sucked in a breath, his voice even and calm now. "What about work?"

"It's okay." I was off for the next few days, and I did have some sick hours left to use.

Good God, I hoped my boss wouldn't fire me for requesting time off at the last minute. I was risking things here, but I had to be there for him, be where he was. I had to help him through this.

"I'll call our PA right now to book you an airline ticket. I'll have Tilton go and pick you up when you arrive, all right?"

I stood and moved about the room, getting out my duffel bag. I wasn't sure how long I'd be gone, so I needed to pack accordingly. "Okay."

"We're in Seattle, so he'll be there waiting for you."

"Okay," I said as I threw a few outfits into the bag.

When he hung up, my jaw clenched as I remembered Josh. My stomach dropped at the thought that he had left without saying good-bye. But, when I walked into the kitchen, I saw a blur of brown hair with oven mitts Josh was bending down to put the cake in the oven. When he met my eyes, his sullen demeanor told me that he'd heard my whole conversation.

Damn . . .

"You're done?" I was at a loss for words, feeling guilty as hell.

But he knows I'm with Hawke, I reminded myself.

"That, I am. I set the timer for you." He peered up with a tight smile, picking up a dish rag.

I swallowed hard. I hated leaving him, but I had to be with Hawke.

"I've got to go," I said quietly.

He nodded and averted his stare. "Figured."

He wiped off the kitchen island and then tossed the rag into the sink. The thud from the cloth hitting the steel echoed as silence filled the space between us.

"Now, all it will need is frosting," he said, his voice low and disappointed.

He proceeded to gather his belongings, and I watched him slip on his North Face jacket.

"Josh—" I started to apologize.

But he raised one hand, stepped toward me, and pulled me into an embrace. The look of longing was evident on his face. He was a whole head taller than me, and he leaned in, pressing his lips to the hair above my forehead. The kiss was chaste and sweet and signature Josh.

"I hope he knows how lucky he is to have you, Sam. Because he is."

When my arms wrapped around his waist to hug him back, his whole body relaxed, but he was the first to pull away this time.

"Call me when you get back." A smile touched his lips, but it didn't resonate in his eyes. It wasn't the typical Josh smile I was used to seeing, the contagious boyish smile. "And save me some of that cake."

With that, he left out the door, and I marched back to my room, packing in a frenzy. With Josh gone, I shouldn't feel this empty space in my heart, but I did. The void was vast and noticeably there.

BEFORE I KNEW IT, I had landed at the private airport in Seattle. When I stepped off the plane, Tilton was near the runway, waiting for me with a limo.

"Miss Clarke." He gave his usual gruff nod and then a head tilt toward the car.

I went in for a hug, but he stiffened, so I settled for a shoulder pat. "Hey, Tilton. Thanks for picking me up."

I'd think, with the amount of times I'd seen him, he would've warmed up to me by now.

I guessed not.

He took my carry-on from my hand and dropped it into the trunk. After I stepped into the car, I asked him about Hawke.

"He's okay." His words said one thing, but the underlying tension in his usually unemotional face had goose bumps forming on my skin, like a bad sunburn.

I clenched my jaw while the traffic formed in front of us. Seattle rain hit my window, the water trickling down like falling tears. My knees bounced with anticipation as I wondered what state Hawke would be in, and I couldn't get to him fast enough.

But, when I got to the hotel music was blasting from the penthouse, the bass bouncing off the walls, like we were at a club. The sight of chaos was in front of me. People were drinking. Drugs were scattered over the tables. Half-naked women were making out with men I didn't know. Over fifty people were in the room, making the massive area look tiny.

I'd never seen Cofi so out of it. I was only a foot away from him, and he didn't even see me—or anyone, for that matter.

I had to sift through the craziness, but finally, I spotted Hawke in the corner, sitting on the couch, his eyes half closed and staring into space, numb to the world and numb to the crowd and numb to my arrival.

"Hawke," I called out loud enough for him to hear me.

But he didn't answer.

Awareness prickled my skin. He was on something. Something strong because he was oblivious of his surroundings. Three girls sat around him, equally high. One was chattering away, but he had no reaction, just the lazy smile on his face. My feet were paralyzed as I took in the scene, like clips from a bad movie.

Tilton grabbed my elbow and led me through the suite.

I jerked away and turned. "Hawke!" I yelled louder.

Still, nothing.

Bile rushed up my throat, the kind you couldn't throw up even though you wanted to, lodged so that you could feel the burn. My eyes heated. My chin tensed. My muscles trembled.

Tilton gripped my elbow with such force that I threw him the meanest look.

"Let go."

"No. I'll bring him to you." He led me to a private bedroom, and before he shut the door, he said, "Stay put."

I paced the room, minutes seeming like hours. When the door finally opened, Hawke slowly strolled in, looking sloppy and incoherent. He staggered in my direction, his arms wrapping around my waist. If this were any other situation, I would've been smiling. But he reeked of hard liquor. And who knew what else was running through his veins?

With two hands pressed to my cheeks, he leaned in for a kiss. "Sunshine."

The softness of his lips was so familiar and foreign at the same time. When he pulled back, the haziness in his eyes increased the dread in every part of my being.

I took his hands and pulled them down to his sides. "What did you take, Hawke?"

"You miss me, baby?" he asked, his voice groggy, his speech slurred. With a step forward, he linked his hands around my ass and pulled me into him. "'Cause, hell, I've missed you."

Normally, desire would flood my veins but not this time. "Hawke, what are you on?" My muscles tightened, and I pushed back my shoulders, my eyes hard. The tension in my body was visible as my anger rose, reddening my face.

"Nothing," he said with his lazy smile.

His ability to lie to me so easily had my stomach turning.

"You're lying."

It was clear he was doped up, and his lie had me doubting everything he'd ever said to me.

This was bringing me back to many years ago, when I'd found my mother in her bed after she found out that my father had left her for good for another woman. She'd looked calm in the moment, but I'd known that she was on something.

When I'd asked her what she had taken, she'd uttered the same word as Hawke, "Nothing."

He dropped his head into my neck, and one hand fell to the top of my jeans. "Is this how we're going to be? This is how you're going to say hi after I haven't seen you in forever?" His fingers undid my zipper.

"No, Hawke. Don't." I pulled back.

He couldn't fill this void with sex, and he wasn't going to use me to forget. That was not the reason I had come here, not the reason I had halted my life in Chicago to be by his side.

Sympathy replaced the doubt, if only for a moment, because it was the main reason I was here. "Hawke, have you talked to your mom?"

My question didn't break his demeanor. He leaned in and dropped his head to the crook of my neck. "Yes," he whispered against my neck. "Stage four cancer."

My heart cracked in half for him. It cracked for the failed relationship that he'd never get back because it was too late. Even though she had wronged him too many ways to count, she was still his mother.

I slumped against him, my arms tightening around his whole body. "I'm so sorry, baby. So, so sorry." I held him in the silence while the chaos of the party boomed just outside the door.

He was unbelievably warm. Hot. As though he were suffering from a fever.

My fingers threaded through his hair, feeling the wetness from his sweat. I pulled back to search his face. "You okay?" I cupped his cheek. "You're burning up." In the softest voice—not accusatory, but with concern—I said, "Hawke, I need to know what you took."

"Just something to calm me down. It's nothing." He swayed forward, looking like he was about to fall over.

"I think we need to call the doctor."

He shook his head and pulled my hand to the bed. "No. Need rest."

I followed his lead as he threw back the covers, dropped onto the mattress, and pulled me into his chest. "Sunshine, all I need is sleep. I'm tired." His eyes fluttered closed. "So tired," he said, tugging my body closer against his. "Tired of everything."

Worry twisted around my heart as I rested my chin on his chest, listening to his heartbeat slow to a sluggish beat.

The sound of the party next door continued, and as soon as I was sure he was asleep, I stormed out the door. Tilton was sitting in a chair against the wall, beer in his hand. When our eyes met, he stood, but I pushed a palm in his direction to tell him to sit down. Not like he'd listen.

He walked behind me as I stalked toward Cofi, who was laughing hysterically, high as a rocket ship.

I stood in front of him, both hands on my hips. I realized in that second, I hated him. Not because of his teasing. Not because of his lack of self-control. Simply because he was a dealer to my boyfriend, who'd been choosing to live the drug-free life so that he wouldn't turn out like his mother.

"Sunshine!"

The powder was spread in neat lines across the glass table. I'd watched enough movies to know what they were doing. You'd think guilt or shame would be written on his face, but no. He had one arm slung over a girl whose eyes were drooping.

I glared at him. "What is Hawke on?"

He then ignored my presence and turned to the girl on his lap.

"What did you give him, Cofi?" I slapped the drink out of his hand.

The copper-colored liquid splattered everywhere, making the

few people on the couch jump up, even Cofi himself.

Tilton took ahold of my wrist, but I tore from his grasp and stepped forward, chest-to-chest with Cofi. I had to tilt my head up to meet his over six-foot frame. He laughed like I was nobody, an ant he could just step on and then move on. Well, I wasn't. Not when people I cared about were involved.

"What did you give him, Cofi?"

"Nothing he hasn't taken before." Cofi sidestepped me, trying to move past. "He asked for it, baby girl. It's what we do together." His laugh was cynical.

I fisted my hands at my sides. The only thing keeping me from punching Cofi was the bouncer wall between us.

"Fuck you!" I shouted.

He turned, his hand slung over the woman's shoulders. Half of her tits were falling out from her deep V-neck tank top, but she was so doped up, she hardly noticed or didn't care.

"I'd love to fuck you, baby. But I don't think Hawke would appreciate that very much."

"You're an asshole!" I propelled myself forward, ready to tackle him, but Tilton held me back, his arms functioning as chains against my waist.

He carried me, as though I weighed as much as a toddler, and dropped me by the door to Hawke's bedroom. I turned toward him, heat behind my eyes. I couldn't remember the last time I'd been so angry.

Gah!

I wanted to take my fist and punch something, anything—preferably Cofi's face.

I shoved Tilton's chest. "If you love Hawke—and I know you do—keep him away from that asshole." I stormed into our room and slammed the door shut, my breathing erratic. Then, I placed my hands on my chest to calm down.

Breathe, Sam. Breathe.

Hawke was sleeping soundly in the California king, and my insides constricted at the sight of him.

His mother was dying. I understood that he was hurting. I understood that he wanted to numb the pain. I just wished I'd been there for him sooner.

A soft sigh escaped my lips as I slipped under the covers. I filled my usual spot against his chest, and when I brought my palm to his face, his skin was no longer hot. His cheeks were clammy, his lips no longer pink but pale.

Adrenaline spiked within me. Sheer terror rushed to the surface. I knelt by his head and brought my two fingers to his neck, feeling for his pulse. It was slow. Too slow. Like a clock gradually dying.

"Hawke." I kissed his face to wake him. "Are you okay?"

No response.

All my muscles tensed. Everything in my body screamed to push the panic button, but I kept steady.

I lifted his head, but it dropped against the pillow.

Then, pure hysteria slapped me in the face. My heartbeat raced. Full-body tremors overtook me.

My hands shook him as I said his name, slowly at first, but then my voice heightened to a crazed tone. "Hawke!"

My head dropped to his chest.

Hearing nothing.

But cold, dead silence.

The continuation of Samantha's story concludes in Book 2 of the Torn Duet—Choosing Forever.

Choosing Forever releases on February 13, 2017.

Dear Readers,

Thank you for allowing this story to have a place on your bookshelf. I'm forever and ever grateful!

If you enjoyed this story, please sign up for my newsletter. My newsletter subscribers are the first to know about my upcoming releases and always have a chance to win an advanced copy of my book before it goes live.

Also, you just never know when some of these characters will stop by.

You can sign up at *www.authormiakayla.com*.

ABOUT THE AUTHOR

MIA KAYLA IS A NEW Adult and Contemporary Romance writer who lives in Illinois. She is the wife to the husband of the year and mommy to three unbelievable cute little girls who have multiplied her grey hairs.

In her free time she loves reading romance novels, jamming to boy bands, catching up on celebrity gossip and designing flowers for weddings.

Most of the time, she can be caught on the train with her nose in a book sporting a cheeky grin because the main characters finally get their happily-ever-after at the end.

She loves reading about happy endings but has more fun writing them.

HERE IS WHERE YOU CAN FIND MIA KAYLA:

JOIN HER READER GROUP:
www.facebook.com/groups/miakaylabooks

WEBPAGE:
www.authormiakayla.com

FACEBOOK:
www.facebook.com/authormiakayla

TWITTER:
www.twitter.com/authormiakayla

INSTAGRAM:
www.instagram.com/author_miakayla

GOODREADS:
www.goodreads.com/author/show/7382805.Mia_Kayla

ACKNOWLEDGEMENTS

IT TOOK AN ARMY TO get this done and to final form and I wouldn't have been able to do it without the help and encouragement of the following people.

First and foremost I want to thank God for that creative side of me that can't keep quiet and for the stories in my head that I have to share with the world.

To the real rockstar in my life—My husband. I love you because you support me in everything I do. And you watch the kids when I have to write.

To my writer friends that keep me accountable with daily word counts, keep me sane by listening to me vent and help me promote — To Michelle, Tracey, Danielle, El, Laura, Jaimie, Faith, Ryleigh, Celeste and Kristy L. Only writers understand the struggles and insecurities of this journey and I appreciate each and every one of you. A lot of us started publishing around the same time and I'm so glad that we're able to grow in this path together. True loyal writer friends are hard to find.

To my family at Indie Chicks Rock, Alphas & Fairytales and Sassy Savy— To Autumn, Molly, Kaylee, Allison, Willa, Jeanne, Dani, Sasha, Emery, Melanie and Claudia. Thanks for giving me a place to meet new readers, share my ARCs and party.

To my PA—Emily, you keep me organized and sane and happy. I'm so glad I met you. Thank you for all you do for me and our reader group. You are always keeping me on my toes and I appreciate you.

To my friend Jenn—Thanks for helping me from the very beginning. From organizing my sales to pimping my book, I know I can always count on you and your constant support of the Indie Chicks.

To my PR team from Sassy Savy Fabulous—Kristi, you are the bestest from the restest. Thank you so much for helping me market this book and pointing me in the right direction. Marketing is definitely not my strong suit so I appreciate your guidance and support.

To my rock star editing team — Oh my goodness, what would I do without you? Produce crap. That's what!

To my developmental editor, Megan— I heart you so much. So much! Thank you for helping me flesh out these characters and for always being honest with me even when the truth hurts.

To my copy editor, Jovana— You truly have an eagle's eye. Thank you for catching all my repetition and editing this book like it was your own. I'm the queen of repetition and I appreciate you keeping me in check.

To my proofreader, Shawna— Thank you so much for taking on a new client last minute. I'm confident after your last look that this manuscript is in tip-top shape.

To my formatter, Christine—You are the best in the business. Thanks for beautifying my books with your graphics.

To my cover designer—Sommer, you've got talent and an eye for cover hotness. Thank you for putting your magic touch on my covers.

To my beta readers—Hot Tree, Amy, Alyssa, Emily, Lisa, Kaitie, Michelle and Sarah—I appreciate your feedback and also your friendship. Without you, this book wouldn't be what it is now.

To Kristy—Thanks for being my post beta reader and for loving this book as much as you do.

To Margie and my RRR Immersion partners—Thank you for Colorado and pushing me to become the best writer I can be. I continue to learn from each of you.

To the bloggers that have consistently supported me from my very first book to now. I heart you! Thank you for following me on this journey.

Last but not least to my readers— From those who have followed me from my very first book and to the new readers, thank you! thank you! thank you! I write for you.

www.ingramcontent.com/pod-product-compliance
Lightning Source LLC
Chambersburg PA
CBHW050021180626
46810CB00002B/524